Dear Diary,

Today the past reached out to touch me. I recognized the handwriting on the package the moment I saw it. It was the same round, unformed hand I had read on the note pinned to Garrett's shirt all those years ago, begging me to find a home for her babies.

Inside the box was more of the past. Tiny pink and blue sweaters painstakingly embroidered with Lana's, Shelby's and Michael's names, and a ragged-eared teddy bear that could only have belonged to Garrett.

But that's all. Only the mementos and a short note asking me to give them to the Lords. No signature, no address, not even a telephone number.

Terrence and Sheila's children are as dear to me as my own. How will they feel to know their birth mother has stepped back into their lives, and in such a mysterious fashion?

And why after all these years has she tried to contact them at all?

Dear Reader,

There's never a dull moment at Maitland Maternity! This unique and now world-renowned clinic was founded twenty-five years ago by Megan Maitland, widow of William Maitland, of the prominent Austin, Texas, Maitlands. Megan is also matriarch of an impressive family of seven children, many of whom are active participants in the everyday miracles that bring children into the world.

When our series began, the family was stunned by the unexpected arrival of an unidentified baby at the clinic—unidentified except for the claim that the child is a Maitland. Who are the parents of this child? Is the claim legitimate? Will the media's tenacious grip on this news damage the clinic's reputation? Suddenly rumors and counterclaims abound. Women claiming to be the child's mother are materializing out of the woodwork! How will Megan get at the truth? And how will the media circus affect the lives and loves of the Maitland children—Abby, the head of gynecology, Ellie, the hospital administrator, her twin sister, Beth, who runs the day-care center, Mitchell, the fertility specialist, R.J., the vice president of operations, even Anna, who has nothing to do with the clinic, and Jake, the black sheep of the family?

We're thrilled to bring you yet another riveting story, adding one more piece to the dramatic Maitland Maternity saga—*Baby 101* by longtime favorite Marisa Carroll.

Marsha Zinberg,
Senior Editor and Editorial Coordinator, Special Projects

MARISA CARROLL
Baby 101

HARLEQUIN®

TORONTO • NEW YORK • LONDON
AMSTERDAM • PARIS • SYDNEY • HAMBURG
STOCKHOLM • ATHENS • TOKYO • MILAN • MADRID
PRAGUE • WARSAW • BUDAPEST • AUCKLAND

HARLEQUIN BOOKS
225 Duncan Mill Road, Don Mills,
Ontario, Canada M3B 3K9

ISBN 0-373-65074-4

BABY 101

Copyright © 2000 by Harlequin Books S.A.

Carol Wagner and Marian Scharf are acknowledged as the authors
of this work.

Visit us at www.eHarlequin.com

Printed in U.S.A.

Marisa Carroll is the pen name of the award-winning writing team of Carol Wagner and Marian Scharf of Deshler, Ohio. The sisters have had over thirty romance novels published in the past fifteen years.

Their publishing history includes sales to Dell Publishing and *Women's World* magazine. They now write exclusively for Harlequin Books. They are the recipients of numerous industry awards, including the *Romantic Times Magazine* Career Achievement Award for their highly acclaimed SAIGON LEGACY series published by Harlequin in 1991. In 1992 they were chosen by Harlequin Books to do one of a series of six books to benefit Big Brothers/Big Sisters of North America, an honor of which they are justly proud. In 1993 their novel *Loveknot* appeared on the Waldenbooks national bestseller list, and in 1994 their novella *Affair of the Heart* was included in Harlequin's MY VALENTINE anthology, a *USA Today* bestseller. Their latest title, *Winter Soldier,* was a *Romantic Times* Top Pick of the Month.

Carol and Marian were born and raised in northeastern Ohio, pursuing careers in nursing, X-ray technology and the business community before entering the writing field in 1982. Marian is employed at Bowling Green State University in Bowling Green, Ohio. Carol is writing full-time. Both sisters have been featured speakers at writing seminars all over the country.

PROLOGUE

SHE COULD SEE the sign as soon as the taxi turned the corner. It was halfway down the block in a row of sand-blasted brick storefronts. It was pink and blue neon, with a baby cradled in a diaper hanging from a stork's beak. The name Oh, Baby! hung beneath it. The style was nostalgic, in keeping with the twenties-era feel of the street. Trees in wooden planters with waves of red and pink petunias at their bases lined the brick sidewalks, and wrought-iron tables and chairs in front of coffee shops and German delis were shaded by green canvas awnings. People sat at the tables and strolled along the street looking in the windows of art galleries and vintage clothing stores, enjoying the unusually cool and clear early September day.

The neighborhood had a cozy, small-town feel. It was hard to believe she was only three blocks away from bustling Mayfair Avenue in the heart of downtown Austin, Texas, and the noisy lunchtime crowd at Austin Eats Diner.

"Park there, driver," she said, motioning. "In front of the baby shop." The taxi driver maneuvered into the space and waited for her to make up her mind.

He caught her eye in the rearview mirror. "You want to get out, ma'am?" he asked. He'd seen how difficult it was for her to open the heavy door when she went into Austin Eats.

"No, not yet."

She had given him fifty dollars when she got into the cab. She didn't want him to be tempted to leave her stranded somewhere along the route or to worry that she would stiff him for a large fare. "Just let me know when you want to go inside," he said, and settled back in his seat, content to wait.

She didn't know if she was going to go inside. She wanted to, she wanted to as badly as she'd ever wanted anything in her life. But if there was one thing LeeAnn Larrimore had learned in forty-seven hard years, it was that you didn't always get what you wanted.

Forty-seven. Not young anymore, but not old enough to die. She looked at her hands, clutching the cardboard box in her lap. They were skeletal, her wrist bones jutting below the sleeves of her shirt. Her whole body looked like that. She was dying of cancer and she didn't have much time left. But even that sense of urgency couldn't overcome the reluctance she felt at going inside her daughter's store.

What if Lana should recognize her? She didn't know how that was possible, though. The last time she'd seen her daughter, she had been an infant. For twenty-five years LeeAnn hadn't even known what had happened to Lana, or her brothers and sister, after she'd left them on the doorstep of Maitland Maternity Clinic with a note pinned to Garrett's shirt asking Megan Maitland to find a home for her babies.

It wasn't until she had been told her condition was terminal that she had given in to that ruthlessly unanswered need to learn their lot in life. It hadn't been hard. She had gone to the library and searched the Internet for news of Maitland Maternity. Not only the clinic's high-tech and professional Web site, but all the news outlets she could find. And there had been news, lots of it. Maitland Maternity, it seemed, had been embroiled in a scandal throughout the past year.

But none of that tangle of false identities and lost sons returned to their families had meant anything to her after she read of the shoot-out that had wounded Garrett Lord, the adopted eldest son of a prominent Austin family, and Megan Maitland's godson.

Garrett Lord, adopted son and godson. Garrett. Her son's name. Her long-dead husband's name. She had searched further. And there it was, a matter of public record. Four children, infant triplets and a toddler boy, had been adopted by Terrence and Sheila Lord, a well-respected banker and his wife, twenty-five years ago.

God had answered a desperate young mother's prayers and given all four of them a loving home. More than that. He had given them parents who could supply them with all their earthly wants and needs.

But that wasn't enough now. She had to know if the Lords had also given them love. The kind of love that had driven her to give them up in the first place, rather than subject them to the hand-to-mouth childhood she had experienced. And that her circumstances dictated would be all she could offer them if they remained a family. A lifetime of secrecy wasn't an easy thing to erase. And she wasn't strong enough to face the possibility that her children, raised in affluence, wouldn't understand why she had done what she had.

So she had brought talismans with her. Three tiny sweaters, two pink and one blue, painstakingly embroidered with their names, Shelby, Lana and Michael. And a teddy bear, much worn and loved by Garrett, his daddy's pride and joy. But her reckless, handsome husband had crashed his Harley into a concrete light post one dark, rainy night, leaving her with four babies and a mountain of medical bills. So she had given her children over to the care of strangers and gone on with her life, never searching them out until her doctor had pronounced her fate.

Today she'd gone to Austin Eats to try to find Shelby. She had been there, red-haired and vivacious, behind the counter. LeeAnn had ordered a glass of sweet tea and watched her daughter direct the busy kitchen staff and still have time to charm each and every customer with a word and a smile. Then a man came in and sat down at the counter, and LeeAnn's breath had caught in her throat. Garrett? Or was it Michael? His coloring was the same as her dead husband's, hair so dark a red it was almost brown, olive skin and eyes that could see into your soul.

She sat there, hands trembling, for another fifteen minutes, torn between happiness and fear. When the man got up to leave he looked around the room, his gaze flicking over her, assessing and dismissive. It was then she began to realize her fantasy might not play out as she wished. The little love offerings she had kept all these years might not be enough for her children to make up for giving them away. She had gotten up and made her way painfully out of the diner. But she hadn't been ready to admit defeat. Going to Garrett's ranch outside the city was out of the question, but there was still Lana. Still her sweet little first-born daughter.

A young woman turned the corner and walked to the door of the shop. Was this Lana? She had LeeAnn's coloring, auburn hair and hazel eyes and a creamy tone to her skin that never seemed to tan. But LeeAnn didn't have auburn hair anymore, the chemotherapy had seen to that. She raised her hand and touched the inexpensive gray wig she wore. The young woman turned her head, and their eyes met. She smiled. LeeAnn reached for the door handle.

A couple approached. The woman was pregnant, and both husband and wife immediately engaged Lana in conversation about the display of furniture in the window. She was obviously going to be busy with them for a long, long time. LeeAnn's little store of courage gave out. She was so very tired. What if Lana didn't understand her long-ago desperation? What if she hated her for never contacting them?

But she had to let her children know she still cared. Once before, she had trusted in the judgment and caring of a woman she had never met. Her confidence hadn't been misplaced. One last time she would ask that woman to help her. She began to compose a note in her mind.

Dear Mrs. Megan Maitland,
Thank you for finding my babies a good and loving home all those years ago—I knew you would. The teddy bear was Garrett's, and these three baby sweaters have the triplets' names embroidered on them. The only fancywork I ever had time to do. My only wish is for the children to know I loved them.
Yours in gratitude.

"Do you want to go inside?" the driver asked again, sounding a little impatient. LeeAnn glanced at the meter. It was coming up on forty dollars. She gave one last look at the young woman now standing inside the bay window of her store, her hands resting on the carved finials of an antique-looking baby bed.

"No," LeeAnn said wearily. "I don't think I should go inside. But I want to mail a package. Take me to the post office, please."

CHAPTER ONE

THERE IT WAS AGAIN. A baby crying. She was certain of it.

But that was impossible. She was alone in the store, had been for hours. For a split second Lana Lord wondered if someone had left an infant behind unnoticed in a quiet corner of the shop. Abandoned, just as she and her brothers and sister had been all those years ago.

Ridiculous. She placed the miniature Stetson she'd picked out as her brother Garrett's birthday gift to their honorary little cousin, Chase O'Hara, carefully into its box. Beside it was a matching box with little cowhide boots she and her sister, Shelby, had chosen to be their brother Michael's gift. No one had left a child behind at Oh, Baby!, she told herself sternly. There must be a television on in the kitchen of the bakery next door. Or maybe it was a lost kitten in the alley beyond the wall.

She taped the lid of the box securely and added a mass of curling blue ribbon. There, all done. For her own gift she'd selected half a dozen different outfits from the store's inventory, but her favorite was a set of *Curious George* books for his momma to read to him.

A grandson for Megan. And the return of Connor O'Hara, the grown son she had given up at birth. What a tumultuous year it had been for the Maitlands, and the Lords. Scandals and mysteries and more excitement than she cared to recall. Now it seemed as if everything had sorted itself out, and most everyone she knew had found someone to love.

Everyone but her. While all her friends seemed to be making commitments to love and cherish, she was breaking off her engagement. She felt very out of step with the world at the moment.

The faint wailing came again.

Lana looked at the beaten tin ceiling. It wasn't a hungry kitten or a TV show. It was a real, live baby crying somewhere above her, where there was supposed to be nothing but empty office space and storage areas. Or so she had been told when she opened her business three years ago. This had never been a residential building, the Realtor had said. At least not since its heyday in the Roaring Twenties. But it had also recently changed hands. Lana had just gotten her signed copy of the new lease. Maybe the owner was up there looking around, although she doubted anyone from Van Zandt Development Corporation would be inspecting the building with an infant in tow.

But a homeless woman with a child might have found her way upstairs. Someone scared and desperate, with no money to buy formula or baby food. As scared and desperate as her own biological mother must have been to leave the four of them on the doorstep of Maitland Maternity Clinic all those years ago.

Lana stood. She didn't like thinking about her birth mother. It made her feel disloyal to her *real* mother, Sheila Lord. The woman who had taken three infant triplets and two-year-old Garrett and raised them as her own. Years ago Lana had made the decision not to waste time speculating and fantasizing about a woman she couldn't even remember. And she'd mostly stuck to that resolve.

She held very still and listened for a minute or so longer. Yes, definitely a baby crying. She should probably call the police, Lana realized. Let them come and check it out. But that might take hours, and the baby sounded as if it were in real distress. Still, only a fool would head up the staircase at the back of her storage room alone and unarmed. She didn't own a gun, but she did possess a good, heavy baseball bat.

It took her a minute or two to locate the bat and a flashlight and come up with the key to the padlock her brother Michael, the head of security at Maitland Maternity, had insisted she install on her side of the staircase door. She pushed the old-fashioned button-type light switch and was amazed to find that it worked. A low-wattage bulb at the top of the stairs glowed feebly against the dark-painted walls.

Lana clutched her bat in one hand and the flashlight in the other. She knew she ought to at least call her best friend Beth's new husband, Ty Redstone, an Austin police detective, or her brother Michael and tell them what she was doing. But that would involve a lot of explaining and listening to demands that she stay put, and she was too impatient, and too curious, to accept the delay. The good Lord had conditioned womankind not to be able to ignore a child's cries. At least He had this woman, and she kept on climbing.

She loved babies. She couldn't let this one suffer any longer without trying to help. When they were girls, she and Beth had vowed to have half a dozen kids apiece. Beth had gotten her degree in childhood development and opened a day-care center at Maitland Maternity. Now she and Ty were well on their way to realizing that childhood dream. Lana had thought she was, too, until her ex-fiancé told her he didn't really want kids. At least not for a long, long time, and then only one or two. So today, instead of planning the last-minute details of her wedding and throwing away her birth control pills, she was picking out baby clothes and wrapping presents to give to another woman's child.

At the top of the stairs the hall was dark, the window at the far end painted over. It might as well be the middle of the night. What if it wasn't a homeless young mother on the other side of the transom-topped door, but a drug-crazed kidnapper? If that was the case, then she was not only foolish but plumb crazy to do what she was about to do. She put her ear against the panel, heard nothing, then stepped back, took a deep breath and knocked with the end of the bat. If some wild-eyed, wild-haired psycho opened the door, she'd grab the child, kneecap the bad guy with the Louisville Slugger and take off running like a bat out of hell.

She stepped into the shadows and waited.

"Who's there?" A male voice, low and rough with a hint of cowboy drawl, came from behind the closed door.

"Lana Lord." Her hands were shaking, her knees wobbly, but her brothers had taught her the best defense was a good offense. "Who are you and what are you doing here?" she demanded.

The door opened and sunlight spilled out, framing the man standing before her. He wasn't particularly tall, an inch or so under six feet, but broad-shouldered and well-muscled. Strong enough to make short work of Lana and her baseball bat despite the tiny baby he held cradled against his chest with one long-fingered hand. But it was also obvious he wasn't a deranged kidnapper. He was wearing chinos and a blue dress shirt with the collar open and the sleeves rolled past his wrists. The baby was holding a handful of his shirtfront in his tiny fist. The cotton was damp, as though the baby had spit up on him and he'd tried to wipe away the stain.

"I wasn't imagining things. I did hear a baby crying."
Lana couldn't take her eyes off the infant. So tiny, so
fragile, especially in contrast to the hard wall of the man's
chest.

"That's all he seems to do. Cry."

"You're holding him wrong," Lana blurted.

"What are you, some kind of expert?" Dark brows
drew together over eyes whose color she couldn't quite
make out.

"In a way. I own the baby store downstairs. And I've
done a lot of baby-sitting in my day." In fact, she and
Beth had worked summers and weekends at a day-care
center all the way through college. Her hands itched to
reach out and touch the little one. "But that doesn't answer my question. Who are you and what are you doing
here?"

"My name's Dylan Van Zandt, and I own the building."

"You're Van Zandt Development Corporation?"

"In the flesh. Look. Thanks for checking up on us. It's
good to know I have such conscientious tenants. Now, if
you'll excuse me, I have to see to my son."

Lana usually spoke her mind, and this was no exception. "I think it's time you take your son home. Whatever
you're doing up here in the dust and dirt can wait until
tomorrow."

His frown deepened. "We are home."

"What?"

"You heard me. This is our home."

"But...here?" She couldn't quite see over his shoulder
into the room behind him. "No one told me—" She'd
been away from the store since Friday afternoon. She'd
spent the weekend at her brother Garrett's ranch and

hadn't returned to Austin until early that morning to collect her gifts for the birthday celebration.

"I haven't exactly had time to send out engraved announcements." The baby screamed. Dylan Van Zandt didn't budge, just stood there stiff and unmoving.

Lana leaned the baseball bat against the door frame, tucked the little flashlight into her pocket, and held out her arms. "Let me have him."

"What?"

"I said let me have him. He's probably afraid you're going to drop him." She wiggled her fingers. "Come here, sweetheart."

Still frowning, Dylan let her take the child. The infant was tiny, a newborn, light as a feather in her arms. *Where is his mother?* She wanted to ask but didn't. Instead she cuddled him against her breast, one hand under his bottom, one hand gently patting his back. He didn't stop crying. His legs were drawn stiffly up against his belly, his face screwed into a scowl that was a perfect match for his father's.

Dylan Van Zandt stood aside and let her precede him into the apartment. And it was a residence, not unused office space as the real estate agent had led her to believe. The ceilings were high, with ornate plaster cornices. A small marble fireplace graced one wall. Light streamed onto the hardwood floor, dulled by years of neglect, from long windows that looked onto Kings Avenue. The room was empty except for half a dozen cardboard packing boxes piled in the middle.

"This way." Dylan Van Zandt gestured toward another doorway. It led into the kitchen, Lana discovered. Green and white thirties-era linoleum covered the floor. Glass-fronted cupboards reached to the ceiling above a granite countertop. The refrigerator was so old it had a round compressor on the top, but it was humming away. The gas stove belonged in a museum. A brand-new microwave oven was on the counter, probably because the gas had been shut off up here years ago. She wondered if the water was also shut off. There was no way he could take care of a baby properly with no water and no heat or air-conditioning, although it was surprisingly cool in the big high-ceilinged rooms.

The kitchen was long and narrow. A small table and two chairs sat in one corner. An overstuffed recliner, a man's chair, held pride of place by the window. Beside it an end table held a lamp, a combination radio and CD player and long metal tubes that looked as if they contained blueprints or architect's drawings. The bathroom was directly ahead of her. She could see the corner of a claw-footed tub and a pedestal sink with a black leather shaving kit on the rim. The only baby items in view were a diaper bag and a glass bottle of formula with a screw-on nipple top like the ones they gave new mothers when they left the hospital. And a top-of-the-line infant carrier, draped with yellow and blue blankets.

"He doesn't like you holding him any better than he does me," Dylan said over his son's continuing screams. He was standing behind her, and she couldn't tell if she heard frustration or anger in his tone.

She turned. "He's colicky. Does he cry like this often?"

"I don't know."

"You don't know?"

"I...I haven't been around him that much. He's only been out of the hospital two weeks. He was a preemie. He weighed three and a half pounds when he was born."

Lana took a closer look at the baby. "How old is he now?"

"Ten weeks."

"He's so tiny." The sound of her voice penetrated the infant's self-absorbed misery. He opened cornflower blue eyes and stared at her for a long moment while Lana held her breath. He was the most beautiful baby she'd ever seen. Perfect little ears, creamy skin, a button nose and silky hair the color of winter sunshine.

He didn't look anything like the dark-haired, hawk-nosed man in front of her. Maybe he had kidnapped the child, after all.

"What do you do for colic?" Dylan was asking her.

"What?"

"How do I stop him from crying?"

"You really don't know anything about babies, do you?"

"No." There was no smile, no self-effacing shrug to soften the denial.

What if he was a kidnapper, after all? Maybe he was in the middle of a nasty custody battle with the child's mother. It happened. You read about it all the time. What had she gotten herself into? Lana looked at his hands. He was wearing a plain gold wedding band. He caught her looking at him. Followed the path of her gaze. Something of what she was thinking must have shown on her face.

"My mom's been taking care of him. She fell and fractured her ankle yesterday putting up curtains in the nursery. She had to have surgery on it. She's going to be laid up for at least six weeks."

"Where's the baby's mother? Where's your wife?" Lana asked, whispering to avoid upsetting the baby.

Dylan Van Zandt didn't meet her eyes. He looked past her at something or someone she couldn't see. His eyes were storm-cloud gray, she saw, bleak as the hill-country sky after a December rain. "She's dead," he said, not a trace of emotion evident in his words or his voice. "She died two months ago. Ten days after our son was born."

CHAPTER TWO

HE SHOULDN'T HAVE blurted it out that way. Her eyes were as big as saucers. Her grip on Greg tightened perceptibly. For a moment he thought she was going to turn and run, taking his son with her. He saw the thought flash behind her green-gold eyes, then vanish as quickly as it came.

"I'm sorry," she said. "I...I don't know what to say."

"There's nothing you can say." She had guts, he'd give her that. Climbing that dark stairway, confronting him with nothing but a baseball bat. He could have been some criminal. A kidnapper, a drug dealer—a wife killer.

"How did it happen?" she asked. The baby squirmed against her shoulder, as though trying to get closer. She laid her cheek against the top of his fuzzy head and swayed gently the way Dylan had seen his mother do. Greg quit squirming, and his cries trailed off to whimpers. When he didn't answer right away she said, "I'm sorry. I shouldn't be asking such a personal question."

Dylan raked a hand through his hair. "It's okay. It was a car accident. She was on her way to the hospital to visit Greg." *And to get away from me.* Best leave that thought unspoken. Technically he'd been miles away when the accident occurred, but in a way he had killed Jessie, with his accusations and his lack of trust.

"How terrible." The baby stiffened and began to howl again. "Poor little tyke."

"Is he hungry? Would a bottle help?" He had no idea what it was the scrap of humanity he called his son wanted.

She shook her head, moved to the table and set Greg in his carrier. She took one little foot in each hand and stretched his legs out, then pushed them back against his body. She kept doing that, stretching and bending, and after a minute or so his son quit crying. He gave a hiccuping burp, answered with the same sound from his diapered end. A blissful look came over his pinched features. "Now you feel better, don't you, little one." She held out her hand, and Greg grabbed on to her finger as though he'd never let go. "Got rid of all that nasty gas. Yes, that's better. I'll bet you're hungry, too, aren't you, Greggy?" She looked at Dylan and almost smiled. "You did call him Greg, didn't you?"

"Yes. He's named for his uncle. My best friend. I…I have a bottle all ready to go." Dylan rushed to the fridge, afraid if he hesitated Greg would start crying again. He put the small bottle of special formula in the microwave, remembering to take the nipple off. He hadn't last night, and it had melted enough to clog the hole. Greg hadn't been able to get anything to eat, and he'd worked himself into a frenzy before Dylan figured out what was wrong and got a new nipple. "It'll be ready in a minute. He eats every two hours, around the clock. If he's not screaming to beat the band, that is."

"Such a little tummy," Lana crooned, tickling his son there. Her hair, the color of cinnamon and nutmeg, brushed against her cheek, soft and shining. He liked the way she wore it smooth and simply cut. Her makeup was simple, too, lipstick and a little mascara, not much more. Her skin was peaches and cream, she had a nice body. He wouldn't have been a man if he hadn't noticed that right off. Her breasts pushed against the silky apple-green blouse she wore. Her waist was small, her hips rounded. Her voice softened, the crisp boarding-school accent she'd used before melting away into the softened vowels and dropped gs of a native Texan. "It has to be filled so you get big and strong. Then your daddy will start callin' you Bubba and hopin' for football scholarships to come wingin' your way."

Dylan set his jaw. That's exactly what he had fantasized when Jessie first told him she was pregnant, back when he had no doubts at all that Greg was his child. But no more. Now it was hard for him to say the words *my son.* He thrust the bottle at her. "Here's his formula."

"Don't you want to feed him?"

"Do you want him to start crying again?"

If she was startled by the harshness in his voice, she didn't show it. "You really are new at this, aren't you?"

"I've never had anything to do with a baby this small. I've got two nieces and two nephews, but they were big strapping Bubba babies." He tried for a smile and hoped he got it on straight.

"This one's no different." She took the bottle, then set it on the table. She picked Greg up and handed him over. "Here, take him. Show me your stuff."

"What?"

"Show me how you feed him."

"I…" What the hell did she think she was doing? She had no business ordering him around like this. He was about to tell her so when he thought better of it. Greg was his sole responsibility, at least until his mom was up and around again. He set his jaw and did as she demanded, feeling big and clumsy and self-conscious. Greg stiffened as soon as Dylan touched him. His eyes snapped shut, and

his face puckered into a scowl. "He's going to start crying
again."

Lana sighed. "Here, let me show you. Like this.
Loosen up." She touched his arm lightly. He felt the
warmth of her fingers through the sleeve of his shirt, felt
the connection all the way to the marrow of his bones.

"I'll drop him." She didn't seem to be affected by the
contact.

"No, you won't. Just pretend he's a football and you're
a running back."

Automatically he shifted Greg lower into the crook of
his arm, curled his hand around his bottom, cradled his
head. Lana laughed, a bright melodious sound that
warmed his soul the way her touch had warmed his skin.
Jessie had never laughed like that, at least not for a long,
long time. "That's better. I was right. You were a running
back, weren't you?"

He grinned. He couldn't help himself. "A real hotshot
on my high school team, but never better than second
string in college."

Greg started sucking on his fist. "He's hungry. What
football metaphor can you come up with to help me out
there?"

"Don't try and get the whole ten yards in one carry."
She handed him the bottle.

"What do you mean by that?"

She smiled again. "Don't let him drink too fast. And
bubble him when the bottle's half empty, whether he
wants to stop sucking or not."

"You are good at this," he said, relaxing a little. "How
about giving me a few more lessons?" It was the depth
of his need to get a handle on this baby-raising that
prompted him to make such an outrageous request.

"I..."

"I'll pay you."

"Certainly not."

He wished he'd kept his damned mouth shut. She was a businesswoman and a Lord. He hadn't been in Austin long, but he knew the Lord name was a respected one. She was way, way out of his league, and here he was offering to pay her for parenting lessons. For being a god-damn nanny. "Sorry, that was out of line."

"It's not that." She looked at Greg, and he saw her mouth tighten slightly. "I don't have time. I'm late now for a party. My godmother's grandson…it's his first birth-day. I can't miss it. And then there's my business…."

"Just the basics," he said, determined that she not walk out of his life as quickly as she had barged into it. "Just until I can get my feet under me."

"They have excellent parenting classes at Maitland Maternity. Or you could make arrangements to leave Greg at the day-care center there. They accept infants. My friend Beth Maitland—Beth Redstone, I should say—runs it. The care's excellent."

She was babbling. He'd only known her for a few minutes but he'd bet his last cent, and he didn't have much more to bet, that it wasn't like her. She was en-tranced by Greg, he could tell. She wanted to say yes. He decided not to try to charm her. Hell, he wasn't that good with women anyway, never had been. He settled on the truth. "I can't afford full-time day care. Every cent I have's tied up in buying and renovating this building."

"Oh. Then a nanny?" She bit her lip. "No. I suppose that would be even more expensive."

"And what woman in her right mind would want to be here all day?"

"Then it's certainly no place for a baby."

She had a damned good point and he knew it, but he

was between a big rock and a hard place. Not only did he have everything he owned tied up in this place, but he had a big chunk of his parents' money in it, as well. "We're staying here, Miz Lord. For the time being we have nowhere else to go. Look, I'm sorry I asked. You've been a big help. Greg and I will muddle through. Go back to what you were doing. And thanks again." He motioned with his head for her to precede him out of the kitchen. Greg sensed his agitation and began to fuss, pushing the bottle out of his mouth with surprising force. Two seconds later he was crying again.

All the starch seemed to go out of Lana Lord. "See, you're upsetting him because you're upset. You win, Dylan Van Zandt. I'll help you with Greg until you can get the hang of it and get this place fit to raise a baby in."

SHE SHOULD HAVE KNOWN Michael and Garrett would have conniptions when she told them what she'd agreed to do for Dylan Van Zandt. Not even being in the middle of little Chase's birthday party with a hundred people standing around watching them had made a difference. She should have kept her mouth shut until they were all four alone. Michael had backed her into a corner and refused to let her go until she'd told them all the details. When she described going up the staircase armed only with a baseball bat, she thought her brother the security expert was going to have a stroke.

Michael lectured her on the stupidity of that kind of stunt, and Garrett lectured her on her lack of even a modicum of common sense for a good ten minutes, until she had all she could take and told them both to knock it off. If she wanted to help Dylan Van Zandt with his son she would, no matter what her siblings thought of the idea.

Shelby, bless her heart, had been all for it. She thought

it was time for Lana to meet someone new. Garrett had said very little after that, but the set look on his darkly tanned face left no doubt in his sister's mind that if there was anything even slightly out of place in Dylan's life, her brother would make the other man wish he'd never laid eyes on one of the Austin Lords.

Family. She loved her siblings dearly but she could make her own decisions and trust her own instincts. Lana leaned against the headrest and drummed her fingers on the steering wheel. It was hot and humid, and thunderclouds were building up over the hills west of town. If traffic didn't start moving soon, her air-conditioning would give up the ghost. She should have had the car serviced weeks ago, but she'd been too busy.

And if she was busy then, she was going to be even busier in the future.

What had she agreed to? Parenting lessons? What did that entail? Baby-sitting? Probably. She could hardly leave Dylan's son alone up there in the dust and dirt and mouse droppings. No, she'd have to keep him with her during the day. The thought made her heart skip a beat. A baby, one that she could care for as if it were her own.

She sobered at that. Greg wasn't her baby. And she had better keep that foremost in her mind.

There was a parking space in front of Oh, Baby!, and since it was Sunday evening she took it. Mostly she parked around the corner on a little side street to leave room for customers' cars. She sat still for a moment looking at her building, seeing it with different eyes. It was made of brick, old and mellowed. The windows were tall and well-proportioned on the second floor, square and functional on the third. The four stores on the ground floor all had bay windows and oval glass in the doors. She loved the small-town feel of the neighborhood. It looked like Main Street somewhere in the Midwest, not just a few blocks off the main drag in Austin, Texas.

When she'd first opened her store, there had been a little flower shop between the bakery and the vintage clothing store. Along with a New Age bookshop, they made up the other tenants, but the flower shop had gone out of business long since. She hadn't thought about it in years. There had been a curving marble stairway leading nowhere that the owner had used to display floral arrangements and garden ornaments, she recalled. And once she'd glimpsed an old-fashioned metal-gated elevator through an open curtain behind the counter. She hadn't made the connection then—that the space behind the grandiose wooden doors had once been the lobby of an apartment building—but now she did.

And soon it would be again.

That meant people moving into the neighborhood, stabilizing it even more. She liked the idea. Young couples ready to start their families, all of them buying furniture and strollers and bottle sets and rocking horses. She liked that very much.

Lana was smiling when she arrived at Dylan's door at the top of the stairs. It was open a few inches, as though he was expecting her. She pushed it wider and called softly, in case Greg was asleep. No answer. She walked into the empty main room of the apartment, taking a moment to look around. An archway she hadn't noticed on her first visit opened into a hallway that must lead to the bedrooms. She wondered if there were two or three.

It would be nice to be living here, so close to her work, without that long commute and the upkeep on her parents' huge old house. But her parents had loved that house. They'd lived there all their married life. And if she moved in here, the apartment wouldn't be occupied by a potential customer.

Lana walked to the kitchen doorway. "Hello," she said softly.

Dylan didn't answer because he was sleeping as soundly as the baby in the carrier beside him on the table. His elbows were propped on the blueprints of the building, his dark head resting on his hands, a pair of reading glasses dangling from his fingers. Lana hesitated, undecided whether to wake him or to leave as quietly as she'd come.

Greg stirred and sniffled and made adorable baby sounds, and Lana didn't leave. A moment later Dylan opened his eyes, blinked just like his son and focused on her. "You came back," he said.

"I told you I would." She'd explained about the party, that she had to be there. But she wasn't sure he'd believed her when she said she'd come back. "How did it go?" she asked. His beard had darkened, she noticed, and he looked dead tired, despite his nap.

"Okay. I fed him again. Didn't try for a touchdown in one run. Got him to burp like you told me. He fell asleep, and I guess I did, too. Damn, I had a lot of work I wanted to get done." He stood and began rolling up the blueprints.

"Are those the plans for the renovation you spoke of?" Lana asked. She felt awkward standing in the doorway. She felt awkward around him, period. She'd been with Jason Fairmont almost two years, and she hadn't even thought of dating since they'd broken up. But Dylan Van Zandt was a very attractive man, the kind no sane woman could be indifferent to.

"Yes." The frown between his dark brows smoothed out a little. "Would you like to see them?"

"Yes, I would."

He unrolled the blueprints, slipping one edge under Greg's carrier and holding the other flat with the palm of his hand. "There are four apartments on this floor, corresponding to the storefronts below us. They all have two bedrooms, three if you count the maid's room, here." He pointed to a small room at the very back of the apartment layout. "I'm planning to turn those into a bathroom and walk-in closet for the master suite." He circled the area on the drawing with his finger. "Updating the kitchens and bathrooms will be the biggest expense. Have to bring the heating plant and the electrical circuits up to code, too. And the elevator to comply with the disability laws. That could cost me a pretty penny to renovate."

"Do all the apartments have fireplaces? And those beautiful high ceilings?"

"Yes, ma'am. But the fireplaces will have gas logs. They make ones so real-looking you can hardly tell the difference."

"What about the third floor?"

"I figure two big loft apartments. I'm hoping this area of the city will start attracting artsy-craftsy types. It's close enough to the university that that's not too big a stretch."

"And all those Generation Xers who work downtown and at the Statehouse are going to start wanting places where they can spread out a bit, raise a family and still not have the commute they'd get if they moved to the suburbs."

"Exactly what I told my dad when I talked him into putting a chunk of his retirement money into this place." He looked at her and nodded approvingly. Lana felt herself color slightly. She hadn't meant to speak her thoughts aloud. She felt disloyal again, the way she had earlier when she'd been thinking about her birth mother. Her parents had loved their big Tudor in its old established neighborhood with gated driveways and enormous live oaks dotting the lawn. She loved it, too. But it was so much house for a single young woman. And it was a forty-minute drive into the city—on a good day.

"I hope it works out for you."

Greg began to snuffle into his fist.

"Time to eat again." Dylan touched his big blunt finger to the baby's cheek, but the movement seemed forced and wooden to Lana. "Every two hours. Just like clockwork. It's gonna be a long night and an early morning tomorrow, buddy. No sleeping in."

"You're starting the renovations tomorrow?"

He nodded. "Time's money in this business. The electrical contractor'll be here at seven, the plumber at noon."

"That's a lot of noise and confusion for a baby. And what about the paint?"

"Paint? We're a long way from paint."

"No, I mean the old paint. You'll be banging around, knocking it off the walls and woodwork. It looks really old. It's got lead in it, I'll bet. You can't have Greg here, if that's the case."

"Hell, I hadn't thought of that."

"You said you had nieces and nephews. That means you must have siblings. Couldn't one of them watch over Greg for a few days?"

"My brother and his wife are in New Jersey, and my sister's husband's in the military. They're in Germany for the next eighteen months. My dad's got his hands full taking care of Mom."

"Then you'll both have to come home with me."

He spun around. "We can't do that."

Lana had the feeling that her brothers' reactions would

echo Dylan's. They were leery enough of her giving parenting lessons to a complete stranger. When they found out she was inviting him to live under her roof, there would be hell to pay. She almost smiled but didn't, because for some reason her heart was beating so high up in her chest it made her short of breath. "Yes, you can. You want me to give you parenting lessons. Okay, you've got me. But not if I have to worry about Greg being exposed to God knows what up here. Come home with me, or the deal's off."

CHAPTER THREE

"HE'S JUST THE CUTEST little thing." Brittany Carson warbled the words and blew bubbles on Greg's tummy as he cooed and gurgled in his carrier on the counter of the showroom at Oh, Baby! "I could just eat him up."

"It looks like that's what you're doing," Janette Malkovitch, Lana's manager, said. "He's not candy, you know."

"He's better than candy. He's precious, aren't you, sweetums." Greg cooed louder. "He likes me best," Brittany said. In just three days' time he'd become a much happier baby. Lana couldn't help wondering if it was because he spent so little time in his father's company. In the few days Dylan had been living under her roof he'd tried hard, but his heart wasn't in it. He treated Greg like a half-tame baby animal, kept him clean and fed and his diaper changed, but never once had Lana seen him pick his son up just to cuddle and coo over him as Brittany and Janette were doing.

"You have work to do." There was a sharp note in Janette's voice that wasn't lost on Lana. She glanced around the display area. It looked fine. Brittany was a conscientious and focused kid, even if she did have five earrings in each ear and her navel pierced, which fortunately didn't show in the clothes she wore to work. Nor did the two tattoos she'd gotten over the summer.

"Oh, lighten up, Janette," Brittany countered. "We've

sold two of those really expensive solid cherry furniture suites since he's been here. I mean, when customers come in and see him lying in the bed or swinging in his swing, they can't help themselves. They buy the works, even if they just came in to window-shop. I think we should consider keeping a baby here all the time.''

Janette was divorced with three kids and an ex-husband who was six months behind on child support. She was slightly more immune to Greg's charm than Brittany, but only slightly. ''Honey, if you're that susceptible to a man's come-on already, you're in for a lot of heartbreak.'' But she was grinning when she said it, and she bent to give Greg a kiss. ''Men are all alike. They smile and look deep into your eyes and let you think you're their moon and stars. When all they really want is for you to fill their stomach or warm their beds, preferably both.'' Janette ran the tip of her finger along the satiny curve of Greg's cheek. ''Are you hungry, little man? Hmm, I bet you are.''

''He *is* due for a feeding. I'll warm his bottle.'' Brittany looked up as a very pregnant young woman entered the store. It was her responsibility to greet customers. ''Sorry, little guy. You'll have to wait,'' she whispered, moving away from the carrier.

''You go get Greg's bottle ready,'' Lana said, raising a hand to wave Brittany back. ''I'll wait on her.''

''Thanks.'' Brittany picked up Greg's carrier and disappeared into the back room to heat his bottle.

Janette made a clucking noise with her tongue. ''You're spoilin' that girl as bad as this baby.''

''I look at it as an advanced course in domestic studies. When I was her age we had to carry around a ten-pound sack of flour with a beeper attached to it for two weeks. It's not nearly as much fun as practicing on a real baby.''

Lana put down the Beatrix Potter catalog she'd been perusing and smiled at the young woman standing uncertainly just inside the door. "May I help you?"

"Hi. I was told you have car seats...used car seats. The social worker at Maitland Maternity sent me here. My baby's due any day and I won't be able to leave the hospital without one." The young woman was dressed simply in cotton slacks and an oversize T-shirt that strained across her bulging middle. She wasn't wearing a wedding ring, and her face looked haggard and too careworn for someone her age. Another of the single mothers-to-be from a nearby women's shelter who received free prenatal care at Maitland Maternity, Lana guessed. Sent to take advantage of the gently used car seats she collected from customers and friends, and friends of friends.

"Right over here," she said, leading the way to the corner of the store where she kept several of the seats on display with a sign inviting customers to donate their car seats when they were no longer of use. "Choose the one that will suit you best."

"I...I don't have much money," the young woman said.

"That's okay. The cost is whatever you can pay."

"Really?" Her face lit up. "That's great. I...I was really worried about getting a good one. I only have a few bucks..."

"Whatever you can afford," Lana repeated gently. "I think you'd like this one." She picked up a car seat that doubled as a carrier. "This will do wonderfully until the baby's about six months old."

The young mother's face fell again. "But...they told me my baby will need to be in a car seat until—"

"When he outgrows this one, you come back and trade

up to a full-size model," Lana said, giving her best imitation of a used-car salesman. "No extra charge."

"Great! I'll take it."

"Fine, here it is. Janette will show you everything you need to know about fastening your baby in safe and snug."

"Thank you. This is a load off my mind." She followed Lana to the counter.

"You really should let me publicize this little program of yours. I could do a lot more for you if you'd let the PR people at the clinic run with it."

Lana turned to find the regal figure of her godmother, Megan Maitland, standing beside a mahogany reproduction of Prince William's cradle.

"Aunt Megan." Her mother's longtime friend had suggested long ago that the Lord siblings call her that, and Lana still did. "What are you doing here in the middle of the day? I thought you were going to take some time off to spend with Connor and Lacy and little Chase." Megan had recently been reunited with Connor, the grown son she had been told had died at birth.

"I'm on my way home now, but there's something I need to talk to you about." Megan motioned toward the back of the store. "Can we use your office?"

"Brittany's back there feeding Greg. Remember I told you at the party I was giving baby basics lessons to…my new landlord."

"That includes keeping his child here in the store?" Megan looked around.

"It does for the time being. As a matter of fact, he's staying at the house." Megan looked surprised. Lana pointed to the ceiling. "Lead paint. It's not safe for the baby. They're staying in the maid's room."

"Do your brothers know this?"

Lana laughed, but it sounded thin and nervous even to her own ears. "Well, no. And I'd appreciate it if you didn't tell them just yet. Or Shelby, for that matter."

"Certainly, if that's what you want."

Lana was surprised Megan didn't pursue the subject. She seemed distracted, and Lana wondered what she was doing here at this time of day. It must be important. "Come over here. We can be private enough."

Lana led the way to an alcove filled with framed prints and quilts and Noah's ark figures displayed in an antique cupboard. Once they stepped inside they were out of sight of Janette and her customer. "Now, what's up?"

Megan didn't return her smile. "I'd like you to come out to the house tonight."

"You know I never turn down an invitation for dinner with you."

"This isn't just a dinner invitation, dear. I received something in the mail yesterday that concerns you. All of you."

Lana began rearranging the Noah's ark figures on the piecrust table in front of her. Something in her god-mother's voice set off an internal alarm. She flicked the switch on a music box and watched the little animals move around the ark, two by two, as it played Brahms's "Lullaby." Her hands were trembling. Only one person in the world would try to contact all four of them through Megan Maitland. "It's from our mother, isn't it?"

"Yes, apparently it is."

Lana couldn't quite trust herself to speak. After twenty-five years of silence, her mother had apparently just dropped back into her life—into their lives. "Apparently? You mean there's no name on...the letter? Is it a letter? Did she give you a phone number, an e-mail address?"

Megan squeezed Lana's hand. "There was a note and

a box of baby things. The note was just like the first one, Lana. The one that was pinned to Garrett's shirt all those years ago. No return address. No signature. Nothing to identify who wrote it. For some reason, even after all these years, your mother doesn't want you to know who she is.''

"VAN ZANDT DEVELOPMENT." Dylan tucked the cell phone between his ear and his shoulder and went on looking at the schematic for the updated wiring he'd have to install to bring the building up to code.

"Dill Pickle? Is that you?"

"Mom?"

She giggled at his shocked tone. "Oh, dear, did I say that out loud?"

"Yes, you did," he said, turning his back on the drawing, giving his mother his full attention. "You haven't called me that since I was two."

"It must be these painkillers. I swear my head feels two feet across. I had to dial you three times to get the call to go through."

"How are you feeling otherwise?"

"I want out of this bed and this horrible contraption. I can't even get up to go to the bathroom. How could I have been so foolish? I only fell two feet from the second step of the ladder." In his mind's eye he could see her shaking her head, her curly brown hair barely streaked with gray. "I really, really do have to lose some weight. The doctors have all been very nice, but I know that's what they're thinking. 'If you weren't so heavy, Mrs. Van Zandt, the injury to your ankle wouldn't have been so severe.'"

"Mom, you're not fat." But she wasn't skinny, either. He couldn't remember her as anything but pleasingly plump. His parents were both nearing sixty, active and healthy except for his dad's high blood pressure and now his mom's broken ankle. Nevertheless, they were looking forward to turning over the business to him in a few years and retiring. That's why he had to make this project work. They'd put a big chunk of their savings into it and let him take out a loan against the company assets.

"I'm not skinny, either. And I'm bored witless already, as you can tell. How's Greg? How are you two doing? Should I send your father up there to help out?"

"We're doing fine, Mom. And Dad needs to stay there with you and the office. The bids for the new gymnasium at the high school are coming up next week. We've got a good chance at getting the job."

"I know, I know. But there are other things just as important as the school bid. Like my little Greggy. Are you sure he's okay?"

She was beginning to sound tired, her words slurring now and then, but Dylan knew better than to try to cut the conversation short. Even half zonked on painkillers, his mother wouldn't stand for that. She sensed how conflicted he was about his son. She had accepted the little guy wholeheartedly, but Dylan wasn't fooled. His mother could count. She and his dad had to be aware that Greg could have been conceived during the time Jessie had lived apart from him. But it made no difference to Linda Van Zandt. Greg was her grandchild, just as his sister Christy's and his brother Trent's kids were. "He's fine. I...I've got someone to help with him."

"Who's that?" His mother's voice was razor sharp again, just like her wits.

"Her name's Lana Lord. She's the tenant in the store below my apartment. The store called Oh, Baby!"

"I've heard that name."

"It was on the architect's drawing of the new facade, remember?"

"Oh, yes, a baby store. I read an article about one of them in the business section of the *Statesman* once. Supposed to be a real growth industry. Lots of waited-till-it-was-almost-too-late professionals having babies and spoiling them rotten. Did I tell you about it? They have more hair than sense and buy whole new sets of furniture for every baby they have. Thousands of dollars worth. Then they just pitch it and start over." She sounded shocked by the waste. "Why, I still have Grandma Parsons' high chair and crib. It was good enough for me and Billy Joe and Gracie and the three of you. It's good enough for Greg when I get it painted, and someday it will—"

"Mom, do you want to hear about Lana Lord or not?"

"Of course I do. It's the medicine. I just run on and on."

"You always run on and on, Mom."

She laughed. "Okay. Tell me about this woman who's taking care of my Greggy."

"She heard him crying the first night and came upstairs. She's keeping him with her in her store during the day. I've got him with me at night...at her house." He didn't have to tell her that. She wouldn't know where he was if she called on the cell phone. But if she did find out, there'd be hell to pay.

"Her house? You're living with this woman you only met three days ago?"

"We're staying in the maid's room. The house is huge. A big old Tudor monstrosity, cold and damp as the dickens."

"I see. Then she must be one of *the* Austin Lords."

"She is." Dylan didn't elaborate, although his mother's silence told him she wanted more details.

"Well," she said after a silence. "I'm glad Greg's out of that musty old apartment. I mean, the paint has to be lead-based—"

Was he the only adult in Texas who hadn't thought about lead paint on the walls? He cut her short. He could hear someone coming up the steps from Lana's store. Only she had the key. He glanced at his watch and frowned. It wasn't five-thirty yet. Something must be up with Greg. Another bellyache? Diarrhea? "I'll call you back, Mom. Someone's here."

"Okay." There were voices in the background. "My roommate's getting visitors, and this call is probably costing me a fortune. I'm sure the hospital doesn't have a five-cents-a-minute plan. Dylan, you'll give me your number at this woman's house, won't you? I don't like being out of touch."

"You can always reach me at this number. But I'll call you as soon as I get hold of the new one. I'll let you talk to Greg, how's that sound?" he asked, half teasing.

"Wonderful. I miss him so much."

"I know you do, Mom. We'll be out to see you this weekend. I promise."

"Good. Take care of that precious little boy of ours."

"I will, Mom."

He broke off the connection and turned. Lana was standing in the doorway of his apartment, the living room of which was now doubling as his field office. "Hi," she said.

She was holding Greg against her shoulder, against her heart. She was patting his back gently, absently, as though it were the most natural rhythm in the world. He couldn't feel that way when he held the child. He wondered if he ever would. Physically, he was more comfortable with him in his arms, but there was no personal feeling there, no warmth, no connection.

"You were on the phone. I hope we didn't interrupt you."

"No," he said. "I was talking to my mom."

"How is she?" She continued patting Greg's back as she moved around the room, stopping to look at the architect's rendering of the facade of the building where it was taped to the wall between the big front windows.

"Pretty spaced out on painkillers. She was worried about Greg. I told her we were staying with you. I promised to give her your phone number. I hope that's okay." It still felt strange to him to be in her home, even though the place was so big he never saw her unless she came into the kitchen while he was getting ready to feed Greg.

"Of course it's okay. There used to be a separate line running into the maid's room. We can have it turned back on. I'll call the phone company today."

"You don't have to do that."

"I'll be sure to send you the bill." She smiled. He didn't like being in her debt, and she knew it.

"Thank you." He didn't smile back. He couldn't. He never knew what to do, how to react to her teasing. Jessie had never teased him. But then their marriage had been based on her needs and his promise to his dying buddy to take care of his wayward sister. Love hadn't been part of the equation.

"How did it go with the electrical inspector today?" she asked as she wandered over to look out the window at the street below. It was a humid and rainy afternoon. Business was probably slow. Maybe that's why she had brought Greg upstairs in the middle of the afternoon.

"About like I expected. This place is a mess. A lot of

the wiring up here is original. Scary as hell when you look at it.''

She turned, alarm on her face. ''But downstairs—''

''It was rewired about ten years ago. Or at least that's what I've been told.'' He didn't want to worry her, but there were some areas on the ground floor that had been missed or skipped to save money. That wiring would have to be replaced, too. Another twenty thousand dollars he hadn't been counting on.

''We have trouble with the computers sometimes when the air-conditioning is going full blast.''

''I'll look into it.''

''Thanks.''

She didn't make any move to leave or to hand over Greg. Dylan weighed the prospect of asking her out to dinner. He owed her a lot for bailing him out of a tight spot. But it would have to be someplace quick and casual. There was no one else to leave the baby with, unless he got the salesgirl—what was her name, Brittany?—to baby-sit. His mom would have a fit at that. He barely knew the girl.

But if Lana didn't think her employee was competent enough to watch his son, she'd say so. He'd learned that much about her already. She spoke her mind and was confident in her opinions.

She stood there rocking, humming snatches of a lullaby under her breath. Her eyes were closed, her lashes dark against her cheeks. She looked tired. That made up his mind. Taking care of his son on top of running her business and overseeing that big house with only a once-a-week cleaning service and part-time gardener must be taking their toll. Besides, he liked the idea of sitting down to a meal with her, not bringing home take-out to wolf down at the kitchen island with only Greg in his carrier beside him for company.

"Lana."

"Yes." She opened her eyes. They were hazel, he'd noticed more than once. Sometimes more green than gold, sometimes darkening almost to brown. When she was angry or upset they got that way. Lightning in river water, he thought. Like now. She was frowning, too.

"I'd like to buy you something to eat tonight. A little thank-you for all you've done for us this week."

"I can't." Her frown deepened. She must have tightened her hold on Greg, because he began to fuss a little. She shushed him, settling him more comfortably on her shoulder. "I'm sorry. I shouldn't have been so abrupt. It's—"

"No apology necessary." The words sounded perfunctory, and he regretted not being able to keep his chagrin hidden. Fine. She didn't want to go out with him. That was all there was to it. She probably had a date and was trying to figure out how to tell the date she had Dylan and Greg living in her house. He'd never thought of that when he'd taken her up on the offer. On top of everything else he was complicating the hell out of her love life. "Look, if you need to be alone tonight, I'll take Greg to the mall or something."

"No. It isn't that. I mean, if you're asking me do I have a date, the answer is no. But I do have plans." Dylan braced himself and didn't know why. Possibly because he could see the agitation swirling in the depths of those green and gold eyes. Something had upset her. She brushed her lips across Greg's hair, then took a little breath as though she wanted to get it all out in one string of words. "I'm meeting my sister and brothers at my aunt Megan's. We were left on the doorstep at Maitland Maternity twenty-five years ago. Abandoned by a mother we never knew. We haven't heard a word from her since then.'' She shook her head as though she couldn't quite come to terms with what she was about to say. ''Until today.''

CHAPTER FOUR

CHAPTER FOUR

FOR THE FIRST TIME in her life Lana was uncomfortable in Megan's house. It felt alien to her, not the gracious, elegant home-away-from-home it had been for as long as she could remember. She had spent as much time growing up here as she had in her parents' house. She had played with Ellie and Beth, Megan's twin daughters, shared secrets with them, called boys on the phone with them. They had all swum in the pool and played in the yard, a tribe of healthy youngsters watched over by doting parents. Her memories of this place were all good ones.

But tonight it felt different because she was different. She was no longer Lana Megan Lord, beloved daughter of Terrence and Sheila. She was nobody. Alone and unloved. It was as if memories of heartache and loss she'd never known she had suddenly forced themselves into the forefront of her mind. She clutched the little pink sweater Megan had given her tightly between her hands, staring at her name embroidered in crooked letters with darker pink floss. Embroidered by a ghost from the past, a woman of whom she had no conscious memory at all. Her mother.

She looked up. Shelby sat across from her on a matching sofa. They were in Megan's private study, the place they always gathered when they were visiting her. It was a big, cozy room, filled with soft leather furniture and shelves of books and family photos, and almost always friends and members of Megan's large family. But tonight the five of them were alone.

"She says this was the only fancywork she ever had time to do." Shelby quoted from the note Megan had read them as she distributed the gifts. It had been handwritten, short and unsigned. "That sounds so sad."

"I can't imagine ever being this small." Michael had placed the tiny blue sweater bearing his name on a table, as though distancing himself from the woman who had given it to him, embroidered it so lovingly and then walked out of his life. "At least we know now the names pinned to our shirts really were the ones she gave us."

When they were small, the triplets had sometimes climbed into the branches of the live oak tree in the back yard and wondered aloud who they might be. Garrett, older by two years, had scoffed at them. He remembered their names, he'd insisted when they picked others they liked better. He'd told Megan so from the very first day.

But one day when the three of them were ten and Garrett was twelve, they'd quit asking him about memories of their real mother. That was the day he and Michael had gotten into a fight over Garrett's insistence that he could remember nothing about her anymore. And if he did he wasn't going to tell Michael, or Shelby and Lana, either. She had thrown them all away, he'd said. Just like they were toys she didn't want. If she didn't want them, then he didn't want to remember her. That had been the last time he'd spoken of her to Lana. And not long after that Lana had made the same promise to herself.

"Why do you think she sent these things to us now?" Shelby asked, her eyes sparkling with emotion. "Why, after all these years without a word?"

"Who knows." Michael moved restlessly around the room, his hands shoved in the pockets of his pants. The physical resemblance between Shelby and Michael was marked. The same with Garrett. They all had tanned skin and dark auburn hair and strongly marked lashes and eyebrows that had somehow become muted to cinnamon and cream when they got to Lana.

"What if she's in need? I mean, if she never had time for a hobby then maybe she still hasn't got enough money—"

"You can't go by that, Shelby. You can't make any kinds of assumptions from that note. We may be dealing with a real nut case here."

"Mike. You're talking about our mother."

"She's not my mother. My mother was Sheila Lord. I don't intend to go looking for some stranger to replace her." Michael had taken their mother's death hard. Their father had been sick for several months before his death. But Sheila had only complained of a headache, of needing to lie down for a few minutes. She'd died of a massive stroke only an hour later. Some days it was hard for Lana to believe she was gone, even though it had been almost three years.

Shelby winced at the vehemence in their brother's tone. Some of the excitement faded from her eyes. "I...I thought you might want to help me find her."

"Find her? What in hell for?"

"She said she loved us," Shelby whispered. She turned to Lana. "What do you think, Lana? Shouldn't we look for her?"

Lana glanced helplessly at Megan. The older woman smiled her understanding and encouragement. She knew how much Lana still missed her mother. "No," Lana said, placing her little pink sweater on top of Michael's blue one. "I'm with Mike. Let her come to us. She obviously knows who we are, how to find us if she wants to. I won't go looking for her.''

"I'll help you, Shel.'' Garrett was standing with one shoulder propped against the fern-filled marble fireplace. He looked at the scruffy, bedraggled teddy bear that had been his gift from the past. If he remembered playing with it as a toddler, he gave no evidence of it.

"Oh, Garrett, will you?'' Shelby's smile returned, brighter than before.

"It would be easier if you helped us, Mike.'' The words seemed pulled from somewhere deep inside him. Garrett didn't ask favors easily, even from those closest to him.

But Michael was adamant. He was perhaps the most stubborn of them all. "No, bro, not this time. I have absolutely no interest in the woman who didn't care enough about any of us to try and keep us together as a family.''

"But, Mike.'' Shelby tried again. "You don't know that. She left us for Aunt Megan—''

"Yeah, I know she could have turned us over to the welfare people to get sucked into the system, but she couldn't have known we'd stay together. It's only because Aunt Megan knew how much Mom and Dad wanted a family. We were damned lucky, that's all. She doesn't deserve any credit for that.'' He picked up his sweater and Lana's and went to put them in the plain cardboard box in which they'd come. "I don't want anything to do with her.''

"Please, Michael. Don't throw it away,'' Shelby begged. "Lana, you, too.''

He turned to her, the little pink sweater still in his hands. "I wasn't going to throw them away. I'm just not interested in looking at them anymore.''

"Me, too, Shel, honey. I…I just don't want to take it home with me,'' Lana said uncertainly. She'd been on her own for half a dozen years. She was able to take care of herself, but these relics of their past had hit her hard.

Michael handed the box with the three little sweaters to Shelby. "Don't get in a huff, sis," he said with that devastating smile of his that lifted one corner of his mouth higher than the other.

"I'll take yours for safekeeping. I'll take the teddy bear, too, Garrett, if you don't want it." Shelby held out her hand. "You can come and get them whenever you want."

Garrett handed the bear over. "I don't need anything to remind me that I was left on the doorstep of a public building without even a blanket to cover me."

"It was quite warm the day you came to me, Garrett," Megan said. "I remember very clearly. There was absolutely no question of you suffering from the cold." There was a slight note of reproof in her low, cultured voice as she stood and walked from behind the big mahogany desk where she'd been sitting.

"There's always something inside you that's cold when you don't know who you are or where you come from."

Shelby and Lana exchanged looks. They had never heard their brother speak like that before. "I'm going to start looking for her first thing tomorrow," Garrett said. "I could use your help, Mike. But if you don't want anything to do with it, I'll go it alone."

"Like I said—deal me out."

"I'll help you, Gar." There was a note of defiance in Shelby's voice.

"Thanks, sis."

"I've got to be going," Michael announced. "Thanks for everything, Aunt Megan. Shelby, are you ready to leave?" Michael had picked Shelby up at Austin Eats when he left Maitland Maternity. He'd offered to drive Lana, too, but it was more convenient for her to take her own car. And besides, she'd been too upset to deal with introducing her brother to Dylan and Greg. And then having to explain their new living arrangements. Time enough for that when the shock of their mother's gifts had worn off.

"I'll drop Shel off at her place on my way to the ranch. It's not out of the way. We've got some stuff to talk about," Garrett said. "Lana, do you want us to follow you home?"

Garrett didn't ask her again if she wanted to help in the search, and she was grateful. She wanted it all to go away. She wanted everything to be the same as it had been that morning, before Megan stopped by the store. But it was different. And for more reasons than because of these tokens from the unknown past.

She thought of the man and baby waiting for her at home. "No, Gar, thanks anyway. I'll be fine. You'll be going out of your way to follow me and you know it."

"Then we'll all be going." Garrett allowed Megan to give him a quick hug.

"Good luck in your quest, Garrett," Megan said.

"We'll need it," he replied grimly.

"And good luck to you," she said to Lana. Unspoken between them was the knowledge that Megan alone knew Lana wasn't going home to an empty house. "I think you've embarked on quite a different quest of your own."

A QUEST OF YOUR OWN.

A journey to find something wondrous and fine.

A journey to find one's self.

Except she knew who she was. Didn't she?

Megan was reading too much into the fact Dylan Van Zandt was staying with her. It was just a more convenient way to help him hone his parenting skills, and safer for

Greg, too. There was no deeper meaning in having him in the big, empty house she'd rattled around in since her mother died.

She parked her car in the garage, passing Dylan's truck on the way in. Her dad's classic '57 Thunderbird was parked along the far wall, covered with a nylon tarp. Michael kept saying he was going to take it, tune it up and drive it, but he never had. It didn't matter. The garage was big enough for five cars. Now it only held two.

She'd told Dylan to feel free to park his pickup inside, but he hadn't taken her up on the offer. Not even today when it had rained all day and she'd left a spare remote for the garage door lying conspicuously on the kitchen island.

He seemed determined to keep his distance. And, of course, it was better for both of them that way.

She walked slowly along the brick path that led to the kitchen door. The rain had stopped while she was at Megan's, although the air was so thick and humid it made little difference. The heavy scent of the night-blooming jasmine that covered the side of the garage perfumed the darkness. The moon rode high in the sky, peeking out from amid a tatter of fleeing clouds. There was light in the kitchen, and in the maid's room where Dylan and Greg had taken up residence. Lana quickened her step. It made the house look more lived-in. As it had when she was a girl—when there was a family living here, not just one sometimes lonely young woman.

She punched in the code of the security system Michael had insisted Sheila install after their father's death and stepped inside. Dylan was standing by the microwave, watching the seconds count down on the digital display beside the door, Greg propped against his shoulder.

The baby was awake, staring at the door as though

waiting for her to appear. His head wobbled, and he laid it on Dylan's shoulder. He was very weak yet, compared with other babies his age. Lana's heart turned over in her chest. He appeared so tiny and fragile. He had overcome much already, but he had more challenges ahead of him than other children, and not just because he was born prematurely.

Growing up never knowing your mother was a hard thing to do. She had managed because she had loving adoptive parents who had smoothed her way. But Greg had only Dylan, a man who distanced himself from his son as well as everyone else—or at least her.

Dylan turned around. "Hi," he said. He was wearing a blue oxford cloth shirt, hanging open, exposing a muscled chest covered with dark hair. Greg's little fingers were tangled in the curling mat, and the contrast between the man's strength and hardness and the baby's utter helplessness and fragility sent a glittering arc of sensation from Lana's heart to her womb. It wasn't a sexual awareness, she told herself, but something more primitive than that. It was more the receptiveness of the female for the male of the species, the protector, the provider. It was conditioning over a million years, nothing more.

"Hi. I thought you'd both be in bed by now." She wasn't a cavewoman. This was the twenty-first century. Women were just as often the protector and provider as men. She ignored the increased beat of her pulse and moved into the room.

"Greg decided he needed a midnight snack." The microwave beeped, and Dylan turned to remove the bottle warming inside. He secured the nipple and tested the liquid on the inside of his wrist, as she'd taught him. He shifted Greg from his shoulder to the crook of his arm and touched the nipple to the side of the baby's mouth.

Greg turned his head automatically and latched on to the nipple, sucking greedily. It should be his mother's nipple, Lana thought sadly. Did Dylan have such thoughts, too, as he mourned the death of his son's mother, his wife, his lover?

He was frowning slightly as he watched his son. He didn't look sad, only fiercely focused on what he was doing. His hands were big and wide, his fingers long and blunt-tipped. Strong hands that could mold and build, soothe a crying baby, arouse a willing woman. Again she felt that glittering tug of awareness deep inside her. It bothered her. She didn't want to think about making love to any man right now.

And she noticed something else. Dylan was no longer wearing his wedding ring.

Lana forced herself to concentrate on the baby.

"He's certainly hungry."

"He took three ounces his last feeding. If he takes three ounces this time, I'm hoping he'll sleep longer."

"I'd be happy to give him his two o'clock feeding." Lana heard herself say the words. Dylan did look tired. He let her take care of Greg during the day, when he was upstairs overseeing the renovations of her building. But in the evening and during the night, he kept the baby to himself.

"Thanks, I'll take care of it." A rebuff, but a polite one.

"I wouldn't mind, really."

"I know you wouldn't. But I think I can keep up with him."

Lana dropped onto one of the stools arranged around the center island. "Would you like a cup of coffee?" she asked.

He shook his head. "Too late for me. You look right at home sittin' there."

"I spent a lot of hours here. My mother was a wonderful cook."

"Mine isn't," he said, and grinned. "It's a good thing my dad can cook or we'd have all starved."

"I have a limited repertoire, but I'm good at what I do. Great-grandma Bostleman's buttermilk sugar cookies. And pot roast and chicken and dumplings."

"Sounds good."

"I'll make us some the first cool day. But Shelby got all the real culinary talent in the family. Since we're all adopted, she insists she picked it up from Mom through osmosis." She fell silent, thinking of the hours just past, wishing her mother was here for her to confide in.

"How did your evening go?"

She hadn't expected him to ask such a personal question. So far their short conversations had centered on Greg's care, the weather, whether Dylan needed towels or soap or toilet paper for the bathroom. Her surprise must have registered on her face. "You looked kind of shell-shocked when you walked in the door."

"I am." Her arms ached to reach out and take Greg from him, to cuddle the little boy close and take comfort from his baby warmth and softness. She sat up a little straighter. "It's not every day you hear from the mother you never knew. And then to find out she's still as anonymous as she ever was."

"What do you mean by that?" He moved a few steps closer, hooked the toe of his shoe around a stool, pulled it away from the island and settled himself on it without jarring Greg or taking the bottle out of his mouth.

Lana rested her elbows on the countertop and propped her chin on her hands. "My birth mother sent a package to Aunt Megan with a note that what was inside was for us. She obviously found out who had adopted us and that Aunt Megan was still in contact with us.''

''Or at least she hoped so.''

''No. She thanked Aunt Megan for finding us a good home.'' Lana recited the little note, picturing the block lettering in her mind's eye. ''It was printed, as though she wanted to disguise her handwriting. As if she didn't want us to have that small a hint of who she was.''

''Where was it mailed from?''

''Here in the city. I don't know which post office. Garrett's going to try to find out.''

''Garrett?''

''My older brother. There are four of us, you know?''

''No, I didn't know.'' He took the bottle out of Greg's mouth and put him over his shoulder. He patted him on the back, gently, the way she had taught him. The baby burped and immediately began demanding the rest of his bottle.

''Abandoned on the doorstep of Maitland Maternity twenty-five years ago. We're triplets, Shelby, Michael and I. Garrett's the oldest. Shelby owns a diner on Mayfair, near the clinic. Austin Eats. Have you heard of it?''

''No, 'fraid not.''

''We'll go there for lunch someday.''

''Sounds good.''

''Michael's head of security at Maitland. Garrett owns a ranch outside the city. I have the store. We've got cousins scattered around the country here and there, but since Mom and Dad died there are really just the four of us. What about you?'' She didn't want to think of the way her family had changed in the past few hours. She had felt the earth move under her feet when Garrett and Michael squared off about searching for their mother. She didn't want to think how deep a rift it might eventually cause in their relationships.

"One brother, one sister. Both married with kids. Both living out of state. Aunts. Uncles. Cousins. We didn't have much but family growing up. It was a bust time then." Lana nodded. Texas's economy had had a lot of booms and busts during the years it had been so dependent on the oil industry. "My dad nearly lost the business more than once. I joined the Marines when I got out of high school because he wouldn't let me work for him, and I didn't have the money to go to college. I ended up in Saudi."

"You were in Desert Storm?"

"Yes."

"Tell me about it."

For a moment she thought he would refuse, but then he began to talk. He told her of the weather and the vast expanses of sand. Of nights in the desert beneath a sky filled with stars, days spent readying themselves for combat. He talked of his friend Greg, his son's namesake. Dead of cancer at twenty-seven. He didn't mention his wife or how they had met, but surely it must have been through his late friend.

Dylan's voice was low and rough, but soothing, too, like whiskey and honey mixed. She wanted him to go on talking, and she was afraid he would stop if she broke the spell with a question about Greg's mother. The baby watched him and listened, too, his big blue eyes focused on Dylan's face. It must have filled his world.

Greg finished the bottle, and Dylan burped him again. The little boy snuggled his face into Dylan's neck and fell asleep. Lana wished she could do the same. "You're getting very good at that," she said. "He's much more comfortable with you already."

His mouth tightened. "I'm trying."

"You're a natural. Greg's lucky to have you. Even if he has lost his mother he still has family. It will mean a lot to him in the future. I know. I don't have any real roots of my own, only grafted ones. I loved my parents dearly, but sometimes it's a little lonely inside." She didn't know why she was telling him this. It was late. She was tired. She didn't like the sudden darkness that drained the softness from his eyes and hardened his face.

"I'll do my best to give him that, if I can."

"If you can? I just told you you're doing great at this daddy business. He's lost his mother. It's tragic, but he still has you. You're his father—"

Dylan cut her off. "That's where you've got it wrong. I have every reason to believe Greg is another man's son."

CHAPTER FIVE

DAMN IT, had he really said the words aloud? He looked at Lana. Her eyes were dark with an emotion he couldn't read.

"Are you sure?" she asked quietly.

He raked his free hand through his hair. He couldn't remember the last time he'd had a decent night's sleep. Greg had been fussy all evening. Dylan had felt tied in knots trying to soothe the little one. She had said Greg could sense when he was angry or frustrated. As if to prove her right, the baby stirred and frowned in his sleep. Dylan began jiggling him gently, holding him close so he could hear his heartbeat and be reassured. Except his heart was hammering in his chest, thundering in his ears. He didn't think that could be reassuring. He settled Greg a little lower in the crook of his arm.

She was waiting for an answer. "Yes. No. Look, will you just forget I said anything?" He should never have started talking to her. It was late. He was tired. She was too damned good a listener. He'd thought it was safe enough to talk about Saudi. After all, they'd both made it through without a scratch. But memories of his friend Greg and the months of pain and suffering before his death had crowded in.

And with that breach of his defenses came memories of Jessie. Young. Scared. Alone. So pretty. So needy.

"It's not easy to forget a statement like that."

He'd expected an automatic assurance that his words were instantly forgotten. A meaningless gesture, maybe, but one that would get him off the hook for tonight. That's what Jessie would have done. What most women would have done. But not Lana Lord.

"No, I suppose it isn't."

"Do you want to talk about it?"

"No. I never intended to say the words aloud."

"And what about your son?"

"What about him?"

"Will you let it keep on affecting the way you feel about him?" He wondered if she was as good a shot with a gun as she was with words.

"I can't answer that."

She looked away. She folded her hands on the counter and stared at them. The overhead light picked out streaks of cinnamon and gold in her hair. He could smell her perfume, light and flowery. If he leaned a few inches closer he would feel the warmth of her skin radiating through the space between them. "I'm sorry to hear that. I don't want Greg to suffer what I did as a child."

"Suffer? I don't understand." But he thought he did, a little, anyway.

"Wondering why my mother left us on the doorstep of the clinic. Wondering what we'd done wrong that she would leave us all that way."

"You said your adoptive parents loved you." He didn't love Greg. Couldn't love him as a father should, and that ate at him. She was right. Kids could sense that kind of thing, no matter how hard you tried to hide it.

"They did. And it helped me put those doubts aside. But it never completely made them go away. I would hate for Greg to have those same doubts."

"I told you I never intended to speak of it to a living

soul." Her adoptive parents had learned to love her. Maybe that was the key. Maybe he could be taught to love his son.

"You will try not to let it come between you and Greg."

"I try every day of my life."

She wasn't looking at him, but at the baby he was holding. Her thoughts were all for Greg. For a moment Dylan was jealous of the sleeping infant. Lana was a woman who knew her mind and her heart, not like Jessie, who was buffeted by every passing emotion. Lana was fiercely loyal and fiercely dedicated to those she loved. It would be a lucky man who earned that love for his own. Was he hoping to be that man? Was that why he'd taken off his wedding band after all these weeks?

"What was she like?" she asked softly.

"She was twenty-four when she died, twenty-one when we married. It was a few weeks before Greg died. He had bone cancer. It went fast and it was pretty brutal."

"You comforted her and perhaps you mistook her gratitude for love?"

"I knew there was another man," he said, and heard the old anger in his voice. He swallowed hard and went on. "She was coming off a bad relationship. He was older, married. He broke it off and went back to his wife. Then Greg got sick. She was a wreck." He hadn't meant to be so blunt. This conversation was getting out of hand. Before he knew it he'd be telling her everything.

"And you were the one who was there to pick up the pieces."

He considered not answering, turning away and walking out of the room. She wouldn't follow him. She wasn't that type. But if he stayed put, she'd keep asking questions as long as he kept answering them. And someplace inside him, a part of him wanted to keep talking, to maybe find out a few answers himself.

"I watched her grow up. She was just a kid when we went to Saudi. She sent tapes and letters. She was so young she dotted her *i*s with little hearts and drew smiley faces in her *O*s."

"But when you got back it was a different story."

"Yes. She wasn't a little kid any longer. She'd been living with an aunt. All the family they had left. And, well, she was a little wild." She'd had a lot of problems with commitment and fidelity, too, but hell, he hadn't known any of that until it was too late for both of them. She was cute and playful, and he'd fallen head over heels in love with her the first time he saw her. But he hadn't told Greg. She was too young for him, and Greg had come to work for his dad. It would have complicated things.

He was Greg's buddy, nothing more. Too old and too serious for her.

"You fell in love with her," she prompted in that quiet voice of hers.

"Maybe a little."

"Maybe a lot?"

"Maybe."

"But you were just her older brother's buddy from the war."

"Yep, that was me. She went off to college and fell in love with her mystery man. Greg didn't like it, but she was of age and there was nothing much he could do."

She nodded. "Then Greg got sick. The love affair soured. Dylan to the rescue."

"Semper Fi."

"The Marine Corps motto."

Semper Fidelis. Always faithful. He nodded. "Greg was my best friend. Jessie's future was the most important thing in the world to him.'' And he'd failed to keep her safe and happy. Instead, he'd contributed to her unhappiness and her death.

"But surely that doesn't extend to—"

What was she going to say? He beat her to it. "A marriage of convenience? A rescue mission to save a screwed-up kid from herself?" He was angry again, and it showed. Greg squirmed and whimpered.

Lana took it right between the eyes. She didn't flinch or look away. "Yes," she replied steadily. "I guess that was what I was going to say."

"I married Jessica because I loved her." Somehow that seemed important to say. Maybe he thought it would shock him out of his awareness of Lana as a woman, all softness on the outside and steely strength on the inside, sitting there before him. Still, it was the truth. At least it had been for a while. But not at the end. Not for a long time before the end.

"But she didn't love you back."

"That's the bottom line." It wasn't working. Lana was still desirable as hell. He wanted to hold her in his arms instead of his son. He wanted to kiss her into silence, into surrender. He stood up. "It's late. I need to get Greg to bed."

She stood up, too. The top of her head was at eye level. She had to tilt her head a little to make eye contact. The line of her throat was pure and sweet. Her skin looked as soft as Greg's. "But your wife loved Greg?" There was just enough of a rise at the end of the sentence to make it a question. The abandoned child in her wasn't so far beneath the surface, after all.

"Yes, she loved Greg." But she wasn't above using him as a weapon. She had threatened to take him to the man she claimed was his father when he was released from the hospital. She wanted the man to raise Greg, not Dylan, not her husband. Not the man who had thought until that day that this child was his.

Lana took one step closer, then another. She reached out and traced the curve of Greg's cheek with the tip of her finger. "He's such a sweet baby. My heart goes out to him. I know what heartache never knowing his mother will cause him, no matter how hard you try to save him from it." Her voice was soft and low, almost a whisper. "You will try, won't you, Dylan?"

"I told you I'd do my best."

"Your best?" She shook her head. There was sadness in her eyes and in the tiny sigh that escaped her lips. She lifted her hand from smoothing Greg's hair and placed her fingers against Dylan's lips. Just as it had that first day, when she'd touched his arm, the shock of contact shimmered through him like heat lightning streaking across the high arc of the Texas sky on a summer's night. "No, Dylan, that won't do. Only your best isn't good enough."

"What is good enough?"

"You must give him your heart."

"I don't know if I've got a heart left to give. Maybe I'm asking you for the wrong kind of lessons."

"What do you mean?" She had taken her fingers away from his lips when he spoke. Now she clasped her hands tightly behind her back.

"These first few days I've needed you to teach me how to take care of him. Now I need you to teach me how to love him."

LANA WAS AWAKE before dawn. She lay in bed and watched the darkness fade and the familiar pattern of sun-dappled leaves appear in a square on her bedroom wall.

She'd been watching those same patterns superimpose themselves on the ivory and gold striped wallpaper for years. She had picked the paper herself, feeling very grown-up and sophisticated, the summer before her eighteenth birthday.

Her birthday. Something else that really wasn't her own. There was no telling when any of them had been born, although Sheila, Terrence, Aunt Megan and the staff at Maitland had taken a good guess. In the end they'd chosen the date six months prior to the day the babies had been found. March twenty-seventh.

For Garrett, who appeared to be about two, their parents had picked the day they'd first seen him for his birthday. Goodness, that was in a few weeks. She wondered if she ought to call Shelby and plan something for the four of them to celebrate the day? She wondered if he would even bother to come. He'd grown so reclusive of late, since the shooting. And Michael. She was afraid he still blamed himself for Garrett's being involved in the hostage situation that had resulted in his injury. She worried about him, too.

She wasn't going to change her brothers. Not at this late date. She would just have to have faith that they would both be okay. That Garrett knew what was best for him to heal and grow strong again. That Michael would trust in himself again.

And she wasn't going to be able to avoid facing Dylan by lying here with a pillow over her head. Lord, what a fool she'd made of herself last night. Her fingers curled into her palms. She could still feel the heat of his lips against her fingertips. Thank God she'd been able to keep her response to herself. It was physical, that was all. She hadn't had that much experience in matters of the heart, especially in the happily-ever-after department, but she knew when she was attracted to a man. And she was very attracted to Dylan Van Zandt. And he was a bad risk in the happily-ever-after department if she ever saw one. A man with a child he didn't think was his, still grieving for a woman who'd married him but didn't love him. Not a good risk at all.

She dawdled in the shower, spent an extra ten minutes on her hair and makeup and hoped he'd be ready to leave the house by the time she got downstairs to the kitchen.

No such luck, it seemed. The kitchen was deserted. There was no neatly rinsed cereal bowl in the sink. Not a bread crumb around the toaster. The coffee hadn't been made. She was already beginning to take that for granted—that he would make the coffee—even though he'd only been here a few days. She did hear water running in the shower in the bathroom that lay beyond the kitchen wall. Evidently, Dylan had overslept, as well.

As she headed for the cupboard where the coffee grinder was stored, the phone in Dylan's room started to ring. It was old-fashioned and shrill, and she jumped at the sudden noise. She took down the grinder and the beans and heard Greg begin to cry. Two more rings and she was standing in the doorway of Dylan's room. She could no more ignore a ringing phone than she could a crying baby. Now she was confronted with both.

Lana averted her eyes from the unmade bed, the imprint of Dylan's head still on the pillow, the pair of jeans draped over the straight-back chair beside the bathroom door, and picked up the phone. "Hello," she said, cradling the receiver between her ear and her shoulder as she crossed the room to lift Greg out of his crib. His diaper was dry. He smelled of baby soap and powder. He had on a one-piece sleeper with tiny figures of Mickey and Minnie all over it. Dylan may have been running late this morning, but he'd managed to get Greg ready to face the day.

"Hello?" a woman's voice replied. Lana wasn't surprised. As far as she knew the only person Dylan had given this number to was his mother. "I'm trying to reach Dylan Van Zandt. Who am I speaking to, please?"

Lana felt a tickle of laughter in the back of her throat. Dylan's mother was very obviously not expecting a woman to answer the phone.

"This is Lana Lord."

"Oh. Miss Lord. This is Linda Van Zandt. I'm sorry to disturb you. I was told I could reach my son at this number."

"You can as soon as he gets out of the shower, Mrs. Van Zandt."

"The shower? You're in his room and he's in the shower?"

"Well, yes, I am." Lana deliberately turned her back to the bathroom door. She could come into Dylan's room and console his child and answer his phone. But she wasn't prepared to see him step naked out of the shower.

"I see." But the rising inflection in the older woman's voice made it sound as if she didn't.

"Greg was crying," Lana explained. "I came in to pick him up and the phone rang."

"Oh. Why, thank you. How is he? How's my little sweetie?"

"He's fine. I think he's grown just since he's been here."

"He was so little. All my other grandchildren were big, healthy babies. Greg's such a tiny mite. How much formula is he taking? Is he still so colicky?"

"He's eating well," Lana assured her. "He still gets fussy every evening, but it's getting better. I think he's going to outgrow it soon.'' She turned her head and kissed the top of Greg's head. He was rooting at the curve of her shoulder, eyes half shut, searching for something to eat. Her breast tightened, and that newly familiar silvery arc of sensation shot along her nerve endings to the very center of her womb. She wanted a baby. Her own baby to love and care for. She didn't want to be a nursemaid to help out a grieving and conflicted man.

''I worry so about him and Dylan,'' Linda Van Zandt said. ''Is he eating properly? Dylan, I mean?''

Lana opened her mouth to make a polite but noncommittal reply when Greg let out a wail.

''Oh, I bet he heard me talking. Let me say hello to my baby.''

Could it be Greg already recognized his grandmother's voice? Lana didn't know if that was possible, but she wasn't going to make an issue of it. She struggled to get Greg into the crook of her arm and the phone close to his ear.

The bathroom door opened, and steam swirled into the room. A few seconds later Dylan appeared at her elbow. ''What the devil?'' he asked.

Lana kept her eyes on the baby. She could feel her face getting hot. What had possessed her to come into his room when she knew he was taking a shower? ''It's your mother.'' She gestured with the phone. ''She's talking to Greg.''

''It's all right,'' he said very quietly so his mother couldn't overhear. ''I'm decent.''

She chanced a look out of the corner of her eye. Just barely decent. Lana took a deep breath. His chest was bare, but he was wearing the jeans she'd seen on the chair. He had a white towel wrapped around his neck. He smelled of soap and warm skin and just plain male, an aphrodisiac if ever there was one. Moisture glistened in his hair. His chest was sun-browned. His stomach was flat and lightly muscled. The jeans were zipped but not snapped, and a dark arrow of hair disappeared below the waistband, drawing her eyes lower. He had long legs and strong, hard thighs, and—

Lana dragged her gaze to the level of his chin and kept it there. "Here's your mother. I was making coffee." She rushed to explain. "And I heard the phone. And Greg was crying."

He nodded understanding. "Thanks." He took the phone. "Hello, Mom. It's me. Is everything okay? Why are you calling so early? You are? So soon? That's great news. Yes, I'm sure you'll sleep much better in your own bed."

Lana wanted to move past him but she was trapped by the phone cord that had somehow gotten between them. Dylan lifted it with one hand, and she ducked under. He went on talking to his mother, and she tried not to eavesdrop as she looked for Greg's bottle.

"Of course I'll come Sunday. I know you miss him. What? No. I don't think that's a good—" he stopped speaking abruptly. Lana located Greg's bottle on the top of the dresser. There was still a little formula in it, so she picked it up and put the nipple in his mouth, then turned. Dylan was watching her with a frown. His eyebrows were drawn together above his gray eyes and he had his hand over the phone's receiver.

"She wants you to come for Sunday dinner."

"But she's in the hospital," Lana said.

"She's going home tomorrow. My dad will cook."

Spend the entire day with him and Greg. Like a family. No, she couldn't. She didn't dare start living her fantasy like that. "I don't think—"

The furrow between his eyes deepened. The irises went from smoke to charcoal. "Mom, Ms. Lord's a busy woman. I'm sure she's got plans." He fell silent again, but his mother did not. Lana could hear her talking a mile a minute. "Yes, ma'am." He held out the phone. "She wants to talk to you."

She passed him Greg, bottle and all. The transfer went smoothly. They were getting good at this. Too good. It felt so right, and that couldn't be. Dylan and his son weren't for her. "Mrs. Van Zandt?"

"I want to invite you to come visit us on Sunday when Dylan brings Greg out."

"That's so kind of you to ask me," Lana began, moving smoothly into the good-mannered refusal her mother had drummed into her head years before. "But—"

"I really would like to do something to thank you for helping Dylan out with Greg."

For the first time Lana heard the underlying anxiety in Linda's voice. She truly was worried about how Dylan was coping with the child. Did she have her suspicions about Greg's parentage, as well? And she deserved to meet the woman who was taking her place, no matter how temporary that situation might be. "I...I'd be happy to come. Thank you so much for asking me," she heard herself say, and was rewarded by the relief that sounded in Linda Van Zandt's next words.

"Wonderful. But it'll be pot luck, I'm afraid. I'm not the world's greatest cook even when I'm not laid up in a wheelchair."

"I won't hear of you cooking for me."

Linda laughed, a light, bubbly sound that caused Lana to smile in return. "I won't be. My husband's the cook in this family. He'll throw a couple of steaks on the grill."

"Then please, let me bring the rest of the meal."

"Oh, no. That's far too much trouble for you to go to."

"It won't be any trouble at all. My sister owns a restaurant. You just leave everything to me."

"Why, thank you. Thank you very much. I'll see you Sunday, then. Oh drat, the nurse is here for my bath. Tell Dylan I said goodbye, and give Greg a kiss for me." She hung up before Lana could hand the phone to a scowling Dylan.

"It seems I'm going to meet your parents on Sunday," she said.

CHAPTER SIX

"OKAY, everything you'll need is in the cooler. There's a sweet potato soufflé and a spinach and goat cheese salad. I put in the raspberry vinaigrette dressing but there's also some buttermilk ranch for the guys. If Dylan Van Zandt and his father are anything like Garrett and Michael, they'd rather starve to death than eat raspberry vinaigrette dressing." Shelby opened the lid of the insulated cooler she'd brought from the diner and peeked inside, assuring herself nothing had been forgotten. "There's red pepper butter for the bread, and rhubarb rice pudding for dessert."

"The stuff you make with the brulée topping?"

Shelby nodded, giving Lana a wicked grin. "I made it especially for you. Michael stopped by, and I let him wield the blowtorch. You know how much he likes to do that."

"And you know how much I like that stuff."

"I thought you might need a little comfort food. Meeting his parents already and everything."

"It's just a courtesy call, Shel." Lana knew her sister wouldn't believe that for a moment.

"Sure. Sure. Now, I've packed all the linens and silver and glassware you'll need in the basket over there. If his mother's in a wheelchair, she isn't going to want to be polishing the good silver to impress you. Oh, and I put a really nice bottle of Burgundy in the bottom of the hamper. That should cover all your bases.''

''Thanks, Shel.''

''My pleasure. So when am I going to meet this mystery man?''

Shelby was standing with her back to the short hallway that led to the old servant's room. She didn't see Dylan as he entered the kitchen, Greg in his arms, a camouflage-patterned knapsack that served as a diaper bag slung over his shoulder. He was wearing khaki pants and a light green short-sleeved shirt that complemented his dark hair and gray eyes. He still looked tired and wound too tight, but no longer like a man who was pushed to the very edge.

Something in Lana's face must have alerted her sister to his presence. Shelby arched her brows in a question. ''He's here?'' She mouthed the words without making a sound. Lana nodded once. Shelby turned. ''Hello,'' she said, drawing the word out an extra syllable. ''Let me guess. You must be Dylan Van Zandt.''

''That'd be correct, miss,'' he replied, the little hint of cowboy drawl that sometimes seeped into his speech becoming more pronounced.

''I'm Shelby Lord.'' She held out her hand. He shook it politely.

''I want to thank you for bringing the food all the way out here today.''

''No problem. I've been wanting to meet you. It's just been so busy at the diner that I haven't been able to get away any sooner.''

''It can get that way when you own your own business.'' Dylan indicated the cooler and the hamper. ''I'll take these out to the pickup, if they're ready to go.''

"All set." Shelby held out her hands. "May I hold him? He's just about the cutest baby I've ever seen."

"Thank you."

"Such big blue eyes. And what pretty blond hair. Does he take after your side of the family, Mr. Van Zandt?"

"Call me Dylan," he said, sidestepping the question.

"And please, call me Shelby."

"I'd be honored to."

Shelby didn't seem to mind that he'd changed the subject. She appeared to be totally entranced by Greg's blowing bubbles. "And what's your name, little man?"

"Greg," Lana said, before her sister could ask any more questions.

"Gregory Reilly Van Zandt. He's named after his late uncle. My best friend," Dylan added stiffly.

"What a good, strong name for a handsome little guy."

"I'll get these out to the truck."

"Be careful with the hamper. There's a bottle of very good Burgundy in the bottom."

"I'll do that." He picked up the hamper, set it on the cooler and lifted them both. Lana hurried to the door and opened it for him.

"We could take my car," she said.

"Did you get the air-conditioning checked yet?" he asked, a hint of a smile curving his mouth.

"Well. No."

"Then I'll drive. It's going to be a scorcher." He turned and walked out the door, carrying the heavy cooler and wicker hamper as though they weighed no more than Greg.

Lana turned to face her sister's curiosity.

"He's living here, isn't he?" Shelby asked.

"Shelby—"

"Isn't he? That's why he's here already. That's why he

came out of the old maid's room. I mean, if he'd just asked to use the bathroom you'd have sent him to the powder room under the stairs.'' She spun on her heel and disappeared through the archway.

"Shelby Anne Lord, come back here," Lana ordered. She didn't know how long it would take Dylan to load the truck, but she suspected he would be as efficient at that as he was at everything. "I'll die of embarrassment if he catches you snooping through—"

"Ah, I was right," Shelby called over her shoulder. "He's living here. In the maid's room." She was standing in the doorway looking at Dylan's things.

Reluctantly Lana came to stand by her side. The room was neat, the bed made, a little pile of Greg's sleepers and tiny T-shirts folded neatly on the bedside table. There was nothing of Dylan's to be seen beyond a travel clock and a rolled tube of blueprints leaning against the bureau.

"Neat as a pin, isn't he?" Shelby said.

"Shelby, come away. I don't want him to find us snooping."

"How long has he been staying here?" she asked, but didn't resist Lana's hand on her arm, urging her away.

"Since the night of Chase's birthday party."

Shelby's eyes widened. "You've been together for over a week and you didn't tell me?"

"We're not together," Lana said too quickly. "You should see those apartments above the store. They're dirty, and there's dust and mouse droppings and lead paint on the walls. Dylan's invested everything he's got in them. He hasn't got money to rent a place of his own right now. And it's an hour's commute from his parents' place in Cartersburg."

"Where's Greg's mother? I mean, even if they're divorced—he is divorced, isn't he?" she demanded.

"He's a widower."

Shelby sucked in her breath. She wrapped her arms more tightly around Greg as he surveyed the kitchen from over her left shoulder. "How did she die?" She'd lowered her voice as though Greg might hear and understand.

"A car accident, I think. I...I don't know the details. I only know she died when Greg was ten days old."

"How terrible. No wonder the man looks as if he's been to hell and back. You poor little thing," she said to Greg, and gave him a kiss. "Do Garrett and Michael know about him staying here?"

"Of course not. Do you think he'd still be here if they did?" Lana was glad enough to steer the conversation in another direction, even one as potentially explosive as this one. She didn't want to think about Dylan mourning his wife.

Shelby chuckled. "I suppose not. But they're bound to find out sooner or later."

"I'll tell them as soon as I see them." She didn't like keeping secrets from her siblings. True, Garrett and Michael's protectiveness rankled sometimes, but both Lana and Shelby knew their brothers acted from the heart.

"Michael hasn't been around the store lately?"

"Not lately."

"He's been avoiding the diner, too. I think he's afraid I'm going to try to get him to help with our search for...her." Shelby fumbled for a word, as if she couldn't quite bring herself to refer to another woman as *mother* in front of Lana. Shelby knew how much Lana mourned their parents, especially their mother. There wasn't a day that passed that she didn't think of something she would have liked to share with Sheila Lord, ask her advice about, laugh with her over.

"Has Garrett found out anything yet? About our biological mother?'' Lana said it first so Shelby didn't have to keep trying to avoid the word. There was nothing wrong with calling her that. Sheila Lord had been a strong, intelligent woman. She wouldn't have been threatened by Garrett and Shelby's quest. At least, not outwardly. But in her heart of hearts she would have been hurt by the search, Lana was convinced of that.

"Not that I know of. Except she mailed the package from the post office branch on Kings Avenue. That's only a couple of blocks from you. She might have been at the store. Do you remember having a customer last week that could have been her? She has to be in her late forties, at least, I suppose. Young grandmother types, maybe?''

Lana shook her head. "I don't recall. No, I don't think so.''

"I didn't see anyone I thought might be her at the diner, either. I've racked my brain trying to remember everyone who came through the door.''

"Shel, you have hundreds of customers a week in there. How could you remember each one?''

Shelby shifted Greg higher on her shoulder and began to sway with him in her arms, as Lana often did. She found the action as comforting for herself as for the little boy. Evidently, Shelby felt the same way. "It's crazy, isn't it? But I thought I would *know* her if I ever saw her.''

Lana sighed. "I thought so, too. But how could that be? We were so little when she left us.''

"Dumped us on the clinic steps, you mean. Even if it all did turn out right.''

"Thanks to Mom and Dad, we've done just fine,'' Lana reminded her.

"And I know that's where your loyalty lies. Don't worry. I'm not going to come crying to you to ask for help. Garrett and I will do this on our own. We've decided to start searching out triplet births. I mean, how many sets could there be, born at the same time, even in a state this size?''

"I know. I've often wondered why someone didn't come forward when we were found. After all, multiple births were a lot less common in those days. We did make the front page of the paper.''

"Maybe we were born at home?''

"Or outside Texas. But you have to start looking somewhere.''

The back door opened, and Dylan stepped inside. "The truck's loaded. We can leave whenever you're ready.'' He looked from one to the other of them. "If you ladies have something to discuss, I'll take Greg for a walk in the garden.''

"No. I was just leaving,'' Shelby said hurriedly. She lifted Greg away from her and gave him a kiss on the forehead. She held him out to Dylan. "He's a wonderful baby. You must be so proud of him.''

"Thank you.'' Again Shelby appeared not to notice the edge of restraint in Dylan's voice, but Lana did. He was doing better with Greg, but still, he held himself back, aloof from the infant.

"Have a good day, you two.''

"We will,'' Lana said. "Shel, I'll call you. And…you call me if you have any news.''

Shelby looked over her shoulder from the doorway. "I will. I always intended to.''

"YOU BE SURE and come back again real soon. I enjoyed meeting you so much.''

"I enjoyed it, too, Linda.'' The two women had been

on a first-name basis from the minute Dylan introduced them.

"And thanks for all the help you've given Dylan. He's so much more at ease with this little mite." His mother had lowered her voice on the last sentence, but Dylan heard her as he stowed the empty cooler and hamper in the back seat of the truck. As he started to the porch, his mom lifted Greg from her lap and hugged him tight. "I miss you, little fella. Come back to visit Grandma soon. When I get my leg out of this darned ol' cast, I'll take you for a walk to meet the neighbors."

Roger Van Zandt was a shorter, grayer, solider version of his son. "Like Mother just said," he repeated, "you come back real soon. And bring your sister. Any woman who cooks like she does is welcome in my house." Roger was beaming as he leaned over the back of his wife's wheelchair to give Greg one last tickle under the chin.

It struck Dylan that his dad had never talked so much around Jessie. But then, she hadn't cared about anything he had to say. Lana did, or appeared to. She had an opinion about everything, sports, the weather, the goings-on at the state capitol and in Washington. She'd helped his dad grill the steaks and she'd discussed Greg's schedule and feeding habits and next trip to the pediatrician with his mom. She'd looked through photo albums with every indication of interest and didn't say no to a cold beer when they were all settled on the deck to watch the sun go down.

"Better yet," Lana said, as Dylan took Greg from his mom and started to the truck, "I'll take you to Austin Eats when you come to town. How's that?"

"Consider it a date," Linda called, blowing a kiss to her grandson. "Drive safe, Dylan. And call me."

"I'll let you know as soon as I get an appointment for

Greg with one of the pediatricians at Maitland. Lana's got an in there. She'll fix us up with the best they've got," he assured his mother as he strapped Greg's carrier into the seat-belt harness.

"If Dylan doesn't call you, I will," Lana said.

Linda smiled and nodded. "Thank you. Goodbye, Lana."

"Goodbye."

Dylan waved as he backed the pickup out of the driveway and headed east toward the highway. The September twilight had shaded into night. Not that you could see many stars anymore. It was still the big, high-arching Texas sky overhead, but the lights of Austin were a pink glow against the eastern sky, and there were streetlights reaching halfway to the city along the back roads where he and his high school buddies used to drag race their salvage-yard pickups, without headlights, on full-moon nights.

Dylan chuckled ruefully. It was a miracle one of them hadn't been killed. No wonder his mom and dad had worried themselves half to death over him and his brother and sister growing up.

"I'm sorry, did you say something?" Lana was sitting with her foot propped on the dash, her hand dangling over her knee, her head leaning against the headrest. She was wearing white canvas shoes and white slacks and a peach-colored cotton blouse. No jewelry except for a watch and small gold hoop earrings, and not much makeup. She looked as fresh and crisp as she had when he laid eyes on her that morning, although it had been hot enough to fry eggs on the sidewalk in the afternoon. Her hair fell away from her face, and he could see the curve of her ear and the soft line of her jaw and wondered how it would feel to kiss her there.

Instead, he said, "I was thinking how fast Austin's grown in the last ten years. Used to be there was nothing but ranch land and little country towns like Crystal Creek and Cartersburg between here and the state capitol. Now it's just one big strip mall."

"Didn't Van Zandt Development build one or two of those strip malls?" she asked with a grin.

His smile turned a little sheepish. "Yeah, but you've got to admit they're the classiest ones."

"I hope you get the bid on the Cartersburg school gymnasium."

His dad had told her all about the project as he grilled the steaks. She'd listened as if it were the most important deal in the world. "Thanks. I think we've got the inside track. We're local. And Dad's reputation is solid gold around town."

"I liked your parents." If she had felt out of place in their company, she hadn't shown it. He thought about the difference between the near mansion she lived in and his parents' twenty-year-old split-level on its two-acre plot. There was no comparing the two houses. But his parents' home was filled with love and clutter and a lifetime of memories. He supposed those things were in Lana's house, too, somewhere beyond the intimidating public rooms—the only ones he'd seen besides the kitchen. But downstairs it was more like a museum than a home. And a small-town ex-Marine with only a two-year college education didn't belong there. At least, not on a permanent basis. The thought sobered him, made him restless.

"They liked you, too. I wanted to thank you for not using that finishing-school tone with my mom."

"Finishing-school tone?"

"Yeah, that snotty one you laid on me the first time we met." *Hell, why had he said that?* He didn't know what had gotten into him, even speaking the thought aloud, except he was disgusted with himself for noticing everything about her, from the jut of her hipbone beneath her slacks to the flowers and spice scent of her perfume. Jessie would have burst into tears at the thoughtless remark or turned cold and pouted for days. He was getting ready to apologize when Lana began to giggle.

"Oh, dear. I should hope not. I try so hard not to let that happen. I always sound like that when I'm scared or nervous. Shelby says it's because I was so traumatized by being sent away to school that year."

"I was right. You did go to finishing school."

"Well, boarding school, anyway," she admitted. "But only for one school year. When we were fifteen. It was the thing to do in those days. And it was in Illinois. Not back East, or Paris, or anything like that. We hated it, Shel and I. And Michael got into all kinds of trouble while we were away. He and Garrett were as homesick as we were, even though they were here. Dad nearly shipped Michael off to military school before we came home. I don't think he's ever forgiven us for that."

"I would never have guessed it was a defense mechanism. The way you stood up to me that first day in the apartment, I just figured you were high class and tough as nails."

"Should I take that as a compliment?"

"If anything I say strikes you as a compliment, it is one."

"Intelligent man. But while we're on the subject of each other's personality traits, what's that little bit of cowboy twang I hear every now an' agin?"

She gave as good as she got. "Hey, I come by that naturally. My grandpa owned a spread west of here. Closest town's a place called Crystal Creek. Ever heard of it?"

"Can't say that I have." She scooted around in the seat to check on Greg. Dylan did the same, using the rearview mirror. The baby was awake, sucking happily at his pacifier. It was a special one, made for premature babies. Dylan had accidentally left it when he came to Austin and had tried to replace it with a regular-size one. It hadn't worked. But now Greg was happy as a clam, tucked up in his seat and sucking noisily.

"My brother Garrett runs a ranch. Three thousand acres. About two hundred head of cattle."

"Nice little spread."

"I take it from your tone your family's ranch is bigger?"

"Some bigger," he said. Actually, a lot bigger, but why brag? The Van Zandts weren't in the same league as the Lords no matter what kind of moneymaking you were talking about. "My uncle and two cousins run the place. I used to go there every summer and work my butt off until I was sixteen. Then I went to work for Dad. I earned my cowboy twang, missy," he drawled, laying it on thick.

"How come I never see you in boots and a Stetson, then?"

"No need to gild the lily. There are too many drugstore cowboys in the city these days. Don't want to be mistaken for one of those. And hand-tooled ostrich-hide boots don't do you much good if you drop a steel I-beam on your foot." She laughed again, and he laughed with her. They fell silent after that. Traffic was light heading into the city. Dylan took the expressway and skirted downtown. Lana had been silent so long he thought she was asleep. When he slowed for their exit, however, she roused herself. She turned her head and peered into the back seat. "Greg's asleep," she said.

"Good. Hope he stays that way until we get home."

"Home," Lana repeated, still sounding a little sleepy. "My home."

"Look, I didn't mean anything by that. It's just a figure of speech."

She looked at him, then reached over and touched his arm. Even through the material of his shirtsleeve he could feel the warmth of her skin. As always, it communicated itself through tissue and bone into his bloodstream, straight to his groin, and higher. If he didn't know better, he'd say straight into his heart. "I'm sorry. I didn't mean anything, either. It's just that I've been mulling over the possibility of moving to one of your apartments when they're renovated. It would be so much more convenient. And Mom and Dad's house is so big. I just rattle around in it. But when you said that, I realized that old pile of brick and stone really is home to me."

"Someday you'll have a husband and a houseful of kids to fill it up."

For a brief moment Dylan pictured himself in that role. Husband. Father. A real husband to a woman like Lana, not a cuckold. Then he pushed the thought away. He wasn't ready for any kind of relationship. Not now. Maybe never.

"That's what I've always wanted. But I'm not doing too well on that front. You can't get a husband or kids if you break off your engagement six weeks before the wedding."

"Do you regret it?" It was the most information she'd volunteered about her broken engagement.

"No. He wasn't the man I thought he was. He wasn't the man for me, and I'm grateful I found out in time."

They'd passed the gates to the country club. He turned onto the winding, tree-lined street leading to her house and parked the truck under the oak tree that overhung the garage. "What did he do to you, Lana?" He had no business asking that of her. Not when he had so many secrets of his own to keep.

"Nothing, except stomp on my dreams with his hand-tooled, custom-made, ostrich-hide boots." She spoke lightly, but he could see the hurt in her eyes even in the near darkness beneath the tree.

"What dreams did he kill?" he asked, leaning toward her, drawn by desire that had grown stronger, like a tightening spring inside him, since the day they'd met.

"Just ordinary, everyday ones," Lana said, drawing slightly away from him, as though she, too, sensed the attraction and was afraid of its strength.

"I imagine your ordinary, everyday dreams are a lot different from mine," he returned in an attempt to bring his wayward senses under control. She wasn't for him. She was a Lord, an Austin Lord, born to privilege and wealth.

She was quiet a moment, then said very softly, "I don't suppose they're all that different. I wanted a husband and a home and babies to fill it up, just like you said. But Jason didn't. He was considering getting a vasectomy and not telling me about it. He figured he could talk me out of wanting babies after we were married. He'd even made the doctor's appointment. If he hadn't gotten himself drunk one night and spilled the beans, I'd be married to him right now, and probably miserable."

"He's an idiot, then, if he'd deny himself the pleasure of making babies with you."

She smiled, and some of the sadness left her eyes. "Thank you. I decided the same thing."

Dylan smiled, too, and then he leaned forward and kissed her. Her lips were stiff under his. For a moment he thought she was going to pull away. Then she softened, her lips opened and she lifted her arms and wound them around his neck. She leaned into him and kissed him back. A kiss that went on and on, and that he began to hope would never end, but did, long before he was ready.

"I'm sorry, Dylan," she said, resting her forehead against his. She loosened her arms, but he caught her hands in his and wouldn't let her pull completely away. "I shouldn't have taken advantage of you like that."

He leaned back so he could see her face, but she was looking down and wouldn't meet his eyes. "I was under the impression that was supposed to be my line," he said, striving to keep a light note in his voice even though his heart was beating like a kettledrum inside his chest. He reached up and lifted her chin with his knuckles. "I'm not a bit sorry I kissed you. I'm more than a little glad you kissed me back."

"But you kissed me for the wrong reasons. And I let you."

"Why is that?"

"You felt sorry for me."

"What?" It was the last thing he'd expected her to say.

"You're that kind of man, Dylan. You want to make things right. I'll be fine. You don't have to try and make it right for me."

"That's not—"

She looked him straight in the eye. "I don't want to be like Jessie was. You fell in love with her because she needed you, didn't you? Now you need to find someone else to take care of, to help make the guilt and the hurt go away."

"That's not true, Lana." She was wrong. He was attracted to her because she was so different from Jessie, so much her own woman, but he couldn't tell her that after what she'd just said. She wouldn't believe him.

"I'm strong enough to get over one broken heart. But I'm not sure I could survive two. I think we'd better not let this happen again. Good night, Dylan." She opened the door of the truck and closed it very softly behind her. In a few seconds she was swallowed up by the darkness. By the time he got Greg unloaded and in the house she had gone upstairs. She seemed determined to keep some distance between them.

And he'd already learned enough about Lana Lord to know that if that's what she intended to do, it was as good as done.

CHAPTER SEVEN

"LANA?" Brittany stuck her head around the door of Lana's office cubicle. "Your brother's here asking for you." She was whispering in case Greg was asleep. But the baby was wide awake, sitting in his carrier, staring cross-eyed at his fist and making gurgling sounds of happiness in the back of his throat. His other hand was wrapped around Lana's finger. She'd been staring at that fist, the little fingers, the tiny, perfect nails, the ledger sheets in front of her forgotten.

He'd changed a lot in two weeks. He was still so small, not even seven pounds. They'd weighed him yesterday on one of the new digital scales that had arrived in a shipment that morning. That meant he'd nearly doubled his birth weight. A very good sign. His cheeks were fuller, his eyes brighter and no longer the dark, dark blue of newborns, but lightening to the color of a Texas twilight. She wondered if they might be gray in the end, like Dylan's. She wondered if he could be Dylan's child, after all.

He was taking more formula at each feeding, and he sometimes skipped a bottle during the night. At least, that's what Dylan had told her, one of the few times they'd been alone at the kitchen island before she left for work. Four whole hours of uninterrupted sleep, he'd announced, grinning.

Lana wished she could say the same for herself. She

hadn't been sleeping well at all since the night they'd kissed. She was far too attracted to him. And for as many of the wrong reasons as he was attracted to her. She was well aware that her yearning for family, for babies of her own could land her in the same no-win situation she'd encountered with Jason Fairmont. And deep inside she knew that this time, if something went wrong with the relationship, she wouldn't come out of it with just a cracked and bruised heart. She'd have a broken one.

"Lana, did you hear me?"

She turned her head at the sound of Brittany's voice. "No, I'm afraid my mind was somewhere else. What did you say?"

"Your brother's here. Garrett. He's asking for you."

Now, what had brought him into town on a weekday in the middle of September? It was a busy time at the ranch. He should be getting ready for the fall roundup. "Tell him to come on back." The lace and ruffles and fragile china figurines that dotted the showroom made Garrett nervous. He had told her standing among the baby-size furniture made him feel like a bull in a china shop.

She disengaged her finger from Greg's grip. The movement startled the infant, and he began to fuss. Lana unhooked the carrier's harness and picked him up, soothing him with a kiss and little shooshing noises.

"You look real natural that way."

"I've been getting a lot of practice these last couple of weeks." She turned and smiled at her big brother. And he was her big brother, tall, broad-shouldered, with hair so deep a red it was nearly brown and strongly marked eyebrows as dark as night. He hadn't shaved in a while, and in Levi's and boots, with a black Stetson in his hand, he looked like the answer to an adman's dreams of the Marlboro man.

"So I hear."

"Garrett—"

Brittany was back. "Your other brother's here, too," she said, and skedaddled.

"Tell me this is just a coincidence?"

Garrett had the grace to look sheepish. "I asked Mike to meet me here. I thought it was about time we were formally introduced to this guy you're keeping company with."

"I'm not keeping company—"

Garrett's eyes narrowed. He no longer looked sheepish, just downright skeptical.

Lana gave up. It had to happen sooner or later. "All right. He's upstairs. Let me put Greg in his carrier and take him out to Brittany. I don't like to take him upstairs until they get the lead paint off the walls. There's a lot of dust—" She stopped talking when Brittany sauntered into the room. Evidently, she hadn't skedaddled far.

"Did I hear my name? Does this mean I get to spend some time with my Greg-man? Huh, does it?" She leaned over the carrier and tickled Dylan's son under his chin. "I never get to hold you anymore. No, it's always the boss lady who's got you, isn't it, big boy?"

"Brittany, would you tell Michael to come on back?"

"I'm already here." Michael pushed aside the beaded curtain that divided the storage area and office from the showroom. "How can you expect a guy to walk through this place without tripping over something? You've got more merchandise per square foot than any place I've ever been in."

"Babies are a growth industry," Lana said in a voice

that meant if they weren't all too old for that sort of thing, she would have stuck her tongue out at him.

"Very funny." She'd always felt more at ease with Michael than with Garrett. Maybe it was because they were triplets, or maybe because Garrett was her big brother and always would be. Michael had had enough teasing. "Where's Van Zandt?"

"I was just telling Garrett. He's upstairs." She led the way. She'd just as soon this interrogation didn't continue with Brittany listening with interest to every word. "We won't be long, Brittany."

Her employee took the hint, although reluctantly. "We'll be fine. We're going to try out that new Beatrix Potter swing, aren't we? If our timing's right, some mama-to-be will walk in and buy it just 'cause you're the cutest thing she's ever seen."

Garrett looked at Greg, then at Michael. He lifted his shoulders in a shrug. "What is it about those things that makes perfectly rational human beings talk like they're addled in the brain?" he asked the other man.

"Must be because they're little and they've got big eyes. Just like Disney characters."

"Oh, stop it, you two. Come on." Lana led the way up the stairs, but she wasn't as calm as she seemed. Her brothers were not only overly protective of her and Shelby, they also held strong opinions about most other things, as well. And the fact she had a man living with her was one of the things they were most liable to take exception to. "There's something I should tell you," she said as they got to the top of the stairs.

Michael wasn't listening. He'd already stuck his head in the door of Dylan's apartment. "Hmm, nice proportions. Does the fireplace work?"

"I have no idea. I think so. But Dylan wants to convert them to gas."

"Probably a good idea. Lot less fuss and bother when all you're really using it for is atmosphere."

Garrett nodded. "How many bedrooms?"

"Three." He looked at her sharply. "I think three. I've never seen them." She swallowed a little lump of nerves that had risen into her throat and hurried along the hall to the landing above the lobby. It was proving harder than she'd planned to tell them she wasn't only giving Dylan lessons in baby care—she was doing it while he was living under her roof. Maybe it wouldn't have bothered her as much before they kissed, but it bothered her now. "Dylan's probably working around here somewhere. They started on the apartment above the Crystal Unicorn." That was the name of the New Age bookshop at the other end of the building.

The elevator doors were open. A man in coveralls and a yellow hard hat was talking to Dylan as he peered down the shaft. Dylan was in Levi's and a light blue work shirt, and he, too, was wearing a hard hat. Lana caught a glimpse of men in spacesuit-like outfits complete with helmets moving around behind a thick layer of plastic that sealed off the hallway beyond the landing. A generator chugged away somewhere in the distance.

The elevator man pointed to where Lana supposed the cables were, and shook his head. "Not lookin' good, Mr. Van Zandt," she heard him say. "Goin' to have to replace the whole shebang. Goin' to cost a pretty penny more than we thought before."

"Damn, that's what I was afraid of." Dylan rubbed the back of his neck as though to loosen knotted muscles there. "Do what you have to, Hiram. We need to have handicap access to bring the building up to code. The elevator's a must.''

"Yes, sir.''

Dylan looked around and saw them. "Lana.'' The frown that had drawn his eyebrows together cleared a little. She thought he might be going to smile, but then he didn't. He had caught sight of her brothers.

"Hello, Dylan.''

"Is everything all right with Greg?''

"He's fine,'' she assured him. "I...I just wanted you to meet my brothers. Have we come at a bad time?'' It wasn't surprising he'd ask about Greg first. She'd done her best to avoid Dylan since their kiss. She hadn't ventured upstairs at all since that night.

"Most anytime's a bad time these days,'' he said, and he smiled, a twist of his lips that never reached his eyes. "I'm Dylan Van Zandt,'' he said, stretching out his arm.

"Garrett Lord.'' The two men shook hands briefly.

"Michael.'' The handclasp was repeated. "Pleased to meet you.''

"Same here,'' Dylan responded.

"Lana tells us you're fixing this place up.''

"Trying to. Hasn't been occupied for over fifty years. Coming up against a lot more problems than I'd planned on.''

"Asbestos?'' Michael asked, nodding toward the sealed-off portion of the hallway.

"No. That's one we avoided. About the only one,'' he added under his breath. "But the paint's lead-based. They're taking it off the walls and ceiling and woodwork. Should be done with these rooms and ready to start on the other side next week.''

"Will any of the dust get into the store?'' Lana asked.

"I have pregnant women and little ones in and out all the time. Not to mention Greg."

Dylan held up a restraining hand and smiled. "No problem, Lana. All the dust and dirt and paint chips are sucked up into a big vacuum. It's perfectly safe."

"If there's lead paint on these walls, then there's probably lead paint on the downstairs walls, too," Garrett commented.

"More than likely. But there's no immediate danger. When I get this floor renovated, I'll start working on updating the stores downstairs."

"I had the walls sealed before I signed the lease," Lana told them. "It wasn't the perfect solution, but it's all I could get the former owner to agree to."

"I still plan to strip the downstairs when I'm finished up here. I'll do it when we upgrade the wiring."

"Sounds like you've got a lot of unexpected expense with this project," Michael said, folding his arms and lowering his chin a little.

Her brother's stance was combative. Lana felt the back of her neck grow warm. "Michael, Dylan's business affairs are no business of yours."

"It's okay, Lana." Dylan held up a restraining hand. "I've run into some problems, but nothing that's a budget breaker."

"A mite overextended, are you?"

"Michael, that's enough." Lana almost stomped her foot for emphasis but thought better of it just in time. She was so embarrassed she couldn't even look at Dylan.

"He hasn't said anything that isn't public knowledge," Dylan said, locking eyes with the younger man. "He's right. Van Zandt Development's got a lot of irons in the fire right now. But I'm still on budget and still on deadline. These units will be ready to put on the market by the end of the first quarter of next year.''

"Will you *keep* on livin' here?" Garrett asked without raising his voice.

Lana couldn't decide if she heard the emphasis on the word or only imagined it. She was beginning to feel the same stirring of resentment for Garrett that Michael's prying questions had engendered.

Dylan swung his eyes to Garrett's face. "I haven't thought that far ahead."

"'Course if you've got yourself someplace better picked out..."

Dylan's hand balled into a fist. He took a half step forward, then stopped himself.

"What are you getting at, Lord?" he asked, his voice as hard-edged as she'd ever heard it.

Lana had had all she could take. "All right. Enough. Garrett. Michael. Dylan isn't living here, as you probably already know. He's been staying with me for the past two weeks. I invited him after Chase's party. I don't want Greg exposed to the dust and dirt up here. I didn't ask your permission then, and I'm not about to now. He's my guest. He's welcome to stay as long as he wants, and that's the end of it. Do you understand? Both of you?"

Michael tilted his head to look at his brother. Garrett opened his mouth as if to say something. Lana didn't know how she'd respond if they continued the argument. She didn't like being at odds with her brothers, but Dylan living under her roof was only a small bone of contention compared with the schism developing between the four of them over the search for their biological mother. At any other time this argument wouldn't be a serious one. Her brothers were quick-tempered but inherently fair-minded.

Given the present circumstances, though, she was afraid any disagreement could drive a real wedge between them.

"Hello? Anyone up there?" It was Shelby's voice, but it wasn't coming from the stairs. It sounded as if she was directly below them, in the old flower shop that was on its way to becoming the building's lobby once again.

"Who's there?" Dylan leaned over the ornate brass railing that rimmed the upper lobby. A flimsy fake ceiling that had hidden the upper level from view when the flower shop was in operation had been removed to facilitate the workmen bringing equipment in and out of the building.

"It's me. Shelby Lord. I'm looking for my—" Shelby put her hands on her hips and looked up at them. "There ya'll are."

"Hi, Shelby," Lana called. "What are you doing here?"

"How did you get in here?" Dylan wanted to know.

"A guy from the elevator company let me in," Shelby said. "Are the stairs safe?"

"They're marble," Dylan said. "They're safe."

Shelby started up, her bright eyes going from one sibling's face to the other. "Looks like the Inquisition's in session up here."

"Michael and Garrett wanted to meet Dylan," Lana said carefully.

"Um. Well then, I guess I'm too late to warn you they're both in the neighborhood." She glanced from one scowling face to another. "I don't suppose this is a good time to invite all of you to come back to the diner and try my new shiitake and sun-dried tomato pizza?"

DYLAN WAS MAKING an omelette and talking to Greg in his carrier on the kitchen island. He wasn't sure when he'd started doing that, talking out loud to the baby. Probably it had just rubbed off on him, listening to Lana and his mother and every other woman who came in contact with the little guy ramble on and on. But however it had happened, it seemed like the natural thing to do. And Greg appeared to like it. He moved his head back and forth and wiggled and made cooing sounds.

"This thing's as big as a Mack truck, buddy," Dylan observed of the restaurant-size range. "Get a load of this. Eight burners. A griddle. Three ovens. Your grandma'd have an apoplexy over that. She hates cleaning ovens. The Lords must have done a lot of cooking in their time. Big parties, fancy dinners. They probably had a cook who lived in.

"There are two other rooms in the servants' wing, remember? I showed them to you that night you had the tummyache and we were up wandering around at two a.m. Why didn't she tell her brothers we're staying back here about as far from her as if we were in another county?"

He shook the skillet he was holding a lot harder than necessary to move the melting butter to the edges. Damn, he should have realized Lana hadn't told her brothers he was living here, but the two of them hadn't needed to act as if he were some kind of con man out to get her money.

Hell, he wouldn't have been nearly as mad at them if they'd accused him of being on the make for her body, because that was damned near the truth. But her money? Sure he was overextended. But the last thing in the world he'd do was ask Lana Lord for money. The very damned last thing he'd do.

"Dylan?"

He almost poured the beaten eggs onto the floor instead of into the skillet at the unexpected sound of her voice. "We're in here."

She stuck her head around the swinging door that led to the front of the house. "Mmm, that smells good."

"There's plenty. Greg just told me he's not too hungry tonight." He was determined to keep this light. He didn't want to talk about the argument with her brothers. He didn't want to talk about their kiss. No good could come of either subject.

"Oh, no, I couldn't. It's your supper."

"What did you have? Did you go down to the diner with your brothers and have the pizza?"

"No." She kept her gaze focused on the omelette cooking in the skillet. He added plain old sautéed button mushrooms and onions and peppers he'd been keeping warm on one of the back burners. No fancy Japanese mushrooms and sun-dried tomatoes for him. "It smells good," she repeated, sounding a little wistful as he sprinkled some hot sauce over the whole concoction.

"Make some toast. Coffee's ready. It's decaf," he said, forestalling her objection.

"Okay." She looked around the shadowy room. It was getting dark earlier now that they were almost past the middle of September. "But let's eat in the family room."

"Family room? Somehow I hadn't pictured this place with a family room. Maybe a picture gallery," he said, letting his accent thicken.

"Oh, it's a real family room, all right. Complete with ratty old sofas and a big-screen TV."

"Okay. I'll bring the food. You take Greg."

"I like that deal," she said. "Dylan, about—"

"Go on. I can find a tray and the silverware. Greg's been dying to hear about your day. He just got done telling me so."

Her eyes, more golden than green tonight, widened with

surprise. "You've been having a conversation with the baby?"

"Just a little man talk. What he did all day. What I did all day. Well, with some exceptions, of course."

"I see." She looked at Greg, still chewing contentedly on his tiny fist.

"Men talk, too, you know. It's not just a woman thing." But that wasn't what she was surprised at, and they both knew it. It was because he was talking about Greg. Not just the facts and figures of his feeding, or diaper changes, or tummy rumbles, but about Greg and him. Together. Father and son. The thought spoiled his mood. He turned to the skillet, aware he was frowning, aware she had seen the change.

"Dylan?" she asked, enough hesitation in her voice that he knew she wouldn't press if he changed the subject.

"How about cheese?" he asked abruptly. "Do you like cheese on your omelette?"

"Yes, yes, I do." She scooped up Greg's carrier, and a moment later she was gone.

"Damn. When will I ever stop thinking about the man who really fathered that boy?" he asked the empty room, shoving bread in the four-slice toaster. He didn't have an answer for himself, and if he did come up with one, he suspected it wouldn't be any time soon. Maybe never.

CHAPTER EIGHT

HE ATE as he did everything else, methodically and efficiently, with a minimum of conversation.

Or maybe it was just that he had little to say to her after what had happened that afternoon.

They were sitting at the games table in the family room. It had once been her father's den, in the days before he'd answered the phone call from Megan Maitland telling him she had four abandoned babies on her doorstep. Her father and his best friends had continued to play poker on Thursday nights at this table until just weeks before his death. Lana had changed very little in the room. The worn leather furniture was older than Garrett. The carpet was threadbare in places from years of roughhousing boys and dozens and dozens of sleepovers for the girls. The tall, many-paned windows looked onto the garden. The fireplace that divided them was built of river rock, the stones discolored from the smoke of countless marshmallow-toasting fires. The mantel bristled with trophies inscribed with all their names, some going back to kindergarten track-and-field competitions.

The bookshelves were filled with leather-bound volumes that had belonged to her father's father, packed side-by-side with paperback thrillers from ten years past and the historical romances that had been her mother's favorite pastime until the day she died. But the wide-screen TV was state-of-the-art, and the CD system was brand-new.

A gift she'd given herself the first quarter Oh, Baby! had turned a profit.

Lana pushed her plate aside and picked Greg up from his carrier. He'd been fussing steadily for the last ten minutes. "What's the matter, little fella? Need your diaper changed?"

"I'll do it," Dylan said immediately.

She stood up, waving him back to his seat. "Finish your omelette. I'll change him."

"I'll do it." He was as stubborn as a mule.

"Come on. You cooked. I'll clean up." He kept on frowning. "It's a pun," she said, then sighed. "Not a very good one."

He smiled suddenly and unexpectedly, and it nearly took Lana's breath away. "I know. Yours are usually much better. By far, not your best effort."

"Just for that, you get to do dishes." She whirled away from the table, still holding Greg. "Where's his bag?"

"In our room."

"Oh." His bedroom. His bed. The memory of the kiss they'd shared was never far from her thoughts. She dreamed of it, and in her dreams the kiss went much further. "Maybe you should change him. I'll clean up the dishes."

"Lana, what's wrong?" He rounded the table and took Greg from her, cuddling him in the crook of his arm, the way she'd showed him that first day. But now it was natural, effortless. And it looked so right.

"Nothing," she said hastily.

His eyes narrowed. They were the color of slate tonight, dark and shadowed. "Yes, there is. Are you still fuming about this afternoon?"

"I'm madder than hell at my brothers for the third degree they put you through." It wasn't a lie. She was upset

about that, just not as much as she was about her day-
dreams of being in Dylan's arms. In Dylan's bed. She
piled cups and glasses onto the tray and picked it up. Her
hands were shaking a little. She tightened her grip before
the china started rattling.

"You don't need to be."

"Of course, I do," she said indignantly. "They were
insufferable."

"You're their baby sister."

"I'm not Michael's baby sister. I'm the oldest."

"How do you know that? I thought you were left on
the doorstep of the clinic."

She felt her cheeks growing hot. "I was. I mean we
were. But I'm the oldest. I *know* it."

"You know it?"

"I know it." She raised her chin and met his dark gaze.
He was smiling. "You're teasing me," she said, indignant
all over again. "I'm trying to apologize for my brothers'
bad behavior, and you're laughing at me."

"I'm not laughing at you. Your brothers love you.
They're protective of you. It's a man thing. It's a Texas
thing."

"It's still not necessary. I can take care of myself."

"Then there's something else." Dylan reached out and
placed his hand on her arm. She almost dropped the tray.
He hadn't touched her since the night they'd kissed. She
felt hot, then cold. She looked at her bare arm, surprised
the sensual imprint of his fingers hadn't branded themselves into her skin.

She put the tray on the table and wandered to the CD
player, trying to regain her shattered poise. Nothing in his
voice or expression gave the slightest hint that he felt
anything at all from the contact. She pushed the button
and the sounds of Duke Ellington filled the room. "It's

because of the search for our mother. We all just tap-dance around it. Michael doesn't want to find her any more than I do. But Garrett and Shelby are determined to track her down. I thought we'd all made peace with being abandoned years ago. We never talk about it. Until these last two weeks. And now—'' She shrugged, having difficulty finding the words. "We still don't talk about it. I wish Mom was here. She'd know what to do."

"She'd probably tell you to stop worrying about it until it happens," Dylan said softly.

"I'm a good worrier. It's what I do best." She held out her hands for Greg. He was squirming in Dylan's arms, a frown on his face.

"He's not happy," she said. "But I don't think it's because of a wet diaper. Maybe he's getting a tummyache. Let's sit here and listen to the music."

She sat on the couch and curled her feet under her. Dylan hesitated a moment, then sat beside her.

"Why do you think your mother abandoned you?" he asked, leaning against the cushions.

She let Greg curl his fist around her finger. His tiny feet kicked at her tummy. He rubbed at his ear with his other hand, still frowning. She didn't know how to answer Dylan's question. "We don't have a clue. When we were young we speculated about it all the time. Then as we got older, we stopped talking about it. I made peace with myself. I thought the others had, too. Why did she send those gifts, Dylan? She certainly knows who we are and where we are. Nothing but those little sweaters with our names on them, and the teddy bear, and another cryptic note. Just like the first. She's as much a mystery to me now as she was twenty-five years ago. I resent that. I resent her, and I don't like myself for it."

"Seems like a natural enough reaction to me."

She leaned her head against the couch. "Am I wrong to be against trying to find her? Maybe I'm just scared she'll be someone I don't want to know."

"That sounds natural, too."

"I might be more like her than I want to be. I might be as weak as she was, a woman who could abandon her own flesh and blood to strangers." She leaned forward so her hair fell past her cheek and hid the tears she couldn't keep from brimming in her eyes. She'd never, ever meant to tell him so much about herself.

He reached out and turned her face toward him. His touch was soft, but the tip of his finger was rough against her skin. "Lana, I've only known you for a couple of weeks, but you're not that kind of woman. You're made of a lot stronger stuff than that. Trust me on this one."

"I wish I could be that sure of myself."

"You've got what it takes to be a wonderful mother. You're a natural."

"That's the nicest thing anyone's ever said to me." She couldn't look away from his eyes.

"It's the truth." He leaned closer. He wasn't looking at her as if she were a mother. He was looking at her as if she were a woman. A woman he desired.

Lana's throat closed. She swallowed hard. She focused on his mouth. She watched him come closer until his features blurred and she had to shut her eyes. His lips touched hers, as softly as a whisper. She leaned into the kiss, wanting more. Her lips opened and she tasted him with the tip of her tongue. She reached behind his head, let her fingers sift through the fine, dark hair at the nape of his neck.

He opened his mouth, and her tongue slipped inside. He sucked gently on the tip, mimicking an act more intimate still. His arm came around her, cradled the back of her head. Greg still lay on her lap. Lana could feel his tiny fingers wrapped around hers, but the rest of her was aware only of the man beside her. She could feel the hardness of his thigh pressed against her leg, the strength of his fingers tangled in her hair, the heat of his body radiating between them.

He leaned closer, his mouth devouring hers. She wanted to be closer still, but she couldn't move. That baby was between them, a small weight, but a precious one. She arched her back. Her breasts brushed against his chest. Dylan lifted his other arm, cradled her breast, caressed the hardened peak of her nipple. He groaned low in his throat, and she moaned too, in frustration and desire, a sound that she'd never thought could come from her.

She'd never felt like this when she made love to Jason. Indeed, they seldom made love. Jason had said it was because he wanted to wait until they were married. Now she wondered if it was because he didn't trust her not to forget her pills and deliberately try to get pregnant.

She had known Jason for years before they became intimate. Then they'd dated for two years before they became engaged. She had known Dylan Van Zandt for only two weeks, yet she was ready to give herself to him, body and soul. The unnerving realization brought her up short. Time and space slid into their rightful places. She could feel the insistent thump of Greg's tiny heels against her stomach, the cool breath of the air-conditioning, the scratch of Dylan's beard against her cheek. She wanted him so badly she hummed, she vibrated with it. He wanted her, too. His hands trembled against the back of her neck, her shoulder. His erection was evident, pushing hard against the zipper of his jeans. She pulled back, breaking the kiss.

"God, where did you learn to kiss like that?"

She gave a shaky little laugh. "I don't know. I never thought I was very good at it." At least Jason had given her that impression.

"Well, you sure as hell improved in the last five minutes." He rested his forehead against hers. She didn't protest, didn't move away. She couldn't. She wanted him too much to deny herself the pleasure of his touch. She took a couple of deep breaths, willing her heart to slow down.

He bent his head as if to kiss her again. She put her fingers to his lips, forestalling him. "No, Dylan."

"What's wrong, Lana?" he asked, his voice as rough around the edges as his beard.

"I'm going to put an end to this now, before it gets out of hand."

"Do you mean I have a woman who can't control herself in my clutches?"

She realized he was trying to keep things from getting too intense, and she blessed him for it. If he had insisted the kiss go on, that it become more than just a kiss, she wouldn't have protested for very long. She wanted him that badly. No matter if Greg was fussing on her lap or that one of her brothers or her sister might walk in on them, or that they both had issues that made a physical relationship a big risk. She wanted him at a level that was so primary, so primitive and basic that none of those other things mattered a damn. "It's a distinct possibility. It's not a situation I've had a lot of practice with," she admitted ruefully.

"Is that a compliment?" he asked, brushing his lips across her forehead before putting a little space between them.

"I think it is." She lifted her fingers and drew them down his cheek. "You're a very sexy man, Dylan. I don't seem to be able to keep my balance around you. That's not good for either of us."

"It's good for me."

She shook her head. The ability to think and to reason was coming back, now that he was no longer so close her breasts brushed his chest. "No, it isn't. You're not on any better footing emotionally than I am."

"Don't tell me you're one of those women who analyzes everything to death."

She smiled. "I didn't used to be, but now I think it's better if I am. And better for you, too."

"I'm over Jessie," he said.

Perhaps he had fallen out of love with his dead wife physically, but the burden of guilt he carried and wouldn't share wasn't so easily denied. She could see it in the shadowed darkness in his eyes and the tight line of his jaw.

"I'm not so sure," she said.

"I'd prove it to you if you'd let me. I mean—" He floundered for the right words.

"I know what you mean." She brushed a kiss across his lips. "Maybe you are over loving her. But your memories, good and bad, are still there. If she didn't come between us, she still comes between you and Greg."

"I told you I'd do my best for Greg." He paused as if he might say more. She held her breath. If he told her that he loved the little boy, despite what he believed about his conception, she would be lost.

Dylan remained silent.

"It's getting late. I'm going to put the dishes in the kitchen and go to bed. I think we should call it a night." Greg had begun whimpering again. She picked him up and cuddled him to her breast. She was very, very close to losing her heart to Dylan. She'd already lost her heart to Greg.

"What's between us isn't going to go away, you know," he said, quietly taking Greg from her arms.

"I know. But what's between us can wait. It has to wait until you come to terms with your feelings about Greg."

He looked at the little boy, who was complaining more loudly. "I'm trying to learn to love him, Lana. I promised you that."

She knew he was telling her the truth. She wondered again what kind of woman Jessie Van Zandt had been. Immature and troubled, certainly. But whatever she had done to Dylan had gone deeper than that. She had hurt him badly, and the wounds were not yet healed.

"Good night, Dylan." Lana stood on shaky legs and walked to the table to pick up the tray of dirty dishes. She wasn't in any better position to embark on a love affair than Dylan was. She had her own hurts that weren't quite healed, her own problems with her brothers and sister and their long-lost mother to solve.

It would be easy to find solace in Dylan's arms. But he was still a stranger, and a little pang around her heart warned her so many things could go wrong. The loving would be glorious, of that she had no doubt. But men like Dylan should come with a warning from the Surgeon General. They could be dangerous to your heart.

DYLAN ROLLED OVER in bed and looked at the clock. Nearly midnight. He could have sworn he hadn't closed his eyes, but he must have dozed off for a minute or two because he'd been dreaming. Of Lana. The kind of dream that in his younger days would have driven him into an icy shower. He listened for sounds from Greg in his crib across the little room, but he heard nothing. He rolled onto his back and laced his fingers together behind his head.

Hell, what was he going to do? He couldn't stay under the same roof with Lana much longer. Somehow, tonight the barriers between them had nearly crumbled. Maybe it was because she'd invited him into her part of the big old house. Her sanctuary. Her home. Maybe it was because she'd caught fire in his arms, nearly sending them both up in flames.

Greg let out a cry. Dylan sat straight up in bed. Greg screamed again, a penetrating animal wail. This wasn't his usual bellow for food, his whimper when he was cold. It went beyond all that, lifting the hair on Dylan's arms and the back of his neck.

He swung his legs over the side of the bed, grabbed his jeans and pulled them on, yanking up the zipper as he crossed the room. It was chilly, the air-conditioning as efficient in the servants' quarters as it was in the main portion of the house. But it wasn't just chilly fingers and toes that were driving his son to such anguished cries. Something else was wrong.

Dylan leaned over the crib and lifted the baby to his shoulder, cradling his head and bottom as Lana had showed him not so many days ago. Greg sniffled and rooted at Dylan's shoulder. "What's the matter, little guy?" Dylan crooned. "Do you want a bottle? Is that it?"

He took Greg into the kitchen, fixed a bottle and put the nipple to the baby's mouth. He sucked greedily for a moment or two, then pushed the nipple away, screaming at the top of his lungs again. He felt warm to Dylan, too warm for the number of covers he'd had over him. He wondered if he was running a fever. He had a thermometer someplace, one of those you put in a baby's ear. They were supposed to be accurate and fast. His mother had insisted he bring it with him. He went into the bedroom, jiggling the screaming infant in the crook of his arm, and searched one-handed through Greg's pack.

He found the thermometer but wasn't certain how to use it. He squinted at the instructions, then gingerly placed it a few millimeters inside Greg's tiny ear. The baby screamed so loudly Dylan nearly dropped the expensive thermometer. His heart was pounding, his hands shaking. What had he done? Punctured his son's eardrum, scarred him for life?

He tried once more but Greg batted at the thermometer with uncoordinated hands. He kept on crying until Dylan turned on his heels and headed through the kitchen and into the dark silence of the main house. He had little experience with illness, none at all with sick babies beyond helping entertain his nieces and nephews when they had the sniffles and couldn't play outside. None of that had prepared him for this. Greg was ill. And preemies weren't like other babies. He was dangerously out of his league. He needed help.

Dylan found his way to the stairs by touch and luck, having no idea where the light switches were. Moonlight guided him up the wide, curving staircase. The hallway above him was all darkness, except for one room, where another patch of silvery moonlight spilled out into blackness.

He knew it was her room even before his eyes adjusted to the lesser darkness and he saw her curves beneath the blanket. He smelled her scent, the combination of flowers and sunlight he had come to associate with her. It was stronger here, mingled with other feminine scents he couldn't identify as readily. Greg had quieted as he climbed the stairs, but he began to cry again.

Lana sat up in bed. "Who's there?" she asked, a faint note of alarm cutting through the huskiness of sleep.

"It's me, Lana. Dylan. I need your help. There's something wrong with the baby. He's sick. Very, very sick."

CHAPTER NINE

LANA STRUGGLED to shake off the remnants of sleep. Her heart was pounding, her breath coming fast and hard. "Who's there?" she repeated, or perhaps spoke aloud for the first time. She wasn't certain she was truly awake, that the shape of the man in her doorway wasn't a lingering ghost of her dream.

She had been dreaming. Not a nightmare, but a dream that was almost as disturbing. She'd dreamed of being in Dylan's arms, beneath the hard weight of his body, joined with him in lovemaking like none she had ever experienced in reality. Now he stood in her bedroom doorway, tall and solid against the moonlight—with a screaming baby in his arms.

"Bring him here," she said as the fear in his voice banished the last of her sleepiness and her fantasy. She sat up in bed and switched on the table lamp, scooting over a little so Dylan could settle beside her. She took Greg in her arms. "He's burning up," she said, knowing she sounded every bit as fearful as Dylan.

"I tried to take his temperature. He screamed and screamed. I'm afraid I hurt him. I read the directions but I've never used one of these things." Dylan held out a tapered thermometer, the kind that fit in a baby's ear.

Lana looked at the sobbing infant he had handed her, and her heart rate steadied a little. Greg was rubbing his fist along the side of his head, his little face screwed into a grimace of pain. He was definitely running a fever, but she didn't think he was dangerously ill, at least at the moment. "You didn't hurt him," she said. "Which ear did you try?"

"The left one. The one he's rubbing."

Lana nodded. "Let's try the other side."

"Okay." Dylan sounded doubtful. "My mom made me buy that thing, but I never thought to ask her how to use it. I guess I hoped he'd never get sick."

Lana took Greg's temperature. He stiffened his legs and cried harder. "It's one oh three point four."

"That's pretty high, isn't it?"

"Yes, it is. I think we should get him to a doctor."

"We don't have a doctor yet. I mean, we don't have an appointment with a pediatrician at Maitland until next week. And his surgeon is clear over at Mercy. That's an hour's drive from here."

"I think he's got an ear infection. It happened sometimes with little ones when I was working at the day-care center. What time is it?" Greg wouldn't stop crying. It was beginning to make her frightened again. Unbidden, the shadowy image of a young woman popped into her mind. Her mother, with three babies this size and a rambunctious toddler to take care of. The fear and anxiety would have been multiplied many times. Especially if she had been alone and without money. Was a gnawing fear like the one that ate at Lana this very moment part of the reason her mother had given them up? Had it been just too much for her to handle alone?

"A few minutes after midnight," Dylan said, his voice bringing her to the here and now.

"I'll call Beth Redstone. She's my friend who runs the day-care center at Maitland, remember? She'll know who's on call at the clinic, or maybe she can recommend one of those all-night care places."

"A doc-in-the-box," Dylan said, frowning. "I don't like that idea."

"Okay. Maitland it is. I guess there's no reason to wake Beth, then. I'll call Abby instead. She'll help us."

"Who's Abby?" Dylan asked, standing up, towering over her, seemingly oblivious that he was wearing nothing but an unsnapped pair of jeans that fit him like a glove. He might be unaware, but Lana wasn't, not even with a crying baby in her arms. Her body thrummed with desire, the lingering aftereffect of her dream.

"Dr. Abby Maitland. She's Beth's big sister. And an OB at Maitland. We've been friends forever. I'll give her a call while you're getting dressed. Leave Greg here." She leaned over and grabbed the phone off her bedside table. Dylan was out the door before she had the receiver out of its cradle.

Lana punched in Abby's home number, and after half a dozen rings it was picked up. "Maitland-McDermott residence," a sleepy male voice said.

"Kyle?"

"Speaking."

"It's Lana Lord. I'm so sorry to wake you."

"No problem, Lana. But you'll have to speak up. I can't hear you." Kyle McDermott sounded more awake. He'd been married to Abby for almost a year. He was probably getting used to, or at least resigned to, being awakened in the middle of the night.

Greg was still crying. She held the phone between her ear and shoulder and laid him on the bed, turning her back for a moment so Kyle could hear her. "I need to speak to Abby. As you can hear, I have a sick baby on my hands. He's the son of a friend...." She didn't know why this was so hard. "His father just moved to Austin. He doesn't have a pediatrician yet. I think the baby might have an ear infection. He has a fever and he's rubbing his ear. He was a preemie, and so tiny, Kyle. It's hard to tell what's wrong."

"You don't have to explain whose baby it is. Megan's kept us well-informed. It sounds as if he's really hurting." Kyle's teenage sister had a year-old daughter. He was probably used to ear infections and all the other ailments and bumps and bruises that went with a baby. "Abby's already at the clinic. She has two expectant mothers in labor. She'll be there most of the night, I expect."

"Could you give me her pager number?" She picked Greg up and jiggled him against her shoulder. It didn't help. He was still crying.

"I'll page her and tell her you're on your way. You sound like you've got your hands full."

"I do," Lana said, laughing a little with relief.

"Don't worry too much. Abby'll fix him up just fine."

"Thanks, Kyle."

"Don't mention it. Night, Lana."

"Night, Kyle. I owe you."

"I'll think of something." He broke the connection. Lana looked up to find Dylan in the doorway.

She hung up the phone. "They're expecting us at Maitland. It won't take me a minute to dress."

"You don't have to come with me, Lana." The shadows were back in the depths of his gray eyes, darkening them to charcoal.

"Oh, yes, I do. You wanted baby lessons. Well, this is your final exam. If we can get through your first emergency doctor visit, I'll consider you've graduated with honors." She teased him to hide her uneasiness. Greg was still so small and fragile. What if there was something much more seriously wrong with him than an earache? How could they know for sure?

"Thanks." Dylan took the baby from her.

"I'll be dressed and downstairs in five minutes."

"I'll get Greg's bag and meet you at the back door." He turned to go. She reached out and set her hand on his arm. "Everything's going to be fine."

"I hope to God you're right."

Thirty minutes later they pulled under the portico that sheltered the entrance to Maitland Maternity. The ride had been a nightmare. Greg had cried the entire way. Lana twisted around in her seat trying to comfort him, but nothing had worked. Finally Dylan had pulled the truck over and she'd gotten into the back of the extended cab with Greg. She'd unhooked the restraint and taken him in her arms, securing him with her seat belt, patting and soothing, but that hadn't helped, either. He continued to scream at the top of his lungs. He was so warm to the touch, his skin burned her through his sleeper and blanket.

He was still red-faced and screaming as Dylan pulled into an empty parking space just beyond the portico. Lana strapped Greg into his carrier and unsnapped the seat belt that held it to the seat as his father rounded the cab and yanked open the door. She handed him the carrier, grabbed the diaper bag and half-jogged, half-ran to keep up with Dylan's long strides as he hurried toward the building.

Maitland's specialty was obstetrics. Its staff didn't treat the general population, but the clinic had a small, state-of-the-art emergency room, Lana knew from the time she'd spent there over the years. A security guard behind a high counter asked their names, said they were expected and buzzed them through.

A nurse in pink scrubs and a paper operating cap, patterned in a vivid jungle print, met them on the other side of the double metal doors that led to the interior of the clinic. "Got a little problem, do we?" she asked kindly, indicating a treatment room to the left.

"He's running a temperature. Won't take his bottle. Keeps rubbing his left ear and crying," Dylan recited in clipped tones, all traces of cowboy drawl erased from his speech.

"Dr. Abby will be here in a minute. Let's get a look at him." The nurse held out her hands for the carrier. Dylan made to follow her into the examining room. "I'm sorry, sir," she said. "You'll have to go with Lynn to do the paperwork." Lana hadn't noticed the young woman with a clipboard until she stepped from behind the nurse.

"It will only take a moment to fill out the insurance forms."

"I'm not leaving him," Dylan growled, sweeping both women with his dark gaze. His expression was set. His face appeared carved from stone.

"We can't do anything for your baby until these matters are taken care of," the slender young woman with the clipboard said firmly. She'd obviously been through this before, Lana thought. Anxious mothers-to-be, nervous new fathers, sick infants. "Please, come with me."

Dylan didn't budge.

"I'll stay with Greg," Lana said hastily. "That's all right, isn't it?"

"Certainly, Mrs. Van Zandt."

"I'm not—" Lana began, then decided it wasn't worth the effort to explain. "Thank you," she said.

"We can fill the bloody forms out right here," Dylan insisted.

Just then Abby bustled in. "Hi, Lana. I haven't seen you since Chase's birthday party." She was in scrubs, but hers were blue, and her cap was covered in nursery-rhyme figures.

"Abby, thanks for seeing us," Lana said. Greg was still crying at the top of his lungs. "He's so miserable."

Abby's sharp gaze traveled from Lana's face to Dylan's, taking in the belligerent line of his jaw, the tense set of his shoulders. "Mr. Van Zandt?" she asked, offering him her best smile. She held out her hand.

"Dylan," he said, giving her hand a perfunctory shake.

"Dylan. And please, call me Abby." She turned her smile on Lana, and Lana smiled back. Abby was the closest thing to a big sister Lana had.

"We're kind of in a lull in the proceedings," Abby assured them. "One baby arrived safely about an hour ago. The other one…well, it looks as if he's going to take his own sweet time to get here. Now, what's wrong with this little fellow?"

"We don't know for sure," Lana admitted. "And I know this really isn't your field."

"Kyle says it sounded to him like an ear infection. He's taken to practicing pediatric medicine without a license since Marcie's little girl was born." Her smile grew wider, more luminous. She patted her round belly. "I guess I should be grateful he's a natural. It'll make it easier on all of us when this little one makes his appearance."

"I'd appreciate it if you'd examine him now," Dylan said sharply.

Abby turned her attention to Dylan. Her smile never wavered. "I'm aiming to do just that. But we've got rules that have to be followed, or we'll lose our accreditation. Please go with Lynn and get the paperwork filled out."

He opened his mouth as if to protest one more time, then closed it. He nodded sharply. "All right."

Lynn pointed to another doorway. "I promise. This won't take a minute."

"Go on, Dylan," Lana said. "I'll stay with Greg while you're gone."

THE DAMNED PAPERWORK was finally finished. He'd given the woman his social security number, his insurance card number, his prescription plan number. He'd given her Greg's birthday and birth weight. He'd given her his name and birthday, although he didn't know what the hell that had to do with anything. Then she'd asked for Jessie's name and birthday. And when she'd typed that all into her computer, he'd bluntly added her date of death. The smiling young woman had stopped smiling then.

She'd looked at him with real empathy in her large, dark eyes and told him she was very sorry for his loss.

Some of the impatience and anger had drained out of him in the face of her compassion. It wasn't her fault he was torn up inside with guilt and doubt. He had no one but himself to blame for his inability to get past Jessie's infidelity—or the part he'd played in causing her death. He'd nodded his thanks and answered the rest of her questions as quickly and as accurately as he could. When he was done he stood up, pushed away from the heavy wooden chair and headed for the exam room, where he could still hear Greg crying.

He stopped in the doorway of the brightly lighted little room. Lana, Dr. Maitland and the nurse were crowded around the exam table where Greg was lying naked on a blanket. Dr. Maitland had a stethoscope in her ears and was listening to his heart. She reached down, flipped him over and held him on her palm while she listened to his lungs.

Then she straightened, a hand at her back, probably to

ease the strain of leaning over the high table. She was noticeably pregnant, but not so big that it interfered with her movements. "His lungs are clear," she said when she caught sight of Dylan in the doorway.

"No baby that cries that loud has anything wrong with his lungs," the middle-aged nurse agreed. "Lordy, I've never heard so much noise from such a little one."

"You're sure his lungs are okay?" Dylan asked. Greg was kicking feebly, in the uncoordinated way of preemies whose nervous systems hadn't quite caught up. His eyes were screwed shut against the bright overhead light, his cries still lusty but less intense than they'd been when they arrived.

"Very strong for a preemie," Abby assured him.

Dylan let himself relax a little. "That's what the pediatric surgeon told us." Greg had been spared the complications resulting from undeveloped lungs that many preemies suffered.

"You're lucky. No other problems?" Abby asked, fastening Greg's diaper.

"No."

"I told her I didn't think there were any," Lana said hastily. "At least that's what your mother told me. I was right, wasn't I?"

"Yes, thank God. We were very lucky that way." He had lived in a state of perpetual anxiety those first few days of Greg's life. He'd hardened his heart against the fear after Jessie died, when he looked at Greg and saw not his flesh and blood, but another man's. Tonight the terror and helplessness had returned, and he didn't like being that vulnerable.

Abby continued working on getting Greg's flailing arms and legs in his sleeper. "I'll do that," Lana offered.

Abby shook her head. "I need the practice."

"You're starting to get pretty plump," Lana observed with a teasing lilt to her words. Her voice still held the echo of a tremor. She was looking at his son, tears shining in her green-gold eyes. *She loves Greg,* Dylan realized. Lana loved Greg purely and simply, without the sense of betrayal and anger that muddied his feelings for the little tyke.

"Three more months," Abby responded. "I can't wait. Kyle and I were talking just the other evening about coming by the shop to pick out nursery furniture."

"Boy or girl?" Lana asked as Abby handed Greg to her. His cries quieted somewhat when he was upright against her shoulder.

"We don't know," Abby replied. "We want to be surprised."

"I do, too." Lana colored prettily and handed Greg to Dylan, avoiding looking directly into his eyes. "I mean, whenever I get pregnant."

"You and Beth. Always playing house and wanting a handful of babies apiece," Abby laughed.

Lana changed the subject, her cheeks turning an even darker shade of pink. "Abby says we should keep him propped up, let him sleep in his carrier. It takes the pressure off his eardrum so there's less pain."

Dylan folded his son into his arms, patting him on the back just as Lana always did. Greg no longer felt like an alien being in his arms, even if he didn't yet feel like his son. He had Lana to thank for that. "He does have an ear infection then?"

"Yes. Not a serious one," Abby assured him.

"Nothing else is wrong?"

"He's in good health. Especially for a preemie. Very small for his age, of course." She glanced quickly at the chart on the table. "But Lana says he's gaining weight steadily. Is that right?"

Dylan nodded, not trusting his voice. *Greg is all right. Just an ear infection and fever, ordinary childhood ailments. Thank God.* He tried to relax, pay attention to what Abby was saying, but all he could see was Lana smiling at him, and all he could hear was the relieved pounding of his heartbeat in his ears.

"He's almost doubled his birth weight in three months. Excellent progress for a preemie. I'll write a 'script for some antibiotics for him. Do you have children's Tylenol?"

"No," Dylan said, forcing himself to pay attention. "His doctor didn't want us giving him any medication that he had not ordered, even over-the-counter ones." All those instructions had been given to Dylan's mother, not to Dylan. He hadn't made it to the hospital the day Greg was discharged until the very last minute he reasonably could.

"Good advice, but we want him to be comfortable. It's a very small dose. He shouldn't have any problems with it, but if he does, call me right back, okay? And I can give you some drops to help with the colic. Lana told me he's pretty fussy with it."

Lana didn't quite meet his eyes. "I thought I should tell her everything I could."

She looked at him then, and this time he was the first to look away. He didn't want to see only mother love in her eyes.

He wanted to see the love a woman felt for a man.

And God help them both, he wanted that love to be for him.

CHAPTER TEN

HOME HAD NEVER looked so good. Lana wondered why she thought she could ever move out of the rambling old house where she'd grown up. Of course it was too big for only one person. But maybe, just maybe, she wouldn't always be alone.

She wondered if Dylan would agree to live here with her if—

"We're home." The words dovetailed so neatly into her fantasy that it took a moment for them to register. "Lana?"

"Yes, yes. Home," she said, feeling foolish for parroting his words.

"Are you okay?" he asked, a frown pulling his dark brows together.

"I'm fine."

"Well, I feel like I've been dumped in a cement mixer." He flexed his shoulders, and Lana tried not to look too hard as the material tightened across the muscles of his chest.

"I could use a brandy," she said. She didn't drink much, mostly wine or beer if she was out with friends, but somehow tonight a brandy sounded just right. She got out of the car. "My father always swore by a brandy at bedtime. And a good cigar. I think I'll skip the cigar."

"Greg's sound asleep," Dylan remarked, unfastening the baby's seat from the back of the pickup. "Do you think we should wake him for a bottle? He missed his midnight feeding.''

"No," she said too quickly. "I mean, let him sleep. He's worn out, poor little mite.''

"You're probably right." Dylan hoisted the diaper bag. Lana carried the pharmacy sack containing Greg's medication. Abby had shown them both how to measure and fill the syringelike dispenser that made getting the liquid antibiotic down Greg's throat at least marginally easier than using a spoon.

"Don't put it in his formula," she'd cautioned. "You'll just waste it. He won't like the taste well enough to take it all, and even if he doesn't object to the taste, if he falls asleep halfway through his bottle, or spits up, the medicine is wasted.''

Dylan had nodded solemnly at everything she said. He watched her like a hawk, committing every move to memory. He scrutinized the labels on all the medications, wrote down Abby's pager number and her home phone, even though Lana told him she had them both on her bedside table.

Dylan loved Greg. In her heart she was certain of that. He might not be able to admit it yet, but he loved the little boy, even though he still believed him to be another man's child.

Lana held the door for Dylan to precede her into the kitchen. The island light provided the only illumination in the big room. Dylan sat Greg's carrier on the counter near the stove. He began to fuss immediately. "Oh, no," Lana said. "I guess we were wrong to think he didn't mind missing a feeding.''

"He's probably starved. He didn't eat much all day. Now that he isn't in pain, he's hungry, I imagine. I'll fix him a bottle. You go on up to bed.''

He'd forgotten about the brandy, or dismissed it from his mind. She ignored the twinge of disappointment it caused inside her. "I'm still too wound up to sleep," Lana confessed. "Are you hungry, too? I could fix us a snack." They'd had omelettes for dinner, but that seemed ages ago.

"I'm fine."

"Okay. Why don't you bring Greg into the family room to feed him? I think I will have a brandy." She was reluctant to leave Dylan alone with Greg. What if his fever didn't drop as Abby promised it would? What if Dylan fell asleep, exhausted, and Greg got worse?

He hesitated. "All right," he said. "I'll do that."

"I'll pour you a brandy, too."

"Thanks."

Lana turned on a small table lamp in the hallway as she passed, then one in the foyer. The grandfather clock beside the wide front door with the fanlight struck the half hour. The house was quiet and still. The last of the moonlight danced through the leaf patterns of the magnolia outside the windows before she banished it by turning on a lamp and pulling the curtains.

She went to the bar and poured two fingers of brandy in two glasses, bypassing the hand-blown snifters on the glass shelves. She could remember her father and his friends swirling the golden liquid in the fragile glasses, savoring the liquor, enjoying their big smelly cigars. She smiled. Her mother had complained about the smell for days after one of her dad's poker parties.

"What are you smiling about?" She looked up, caught sight of Dylan's reflection in the mirror behind the bar. He was holding Greg in the crook of his arm, in a way that looked so natural now.

"I was thinking about my dad and his poker parties

and the smell of cigar smoke that drove my mother crazy.''

He nodded. ''My dad and brother are into cigars. Never quite did it for me.''

''My brothers enjoy a good cigar, too. They're both a lot like my dad. I've always known it, but lately I've thought about it a lot more. Families are made up of many, many things. Being blood relations is only one of them. I think you realized that tonight, too, didn't you?'' Exhaustion and release from the stress of the past couple of hours made her bold.

Dylan came closer. Greg was sucking noisily on his bottle, his pain forgotten. His eyes were scrunched tight in ecstasy, his tiny, tiny fingers wrapped tightly around Dylan's littlest one. ''I'm trying, Lana.''

She took a swallow of the brandy. ''I think you love him already. You just don't want to admit it.''

''You're certain of that, aren't you.'' He looked at the child in bemusement. ''I was as scared tonight as I was when he was a newborn and his life hung in the balance— before—''

''Before you learned he wasn't your son?''

''Yes. Do you think there's hope for me yet?''

She nodded, not trusting her voice.

''If I do learn to love him, it will be because of you.''

''I learned something tonight, too.''

''What was that, Lana?''

''That I will make a good mother when I have a child of my own.''

''I don't think that was ever in doubt.''

She shook her head. ''My birth mother abandoned us. Deep down I've been afraid I might do the same thing with a child of mine.'' She looked at Greg, reached out to touch the gossamer softness of his hair. "Like mother, like daughter."

"You're as protective of Greg as a mother lion. I could never see you abandoning a child of your own."

"I could never give up my child. Having Greg here let me learn that much about myself. Thank you, Dylan."

His dark gaze sought hers, drawing her eyes to his by the sheer power of his will. "I could have told you all that forty-eight hours after I met you, Lana Lord. You are a very special woman." He bent his head and covered her mouth with his.

Their bodies were touching nowhere except their mouths. Dylan still held his son between them, but Lana felt as if he'd taken her in his arms and crushed the breath from her lungs. She felt his reaction, felt the jolt to his system as if a surge of adrenaline was released straight into his veins. It matched her own, made up of equal parts of relief and longing and desire. She kissed him back, put her arms around his neck and rose on tiptoe to get closer.

She was falling in love with him. She couldn't pinpoint how or when it had happened, she only knew it had. And she knew just as certainly that what was between them tonight wouldn't end with only a kiss.

SHE HAD NEVER expected to wake up in Dylan's arms. Not in real life, at least. Lana lay very still, listening to the sounds of his breathing. He didn't snore. Not that it mattered. Lana smiled. It wouldn't have mattered if he'd snored like a chain saw. He was still a wonderful lover, passionate and caring.

She hadn't expected to fall in love, not for a long time, anyway. But that had happened, too, insidiously and, she was very much afraid, irrevocably. There was no accounting for such things, she guessed. She had talked herself

into being in love with Jason Fairmont because she had
wanted a home and family so badly after her parents died.
She understood that now. But her heart had taken the lead
with Dylan Van Zandt, and where her heart went, a
woman must follow. That sounded like the title of a country and western song, a hokey one, and Lana's smile
broadened. It might be hokey, but it was the truth.

She stretched, wiggling her toes, feeling twinges and a
little stiffness in unexpected places. She certainly hadn't
anticipated the first time she made love with a new man
to be interrupted by a fussy baby. But it had happened.
And she hadn't minded—well, not much, anyway. But
Greg had fallen into an exhausted sleep at last, and the
second and third time they made love had been everything
she'd dreamed about—and more.

She rolled onto her side. Dylan was sleeping facing her,
his arm heavy beneath her breasts. She liked the weight
of it there, the solidness of his body beside hers, the long
length of his legs beneath the sheet. Waking up beside a
man could be very pleasant, indeed.

She lay quietly a moment longer, then lifted her hand
to Dylan's cheek. He was frowning in his sleep, tiny
worry lines fanning out from the corners of his eyes and
mouth. She hated to wake him. But it was after six. He
would want to be at the building when his workmen arrived. He wouldn't thank her for letting him sleep.

"Dylan." His eyes opened immediately, gray and clear
as a rain-washed morning in the hill country. His beard
had darkened during the night. She remember the rasp of
it against her skin, felt the tenderness still in places that
brought a rush of color to her cheeks.

The frown eased off his brow, but he didn't smile.
"Good morning," he said, his voice husky with sleep.

"Good morning." A tiny frisson of unease slithered

across her nerve endings. Did he regret what had passed between them during the darkest hours of the night? She hadn't had a lot of practice at pillow talk. Jason had never stayed the night. It didn't sit well with his image of himself to be seen driving away from her house, rumpled and disheveled, at first light. "Did you sleep well?" she asked.

"What little sleep I got."

"I'm sorry. Do I snore? Oh," she said. He was smiling. "Oh. I...I see what you mean."

"I'd like to be kept awake like that every night." He levered himself on his elbow, then leaned down and kissed her, and Lana forgot what time it was, where she was, almost who she was.

No. She didn't forget that. He was making her vividly aware of every inch of her body. And she wanted to do the same for him, give and take of love and its sensual pleasures in ways she had never contemplated with Jason.

Dylan's mouth covered hers. He cupped her breast with his big hand, his thumb circling her nipple with tantalizing slowness. She arched toward him, as eager for his loving as she had been the night before. There had been no words between them then. There were no words now. They didn't need them. Their bodies were creating a language of their own.

It scared her a little that she was so in tune physically with this man. They had known each other only a short time. In some important respects they were strangers still. But not now. Not this moment.

Dylan's mouth left hers and replaced his hands on her breasts. Lana ceased to think at all, only to feel. She splayed her hands across his back, feeling the muscles cord beneath her fingers. She felt the heat and hardness of him against her stomach and thighs, and she opened to him, arching her back to bring him closer. Dylan groaned, his breath and beard rough against her breast. He drew her nipple into his mouth, circled it with his tongue. She moved beneath him, letting the rhythm of her movements match the slow thunder of his heartbeat.

Dylan pushed his leg between her knees, nudging them apart. She opened to him gladly, greedy for the feel of him inside her. She reached between them, bold with desire, and guided him to her. He made a sound deep in his throat, part growl, part groan, rubbing against her, prolonging his sweet agony and hers. Lana closed her eyes, anticipating the joining she already craved as though it was a drug. He shifted his weight again, parted her mouth with his. His tongue twined with hers. He pressed against her softness, and Lana held her breath, waiting, needing, ready for him.

He hadn't said he loved her, not yet. But he was loving her with his hands and his mouth. The words would come. She could wait. Now she only wanted to feel him with her, inside her, taking her with him to places beyond herself that she had never been before.

The phone rang.

"DYLAN." Lana's mouth was against his. She tasted as sweet as honey, warm and soft and pliant in his arms. "Dylan, it's the phone."

"Damn." He rolled off her, blood still pounding through his lower body, even harder than through his brain. He'd never thought he could lose himself so completely in a woman's arms. He hardly knew who he was or where he was. And he didn't care.

"Dylan," she said again. "The phone. The one on the bedside table. It must be your mother." She scooted away from him, and the rush of cold air on his skin brought him to his senses. Lana was looking at the old-fashioned Touch Tone as though it were a snake. He could see her face clearly; it was growing lighter in the square, high-ceilinged room as the sun lifted over the horizon.

"Doesn't the woman ever sleep?" His voice sounded gruff and scratchy to his own ears. He cleared his throat and reached for the phone.

"Please. Don't let her know I'm here," Lana whispered, anchoring the sheet more firmly, and more revealingly, around her. "I don't think she'll believe I was only checking on Greg while you were in the shower a second time." She hunched her shoulders, as though she were afraid his mother could somehow see her lying naked in his bed.

He hid the smile he knew she wouldn't appreciate and reached over her to pick up the receiver. "Hello."

"Dylan, is that you?" His mother sounded alarmingly wide awake for six-fifteen.

"Yes, Mom, it's me."

"You sound tired."

"I am." It had been a long day and a longer night. He glanced at Greg's crib. He was sleeping with his cherub face turned toward the bed. Dylan still saw nothing of himself in the little one's blond hair and bluebonnet eyes. But the realization didn't hurt as much as it once had.

"It's Greg, isn't it?" his mother said, apprehension sharpening her voice. "I knew something was wrong. I barely shut my eyes all night from worrying."

"He's okay now, Mom." Dylan didn't belittle his mother's premonitions. She had them now and then, and they were always right. She called it a watered-down version of second sight that came from her Irish great-grandmother.

"Is he sick?" she demanded.

"A little fever and an ear infection, that's all. Nothing more serious. We took him to Maitland Maternity last night and had him checked out. The doctor prescribed some antibiotics and sent us home to bed." He felt Lana squirm a little beside him, and he hurried to amend the sentence. "He slept through the night."

"We?" She never missed a trick, his mother.

"Yes, Lana and I. The doctor we saw was her friend."

"Give her my thanks...when you see her." He might only have imagined the slight pause in her sentence. But then again, maybe not. His mother was one smart cookie.

"I will. I have to hang up now. I want to get my shower before Greg wakes up and wants his bottle."

"You let me know if there's any change. I mean right away. I worry about him so. I hate being laid up here like this. I never thought I'd see the day when I'd hate having your father wait on me hand and foot."

Dylan laughed, as she intended him to. "Have you told him that?"

"Of course not. He might take me at my word. And frankly, I hate walking on these crutches even more than I hate being waited on." She giggled infectiously. "Besides, I'm only now getting caught up on my soap operas." She took a breath, and he was afraid she was going to launch into an up-to-the-minute description of the goings-on in Port Charles.

"Mom, I really have to get going."

"You'll bring Greg out real soon, won't you?" Her voice had turned wistful.

"As soon as I get a few hours free, Mom. I promise."

"Remember to thank Lana for her help for me. And tell her the welcome mat's always out for her."

"I'll do that. Bye, Mom." He hung up the phone.

"How did she know something was wrong with Greg?"

"She claims to have remnants of my great-great-grandmother's second sight."

"Really?"

"Really. She has these hunches sometimes, and they usually turn out right."

"Do you think she guessed I was here?"

"If she did, she didn't let on," he said carefully.

"I'm glad. I don't want her to think badly of me."

He laughed softly and pulled her close, dragging the sheet down to her waist, pressing himself against the softness of her breasts. "She would probably be singing hallelujahs. She likes you, Lana. More than she ever liked Jessie."

She stiffened beneath him.

"I'm sorry," he said, kicking himself mentally for mentioning his dead wife. "I shouldn't have compared you to Jessie. I shouldn't have brought her up."

"No," she said. "I think you should talk to me about Jessie."

It was a subject he didn't want to explore, especially with Lana naked in his arms. His wife's last words to him still lived in a sore spot in his heart. *Greg isn't your son. His real father is a wonderful man. He loves me. He can give Greg everything in the world, and I'm taking our son to him as soon as he can leave the hospital.* All his illusions of what their life together held had come crashing down around him with those words. He had argued with her over her revelation, told her that he would never give Greg up. She had bolted out of their apartment still crying, almost hysterical, and twenty minutes later she was dead, after running into the side of an eighteen-wheeler making a turn off a county road onto a busy highway.

"You're thinking about her death, aren't you?" Lana asked softly. "I'm sorry I brought it up."

He rolled away from her and sat up. "Don't be sorry, Lana. It's my problem, not yours. I should never have let her get behind the wheel that day. She wasn't strong enough to drive alone." It was as far down that dark path as he could go. What they had shared in the hours just past was too precious to sully with confessions of his failings as a husband to Jessie.

"That wasn't an answer."

"I might never be over her death," he said truthfully. "And what about you? Are you over the guy you were going to marry?"

It was her turn to look away. She focused on a spot above and beyond him. She seemed to be looking not at what lay over his shoulder, but inside herself. "I'm over him," she said finally.

He took her chin between his fingers and turned her head so that she had to look directly into his eyes once again. "That's not an answer."

"If you mean, am I sorry about last night? I'm not. But everything's happened so fast. I—"

"I don't want you to be sorry for anything. Last night was wonderful." He leaned down and kissed her. "You don't have to explain any more."

She kissed him back, a more lingering, searching kiss than the one he had given her. His blood ran quick and fast and pooled low in his body, but he made no further move toward her. "I want to," she said softly. She touched his cheek. "That already makes what we have so very different. With Jason I kept most of my thoughts to myself. That was a mistake."

The hurt and anger were there again. He had shared most of his hopes and dreams with Jessie. He had told her how much he wanted a son to carry on the family business. And all the time she knew she was carrying another man's child.

He wasn't ready to share that part of himself again. Maybe he never would be.

Greg was awake, batting his tiny hands at a stray sunbeam that had worked its way between the tree branches and through the window above the bed. Dylan slid out of bed and grabbed his jeans. "The baby's awake," he said unnecessarily. Greg was cooing and blowing bubbles, sucking on his fist. Dylan picked him up and cradled him in his arm. "Good morning, big guy. Are you feeling better this morning? No more earache?" Greg crossed his eyes and waved his hand, then he stuck his fist in his mouth and frowned when his frenzied sucking didn't produce any milk.

Dylan turned to go into the kitchen. Lana held out her arms for the baby. She cuddled him close and touched her lips to his forehead. "No fever," she said, a relieved smile curving her mouth. "That's good. I think he's hungry." Greg kicked and squirmed in her lap, grabbing on to her finger like a limpet.

"I'll get his bottle and his medication," Dylan said.

"You didn't answer my question," Lana said, looking not at him but at the baby. "Did you tell Jessie the things that were in your heart?"

"Yes. It just turns out the things that were important to me weren't as important to her. She had bigger dreams. And a lover who evidently could make them come true for her." He saw her wince at the sharp edge in his voice. He hadn't wanted the words to come out that way, but he couldn't seem to help himself.

"I'm sorry for that. I told Jason things, too. Shared my dreams. They weren't the dreams he wanted."

"Tell me your dreams, Lana." The words came from somewhere inside himself he couldn't control. She touched the baby's cheek, a caress that he wanted to feel on his own skin.

"Someone to talk to. Someone to take care of and who would take care of me. Passion." She looked at him. "And babies. Lots and lots of babies to love and cherish."

He got a grip on himself. "I don't want to hurt you, Lana."

"And you don't want to be hurt again, either."

He nodded, not trusting his voice.

"I think I'm falling in love with you, Dylan." She was waiting for his answer.

She would make a wonderful mother. A wonderful wife. He stood there, mute, raw inside with new longing and old familiar pain. She smiled, and the serenity of it almost took his breath away.

"I know you're not ready to say the words back to me. I don't care. I can wait. And I will wait, Dylan. Make no mistake about that."

CHAPTER ELEVEN

THEY WERE SEATED in the little corner of the kitchen at Austin Eats that was Shelby's own. Somehow, even with everything that went on in a busy restaurant, it seemed an oasis of quiet and solitude. Lana often wondered how her sister managed it, considering how involved she was with every aspect of her business.

Lana was giving Greg a bottle. She looked at the baby sucking industriously on the special preemie nipple, his eyes squeezed shut in concentration and enjoyment. He was a much happier baby, despite his ear infection. He had the stability and routine, the quiet time that all premature infants needed to allow them to catch up with the world. And most healing of all, Lana knew, was the fact that Dylan treated him as his son. If she voiced the thought he would deny it, admit only to doing what he should for the infant. He was still so torn inside over his wife's betrayal that he couldn't trust his own heart.

"You look very natural doing that," Shelby said.

"It does feel right."

"Your wish come true. A baby, I mean." Shelby smiled and reached out to curl her finger around Greg's tiny fist. "And without that pain-in-the-butt Jason Fairmont as a daddy." Shelby paused as though sifting her words through her mind. She looked at Lana, her eyes narrowing. "You've been spending an awful lot of time with Greg and his father."

"Dylan needs my help."

Something in her voice must have confirmed her sister's suspicions. They were triplets, after all, not as closely bonded as identical twins, perhaps, but attuned to each other's emotions more closely than many siblings. Shelby sat a little straighter in her high-back wooden chair, a flea market find that almost, but not quite, matched the chair that Lana was seated in. "Lana, look at me," Shelby commanded.

Lana resisted a moment before doing as Shelby ordered.

"My God." Shelby looked at the baby and then at Lana. "You're in love with Greg's father, aren't you." It was a statement, not a question, and Lana treated it as such.

"Yes," she said.

"But you've only known him—" Words failed her sister, something that didn't often happen.

"Seventeen days." Lana supplied the information.

"Seventeen days! Oh, Lana, honey." Shelby closed the laptop computer she'd been making menu notes on and gave Lana her full attention.

"I'm not on the rebound," Lana replied firmly. "I know what I'm doing." What was in her heart was so different from what she'd experienced with Jason, she felt as if she were another person entirely.

"Are you sleeping with him?"

Lana felt herself flush and wished for the millionth time that she had Shelby's warm coloring instead of her own pale skin.

"You are!" Shelby leaned both elbows on the table, the cookbooks, order forms and coffee mugs stacked at her elbow forming a kind of barrier that cut them off from the busy staff just steps away. "Lana, this isn't like you.

I mean, I know he's healthy, the whole family seems to live forever. So there's nothing to worry about there.''

"What are you talking about?"

It was Shelby's turn to blush. "Nothing. I mean, you know, sexually transmitted diseases and all. It's something you think about. And birth control.''

"I'm still on the pill," Lana said shortly. She didn't want to discuss it. It would only remind Shelby that she'd broken up with Jason such a short time ago her prescription hadn't expired. "But what do you mean his whole family is healthy?''

"Well—" The sound of a spoon clattering on the floor gave Shelby an excuse to look away. It was only a little after ten in the morning, but lunch preparations were well under way at Austin Eats.

"Shelby, what did you mean by that last remark?"

"Nothing. Just that Garrett and Michael—"

"Had Dylan investigated." Lana finished her sentence for her. "I thought Michael wasn't interested in finding our birth mother. But he obviously is interested in snooping around in my private life.''

Shelby had the grace to look ashamed. "Garrett hired a detective to start the search for our mother and... Well, it seemed logical to have Dylan's background looked into. Michael agreed. And so do I, frankly. You invited him into your home when you didn't know him from Adam. He could have been a mass murderer or a con man after your money. You aren't exactly penniless. None of us are.''

"He's not a mass murderer. He's not a con man. And he's not a gigolo." Her last words struck closer to home than she wished. Jason had been as much in love with the notion of marrying a Lord as he had been with her. Shelby knew that, and, to her regret, so did Lana.

"They don't want you hurt again."

"I know that, too."

"They're worried about you, Lana. We can all see how hard you've fallen for this guy. That day Michael and Garrett came to the store—" She rolled her eyes. "You were halfway in love with him already."

"It's not halfway, Shel. I am in love with him." She'd said it out loud, and now there was no turning back.

"And he loves you?"

"I— Yes." Her small wave of confidence evaporated. Shelby would know she wasn't telling the truth. "He hasn't said so in so many words."

"Oh, Lana."

"I'm not walking into another one-sided relationship. Dylan just needs time." She was talking in clichés, but the emotions behind her words were as individual and unique as the woman she was. Dylan did need time. She was strong enough within herself to give it to him.

"He's so recently widowed. And—" Shelby gestured helplessly at Greg, nestled against Lana's shoulder as she patted his back to get him to bubble.

Lana looked deep into her sister's eyes. She saw nothing but concern and love. No hidden agenda, no trick questions. Shelby was only asking about Jessie's death because she was worried about Lana's happiness. Lana relaxed a little, inhaling the powdery sweetness of Greg's scent, potent even though it competed with the stronger smells of garlic and beef stock and a hundred other tantalizing kitchen aromas. "And what?"

"What has he told you about his marriage and Greg's mother's death?"

"I know Jessie and Dylan quarreled before she left for the hospital that day." Someday, perhaps, she would tell

Shelby of Dylan's doubts about Greg's parentage. Someday when she knew all the details herself.

"I'm sorry, Lana," Shelby said, a tiny frown wrinkling her forehead between her strongly marked brows.

"You're telling me Garrett and Michael's detective didn't learn that about Dylan's private life? He must not be very good," she added with a hint of sarcasm that she wished she could have filtered out of her voice.

"Actually, she's very good. She did learn Dylan and his wife were estranged through most of her pregnancy. I just didn't want to say anything more if you weren't aware his marriage was troubled."

"I knew." Something in her voice must have warned Shelby off that particular line of questioning. She changed the subject.

"And did you know that his credit is strained to the limit because of some cost overruns and delays in the renovation of your building? Not to mention the substantial medical bills he still has to pay."

"I suspected as much, although he doesn't discuss his business dealings with me."

"He has a lot of his family's money tied up in the project, too."

"I've known that much since the beginning," Lana said. Greg was asleep. She leaned down and strapped him in his carrier, then placed it on the table between her and her sister. A barrier. A line of demarcation. Shelby's frown deepened.

"You're certain he's ready for a new relationship?" Shelby reached out to straighten a wrinkle in the toe of Greg's Winnie-the-Pooh sleeper.

"No," Lana whispered. "But I told you. I'll wait."

"Be careful, Lana. I don't want you to get hurt again any more than Garrett and Michael do."

"I know you don't, sis. But I don't know how to stop the way I feel. Maybe someday you'll feel like this, too. As though you've found the other half of your soul. I made a terrible mistake believing I loved Jason. He was wrong for me. Loving Greg's mother was wrong for Dylan. But this is right. I just have to show Dylan he can believe in his feelings again, too."

Shelby held her gaze for a long moment, and Lana gave her back look for look. Deep down she did suffer remnants of pain at Jason's duplicity. It was only natural. But she wasn't going to let it stop her from moving on and loving Dylan with all her heart and soul. Even though she was aware that he could wound her far more deeply than Jason ever had.

"Maybe someday I will. I've got a few minutes. Do you want some company on your walk to the store?"

It was a peace offering, and Lana snatched at it. She didn't like being at odds with her sister. "I'd love some company. If I stay here much longer, I'm going to start looking for something to eat. What's that great smell?"

"*Boeuf bourguignonne.* But on the menu it's plain old beef stew. Comfort food is in."

"Mmm...my favorite." Lana turned her back on the bustling kitchen reluctantly. It was a beautiful day. Cool for September, with a cloudless blue sky and low humidity.

"May I push him?" Shelby asked.

"Sure." Lana shoved her hands into the pockets of her slacks and fell into step beside her sister.

"Do you think he's warm enough?" Shelby wanted to know. She was peering through the transparent plastic canopy of the stroller with a little frown.

"I think he's all right."

"I'd hate for him to get sick again."

"Me, too."

They walked in silence for a block or so. "We kind of got sidetracked at the diner, but Garrett had a report on our mother from the detective, too," Shelby said at last. "Or at least some information on sets of triplets born about the same time we were."

"I haven't spoken to Garrett since the day he and Michael came to the store," Lana reminded her sister. "What did the detective find out?"

"You're sure you want to know?"

"Shelby." They had stopped to wait for a traffic light. "We've been through this already. I can handle it."

The light changed. Shelby maneuvered the stroller into the crosswalk as more impatient pedestrians eddied around them, hurrying on their way. Once across the street she shot Lana a quick assessing look. "There were five sets of fraternal triplets born in the state that year with the right configuration. Two girls and one boy."

"So many?"

"It's a big state. Garrett and I are going to check them out when we can track them down. If we find them, we'll have to keep looking further afield. If we only find four of them—"

"Then the odds are good that the fifth set is us. How long will that take?"

Shelby pursed her lips and gave a little shrug. "Who knows? Garrett and I have decided to split the list when the detective turns in her report. It may take a while. Families move. Split up."

Fracture, shatter, Lana thought. She wondered if her sister's thoughts were following the same pattern as her own, because Shelby fell silent again. "Are you sure *you* want to go through with this?"

"Yes." But her sister didn't sound as certain as she

had that night at Megan's, when their godmother had produced the tiny sweaters and Garrett's teddy bear. Talismans from a time too distant to remember. Relics tinged with a sadness that could still be sensed even a quarter of a century later.

"Shel?"

"Well, it is a little daunting. What if we find we have a whole passel of aunts and uncles and cousins we never knew existed?"

"We'll get to know them."

"What if we don't like them? What if they're crooks or rapists or murderers or something?"

"Then we don't add them to our Christmas card lists," Lana said, as lightly as she could.

"What if we're the skeletons in their closets?"

"Then they don't add us to theirs."

Shelby laughed. "Okay. I'm getting a little carried away. It's just…well, at first I thought of it as a quest. You remember the way Aunt Megan described it that night at her house. A way to answer a lot of questions we've never had the answers for. Our medical history, and whether or not our kids will have big noses or crooked teeth or need to wear glasses. What kind of background we came from. Are we Irish? Or Italian? Or who-knows-what? All the things we wondered about when we were children. I don't want my kids to have those same questions. But after that? Well, I guess I thought it would just end there."

"But now you know it won't."

"Yes. And I have to admit it's given me some sleepless nights. I feel a little like Pandora getting ready to open her box."

"Have you talked to Garrett about your second thoughts?"

"No. He's so determined to find her, Lana. I don't think it would make one bit of difference to him if I had second thoughts or not."

"But, if he knew, he wouldn't ask you to help look for these other triplets."

"No, he wouldn't. He'd go it alone. And for that reason, if no other, I'll never breathe a word to him. And you'd better not, either."

"I won't," Lana promised. "But if you ever feel as if you're getting in over your head, you'll come to me, won't you?"

"Don't worry," Shelby said. "I'll holler long and loud if I need help."

They'd arrived in front of Oh, Baby! Lana had turned to help Shelby lift the stroller up the single step into the store when a sidewalk-shaking, window-rattling crash came from the old lobby. Instinctively Lana put herself between Greg and the cloud of dust and debris that rolled through the doorway.

"My God," Shelby breathed. "Was that an explosion?"

"I don't know."

Dylan and his workmen were inside the building. She had to see if he was all right. Lana spun around. "Stay with Greg, please."

Brittany and Janette came rushing out of the store. "What happened? Was it an earthquake or a bomb?"

"We thought the ceiling was going to come crashing down on us."

"Is anyone else in the store?" Shelby asked, pulling Greg's stroller to the curb, away from the settling dust cloud.

"No. We're alone."

"Lana, don't go in there. If it was an explosion there may be another. Or fire. Or God knows what."

"I have to see if anyone's hurt."

"Stay here. I've got my cell phone. I'll call nine one one."

Lana hesitated a heartbeat. "No. I have to see—" She started forward just as three coughing, dust-covered figures emerged from the doorway. "Dylan?" He was coated in plaster dust. There was blood on his cheek from a cut just below his eye. She was beside him in an instant. "Are you all right?"

"I'm fine."

"Your cheek."

"It's nothing."

She laid her hand on his arm. The muscles and tendons beneath her fingers were rock hard with tension. "What happened?"

"The damned elevator cable snapped. The whole car ended up in the basement." He never even turned his head to look at her as he spoke. "Hiram, you okay?"

"I'm fine, Mr. Van Zandt."

Two more workmen emerged onto the sidewalk. "How about you other guys?"

"We're okay." The assurance came from all the men.

"Should we call nine one one?" Shelby wanted to know. She stepped closer to Lana, Greg cuddled against her shoulder.

"No need," Dylan replied. "But we'll have to call the building inspector. And the fire marshal. Hiram, you make the calls. Tell them what's happened. I'm going back inside and make sure the electricity and gas lines are shut off just in case."

"Sure thing. I'll call from my truck. I can't figure out

what went wrong. I could have sworn that cable was okay."

"Don't worry about it now. We'll have plenty of time to figure out what went wrong when the city guys get here."

Dylan went into the lobby, followed by his workmen. Lana followed them inside. She half expected Dylan to try to stop her, but he didn't. He didn't even glance at the wrecked elevator but proceeded to the back of the building. A few moments later the lights went off, leaving the room in partial gloom.

The dust was still thick inside the building, but settling rapidly. Lana coughed and held her hand in front of her face as she moved in for a closer look at the damaged elevator. The ornate brass gate that fronted the shaft was twisted and bulging where the top half of the car was resting against it. A heavy wire cable, frayed and broken, looped over the grill and draped onto the floor.

One section of cable still held, preventing the car from dropping all the way into the basement. Dylan was back, and he'd found a flashlight somewhere. His workmen crowded around him as they surveyed the damage. "What a hell of a mess," one of them said.

"You're damned right it's a mess," a second man said. "It's going to cost a pretty penny to put this right, ain't it, boss?"

Dylan was silent.

Lana wanted to go to him, but she held back. She might have fallen in love with him, but he'd made no such commitment to her. At the moment she felt that omission more strongly than ever before. Still, she couldn't just walk out on him. She touched his shoulder. He turned to her but his eyes were distant, distracted. "Is there anything I can do?"

"No," he said, his voice as hard as the bunched tendons under her fingers. "Go back to the store. See if you have any damage there."

She lifted her fingers to the cut on his cheek, not quite touching him. "You're bleeding."

He dragged his hand across his cheekbone, looked at the blood smeared on his fingertips. "I must have gotten cut by a chip of marble. Hiram and I were standing right in front of the shaft when she fell."

"Won't you at least let me put a bandage on it?"

"It's just a scratch." He seemed impatient for her to be gone.

"No one else was hurt?"

"That's about the only good thing that's happened today."

She wanted to tell him not to worry, but the owners of the bakery and vintage clothing store and the manager of the Crystal Unicorn came rushing into the lobby, demanding to know what the ruckus was about and how long they were going to be without electricity and gas.

Dylan turned away from her to deal with his shaken and irate tenants.

She had wanted to tell him it would all work out. But she wasn't sure that it would.

CHAPTER TWELVE

GREG WAS as restless as Dylan was. He picked up the tiny, squirming bundle of baby and blankets and cradled him. He touched the satiny soft skin of the child's forehead with his lips. He was cool to the touch. No fever. The antibiotics Abby Maitland had prescribed were doing the trick. "Do you have a wet diaper, buddy? Or is the moon keeping you awake, like me?" he whispered, staring at the tiny, scrunched-up features of his son.

Only Greg wasn't his son. He couldn't forget that, not for a moment, no matter how hard he tried.

And it wasn't only the moon keeping Dylan awake.

He cuddled Greg against his chest and wandered out of the maid's room into the kitchen. It was as dark and silent as the rest of the house. Lana had gone upstairs to bed hours ago. He had heard her come into the kitchen about midnight for something, a snack maybe, or a glass of milk, but he hadn't opened the door to his room.

He wasn't in the mood to face her. Not after the way he'd shut her out that afternoon after the elevator fell. He had seen the hurt in her eyes, but he hadn't been able to do anything about it. It took all his willpower not to slam his fist into something to relieve his outrage at this latest stroke of miserably bad luck.

Lana must have thought his anger was directed at her. And in the hours since, he'd done nothing to disabuse her of the notion. He'd been too busy feeling sorry for himself.

His dad was coming into town in the morning to make his own assessment of the damage to the building. Dylan didn't want to face him, either. His dad would stomp around, check this and that. Say it was an accident. Say it could have happened to anyone. Tell him to be thankful no one was hurt and to get back to work.

He wouldn't mention money. But it would be there between them. The need to come up with a new line of credit for this setback. And Dylan was damned if he knew where the money would come from. Van Zandt Development had gotten the bid on the Cartersburg school gymnasium two days ago. When that happened, Dylan's building had moved down the list of priorities about ten notches. He was going to have to come up with the solution for this one on his own.

He pulled Greg's bottle out of the fridge and stuck it in the microwave. Then watched as the little one sucked eagerly on the nipple, taking about an ounce before falling back to sleep between one moment and the next.

Dylan sighed. He wasn't likely to fall asleep anytime soon.

He pushed through the swinging doors and made his way down the dark hallway, guided to the family room by the bars of leaf-filtered moonlight falling through the fanlight above the baronial front door of Lana's house. Other than the night Greg got sick, he'd never ventured into this part of the house without her invitation, but tonight the four walls of the maid's room were closing in on him, and he was reluctant to return.

He had to get his project on track. If he failed, he might not take the company down with him, although that was a damned good possibility. But for certain their credit rating would suffer and make lenders look at future Van Zandt Development projects bearing Dylan's signature with a jaundiced eye.

If worse came to worst, he'd strike out on his own, take the strain off his dad's reputation.

But how the hell he'd make it on his own with Greg to care for was something he didn't want to think about. He could live out of his truck if he had to—alone. But not with a baby to care for. That's how he'd ended up in Lana's house to begin with.

Lana. There was no way on earth he could ask her to be his wife when he had nothing to offer her. He couldn't even let his thoughts go in that direction. Not tonight. Never again.

"It's just you and me, buddy. God's supposed to watch over the little ones. I sure hope He's on the job, 'cause your daddy's not doing such a good job on his own."

He settled onto the sofa and laid Greg to rest on his chest. Such a little mite. So helpless, so dependent. He looked at the sleeping infant. His name was on Greg's birth certificate. In the eyes of the law Greg was his son, no questions asked. And Dylan would do the best he could for him.

He might not be able to give him his unconditional love. But he could give him a sense of family, memories of his uncle...and his mother...

A table lamp beside the door was switched on. "Dylan?" It was Lana's voice, a little sleepy, but not alarmed to find him in her family room after midnight.

He'd been so lost in his thoughts he hadn't heard her come down the stairs. "Greg was fussing. I gave him a bottle and walked him to sleep. I hope you don't mind us being here."

"Of course not." She came to stand beside him. She

was wearing a thin cotton robe, belted over an even thinner nightgown of some fine, pale-green material. He could see the thrust of her breasts and the soft curve of her waist and hips in the shadowy room, and felt himself harden. He wanted her. He wanted to hold her, and love her, and fill her. He wanted to fall asleep beside her every night, and wake beside her every morning.

But he hadn't been able to tell her that when they made love. And he couldn't now. He had nothing to offer a woman like Lana Lord. He could hear the pain in her voice and felt it echo in his patched-together heart. He had taken her body, accepted her love, and had been able to give very little of himself in return. If he was any kind of a gentleman at all, he'd pack up, leave her house and never darken her door again.

"Do you want to be alone?" she asked.

"No." He spoke the word before he could stop himself.

She curled into the corner of the sofa beside him, reached out and traced the outline of Greg's little fist where it lay curled on Dylan's shoulder. He could feel the warmth of her fingertips through the thin cotton of the old T-shirt he was wearing when her hand brushed his chest. She rested her arm along the back of the sofa, close enough that he could smell the lingering scent of flowers on her skin, but not close enough to touch. "Do you want to talk about it?" she asked.

"The accident today?" She nodded. "There's not much to talk about. A cable broke. We don't know why. It was brand new."

"How much will it cost to fix?"

"A pretty penny. The car's a mess. And the dimensions of the shaft aren't standard. We're talking custom-made components." He laid his head against the back of the couch. Greg turned his head, dragging his little button nose across his chest to snuggle trustingly into the curve of his neck and shoulder.

"Do you have insurance?"

"I don't know if they'll cover this. Depends on whose fault it was. That could take weeks or months to settle. I don't have the time to fight the elevator company or the insurance company if they want to be difficult about it."

"Or the money?"

He rolled his head and looked at her across the small space that separated them. The only light came from the waning moon shining through the window and the lamp against the far wall. "Or the money."

"You don't want to talk about money with me, do you?"

"It's not your problem."

"Didn't last night mean anything to you?" Lana asked softly, still holding him with her eyes.

"It meant a hell of a lot to me. But it had nothing to do with what happened today."

She was silent for a long moment, as though waiting for him to say something more. "It had everything to do with what happened today." She lifted her arm and traced the cut on his cheekbone with one long, tapered finger.

"Lana, don't." He could see where this was leading. She was going to offer him the money to finish the renovations on the building.

"Let me help, Dylan. I have the money. More money than I'll ever need."

"Lana, for God's sake." She had offered him her heart and now her money, and he had nothing to offer her in return.

"Don't go all Texas-male on me," she said, smiling a little.

"I'm not going—" He let the air whoosh out of his

lungs in exasperation. *God, did she know what her smile was doing to him?*

"And don't raise your voice. You'll wake the baby."

"Damn it, Lana. Let me get a word in edgewise."

"Okay." Her smile had become fixed, a little strained.

"I'm not taking your money. Period. End of conversation."

"Why not? I've got all kinds of investments. This will just be another one. No strings attached."

"There are all kinds of strings attached."

The little smile died and took all the light and the air from the world with it. "No, Dylan, you're wrong." She stood up. "I meant every word I said to you last night, but I know loving someone doesn't come with a guarantee they'll love you back."

"Lana." He might never have the courage to say aloud the words that clamored for release inside his brain. He'd sound like a goddamned gigolo. *I love you, Lana. I need a hundred thousand dollars.* What a hell of a mess.

"Don't say something you'll regret later."

Could she read his mind? The opportunity to declare his feelings for her had passed the moment she said she loved him and he'd failed to reply. Now that moment might never come again. He stood up, too, wanting to keep her with him despite knowing he should let her go. She took a step out of his reach. "It's late. We should both be getting to bed. Think about my offer. If not for your sake, then for Greg's."

LANA GAVE UP trying to sleep an hour before sunrise. She needed to get out of the house, away from the store, but mostly she needed to get away from Dylan for a few hours. She thought of her promise to care for Greg and discarded the idea. She showered and dressed and was making coffee when Dylan came in, his hair damp and curling at the nape of his neck.

"Good morning," he said formally.

"Good morning." What was she doing involving herself so completely with a man who had made no commitment in return? And Greg? Giving her heart to a baby that wasn't hers. She had thought she loved Dylan enough to wait until he felt free to feel the same, but this morning she wasn't so sure, and the uncertainty gnawed at her.

"It's going to be a nice day." He set Greg's carrier on the island. The baby was bathed and dressed and smelled sweetly of powder and lotion. Lana itched to lean down and kiss him, but held herself back.

"Yes." She made up her mind. "I...I'm going to take the day off. I need to see my brother Garrett. I'll leave a message for Brittany and Janette. They'll be glad to help you with Greg. I know it's terrible timing, what with the accident yesterday and all—" She felt like a heel, but her instinct for self-preservation was overriding all her other responses.

"It's not a problem," he said, so quickly she knew it was a problem.

"I could—"

"No." He held up a restraining hand. "Maitland Maternity has an emergency program at their day-care facility. They gave me a pamphlet on it the night we took him in for the ear infection. They've got his records there now, so it shouldn't be a problem to drop him off today."

"Oh." She felt a sudden illogical spurt of dismay. She wasn't as necessary to him and Greg as she'd thought she was.

"You're a hell of a teacher, Lana," he said, a wry smile tugging at the corners of his lips. "I've done my homework and covered all the bases. Take your day off. I can't keep imposing on you indefinitely, anyway. I'm going to have to make other arrangements for Greg soon.''

"But day care is so expensive—"

"I'll manage, Lana," he insisted in a tone that said more plainly than words the subject was closed. "You have your own life, and I've monopolized it for too long."

He was throwing up roadblocks between them, just as he had last night, and she was no more immune to the hurt than she had been then. "Fine. It will all work out nicely, then," she said, ignoring the sharp little pain in her heart. "I'll be back in time for dinner."

"Don't hurry. Greg and I will eat out."

That hurt, too. She'd come to look forward to their eating together. Like a family. Which they were not, she reminded herself yet again. And never would be, if she let Dylan retreat farther into his shell.

Maybe she did need a day off, or she might lose her resolve to be as patient as Job when it came to loving Dylan Van Zandt.

The drive to Garrett's ranch helped blow the cobwebs from her brain and gave her a chance to think about something other than Dylan—like giving her nosy older brother a piece of her mind. She grinned at the thought, switched the radio to a country and western station and set about to enjoy the drive.

Garrett's ranch sat at the end of a dusty lane. It was a small place as Texas ranches went, only three thousand acres. Cattle grazed along both sides of the lane. There was a rambling stone-fronted house that desperately needed a woman's touch, and a handful of outbuildings shaded by cottonwood trees that lined the banks of a small stream, dry this time of year. She found Garrett in the stables, getting ready to head off to ride a fence line.

"Lana." He looked surprised, his mouth curving into

one of his rare smiles. "What are you doing out here so early? You just about missed me."

"It was a spur-of-the-moment decision," she said as she moved into the shade of the large building. Horses neighed and snickered when she passed. She reached out to pat a sorrel filly on her satiny nose. She was a city girl through and through, but when she drove into the hill country, brown and golden in fall, soft and green in spring beneath the overarching blue Texas sky, she knew why Garrett loved it so.

"Should you be out riding fence line already? Did the doctor say it was okay?" She would never forget how frightened she'd been when she heard Garrett had been shot in a hostage standoff last spring.

"I'm fine, little mother hen. Go find someone else to look after," he said, flicking her chin gently with his knuckle. "Oh, but wait. You have found someone to cluck over," he said wickedly. "I forgot."

"Well, I haven't," she replied, accepting his challenge and the change of subject. Garrett didn't like to talk about himself. And if he felt well enough to ride, then he probably was. "What in heck do you think you were doing, hiring a private detective to spy on Dylan that way? It was unforgivable."

Garrett's green-gold eyes hardened slightly, and the teasing drawl disappeared from his voice. "You're too trusting, sis. He could have been some kind of crook, or worse yet."

"A man with a colicky baby in his arms? I don't think so."

"Think so." He slapped his Stetson against his leg, and the filly Lana had greeted on her way in took exception to the motion and shied, stomping and neighing. Garrett turned to soothe her with a word. She settled down and stuck her head over the half door to be stroked.

"I can take care of myself, Garrett."

"So you've told me before." He looked at her. "Is that the only reason you took a day off work and your nanny duties to drive all the way out here?"

"No," she said, sighing. He had always been able to read her like a book, but she wasn't any more ready to discuss her one-sided affair with Dylan than her overprotective big brother was to discuss his private life. If he found out she was sleeping with Dylan—she didn't want to think what might happen. "There is something else." And there was. "It's about you trying to find our mother."

"I understand why you don't want to look for her, Lana. But I want to know who she was. And why she did what she did. It's time we all learned who we are."

"But that's just it. I know who I am. I'm Lana Megan Lord. That's the only person I want to be."

"It's not that simple, Lana. There are questions to be answered."

She looked out of the double doors that stood open to the morning sun. Somewhere in the distance a motor roared to life. Probably one of the ATVs Garrett's ranch hands used to get around when they didn't want to take time to saddle a horse. "Do you remember anything about her at all, Garrett?" She hadn't dared ask him such a question for years.

"No," he said, lifting a work-roughened hand to gentle the skittish filly once more. "Not really. Only an impression or two. She liked to sing to me, I think. And she had a pretty laugh. And sometimes I think I remember a man. Our father? An uncle? Who knows? But he would take me up on a big shiny motorcycle."

"A motorcycle?" She had never heard him speak of such a memory before. Lana held her breath, afraid if she said something more, Garrett would stop talking.

He nodded, then set his hat on his head. "Yep," he said, slipping naturally into Texan. "I had a dream like that all through childhood. It sure couldn't have been Dad." He smiled again, that lazy cowboy grin he so seldom used, and she felt the jolt of it all through her. Her brother was a lady-killer, no doubt. Someday, somewhere, he'd meet his match, and then sparks would fly.

Lana laughed, too, in charity with him once more. "No. I can't ever picture Dad on a motorcycle."

"A big motorcycle," Garrett repeated, looking past her shoulder with a frown. Looking into the past as far as he could go, she thought with a shiver. "A Harley, maybe?"

"You really want to know about her, don't you?" Lana asked, reaching out to touch his cheek.

He put his arm around her. He hadn't done that, either, for a long, long time. She leaned into his strength, remembering all the times he'd been there for her...for all of them when they were growing up. She forgave him then and there for siccing the detective on Dylan. He had meant well, after all. "Yes, Lana. I really want to know. Who we were. And who she is. And if you and Michael think about it, deep down in your heart you'll realize that you do, too."

CHAPTER THIRTEEN

"How is Grandma's little man? Is he feeling better?"
Linda Van Zandt cuddled Dylan's son against her breast,
her eyes closed, her round face wreathed in smiles. "I've
missed you, sweetie. I've missed you so much. I told your
grandpa if he didn't bring me to town with him today I'd
walk every step of the way if it killed me. Just to see you,
sweetie. Just to see you." She opened her eyes and saw
Lana watching her. Her expression became self-conscious.
"You must think I've lost my mind carrying on like this
over him."

"Don't be silly. Everyone who sees him has exactly
the same reaction, and they don't have the excuse of being
his grandmother."

"There is that. I hate it that we had to drive in for the
reason we did today, but I'm still thrilled to have time to
spend with Greg." Linda shifted her weight on the sofa,
trying to find a more comfortable position for the heavy
cast on her left leg.

"Here, let me get you a stool."

"Don't bother," the older woman insisted, but the fine
lines that bracketed her generous mouth had grown more
pronounced in the half hour since she'd arrived at the shop
unexpectedly in Dylan's father's wake. The two men were
conducting their inspection of the damaged elevator shaft.
The building inspector and fire inspector had declared
there was no structural damage beyond the immediate

area, so for the most part, everything at Oh, Baby! and the other establishments in the building was back to normal.

"It's no bother. I should have thought of it as soon as you sat down." The lumpy hand-me-down sofa had definitely seen better days. But it was still the most comfortable piece of grown-up-size furniture to be found in the nether regions of the shop. Lana hopped up from her desk and looked around. She spotted a sturdy cardboard shipping carton of the right size and pushed it forward. Linda set Greg beside her on the couch and lifted the heavy cast onto the box.

"Thanks," she said with a sigh of pure relief, arranging the folds of her brightly colored cotton skirt over her knee. "I can't tell you how awkward getting around with this thing is. I can't imagine why I was so stupid as to fall off that step stool."

"You had a lot on your mind. Perhaps it made you a bit distracted."

"You're probably right. I'm not usually so clumsy. But I'd been up a lot the night before with Greg. Not that I'm complaining, mind you. It was touch and go with him so often those first few days I told the dear Lord above that if he grew up strong and healthy, I'd never begrudge a moment's care of him." She picked Greg up again. He'd already started to protest at being abandoned so abruptly. "You don't like being laid aside, do you? You're a spoiled little monster aren't you?" his grandmother murmured in loving tones, rubbing noses. "A spoiled, wonderful little monster."

"Would you like something to drink?" Lana asked.

"A cola would be nice. It's so hot and uncomfortable today." The only source of air-conditioning in the storeroom came from an ancient window unit that was too far past its prime to do much good. A hurricane had begun to churn its way north in the Gulf. And although it was expected to turn east toward Florida, already it was beginning to affect the weather. It was hot and muggy with a mutter of thunder in the distance and the promise of storms later in the day.

"That sounds good to me, too." Lana went to the little refrigerator and took out two soft drinks.

"Has he smiled at you yet?" Linda asked.

"What?" For a moment, in her mind's eye, Lana saw Dylan's unsmiling, worried face. When she turned with the colas in hand, she saw Linda's attention was focused on Greg. "No," Lana said, pouring the soft drink into plastic cups. "Not yet."

"The doctors said he would be a little slow at those kinds of things. They said he would need all his energy to catch up with everything else, but I swear he just smiled at me, and it wasn't gas."

Lana added ice to the cups and handed one to her guest. "Brittany, one of my employees, swears he smiled at her the other day. And laughed, too."

"Did you smile at Brittany? Huh? Did you? Are you going to be one to like the ladies like your daddy?" She looked up, chagrin written large on her round, good-natured face. "Oh, dear. That certainly came out wrong. I mean…Dylan's not a ladies' man. He never—"

Lana laughed. She couldn't help herself. "I know Dylan's not a ladies' man."

"Not that he wasn't popular with the girls," Linda added, rushing to her son's defense. "But he never dated that much. He played sports in school and he helped his father on weekends and in the summer. He had girlfriends, but no one serious. I have no idea what kind of women he consorted with in the Marines. But I don't believe half the outlandish stories Greg used to tell. Greg was his best friend. Jessie's brother. This little fellow is his namesake. Gregory Reilly Van Zandt.''

"I know," Lana said. "Dylan's told me about him." She hoped Linda would go on talking about Dylan. Maybe she would say something that would help Lana understand the enigmatic man she was falling so helplessly in love with.

"Sometimes I wish he had played the field a little more," Linda said. "Maybe he would have been more immune to Jessie's charms." She shook her head. "No, on second thought, I don't think he would have acted any differently toward Jessie than he did. Dylan has a great sense of responsibility. And she was such a needy little thing. Well, what's done is done. May she rest in peace. And she did give me my wonderful little grandson. I'll always have a soft spot in my heart for her for that reason alone."

Lana didn't even have to ask if Linda had any doubts that Greg was her grandson. She obviously did not. If only Dylan shared her conviction.

Greg began fussing again, arms and legs moving in uncoordinated whirligig motions. "Are you hungry, little man? If I feed you, will you give Grandma another great big ol' smile?"

Lana glanced at the clock above her desk. "It is nearly time for his feeding. I'll heat a bottle for you."

"Thanks. I've missed giving him his bottle." Linda watched as Lana took a bottle from the little fridge beside the couch and put it in the microwave next to it. "Four ounces already? He is growing like a sprout, isn't he?"

"Yes, and the colic's much better, too. He's only fussy a half hour or so in the evening now."

"Thank goodness."

Lana put the nipple on the bottle and checked the temperature of the liquid on the inside of her wrist. "Just right." She handed Dylan's mother the bottle along with a cloth diaper to put over her shoulder when she burped him.

"You look as if you've been doing this all your life."

"I worked a lot of weekends and holidays in a day-care center. I *have* had a lot of practice." Lana reached down and brushed her fingertip along the curve of Greg's ear.

Linda studied her for a long moment. "I meant, you look very natural caring for Greg. You look as if you enjoy being a mother."

"I've always wanted a large family."

"I'm glad to hear that." Linda sounded pleased with her answer. "You have the touch. Look! He's smiling at you. Isn't that precious?"

Greg was smiling, but Lana doubted that he could focus on her face so far above him. If he was smiling at anything, it was his bottle. But oh, how that round little O of his mouth tugged at her heartstrings.

"I think it's his bottle he's smiling at," she said.

Linda took the bottle and popped it in his mouth. "No. It was you. I can tell. He recognizes you and he trusts you. He's a happy baby. You've done wonders with Dylan, too, you know. He was scared to death to even hold Greg before you took him in hand."

"A colicky baby is a trial to anyone. Especially a first-time father." Lana wasn't sure where the conversation was headed.

"Such a tiny little bit of a thing," Linda cooed, then turned completely serious. "You've been good for both of them."

"I...care a great deal about both of them." She had to

tread carefully here. The topic was an emotional mine field. She had told Dylan she loved him and would wait for him to love her. But inside, in her heart, she wasn't as confident as she had let on. What if he never came to love her as she loved him? What would she do if her heart was broken again?

Dylan's mother watched her closely for a long moment, then bent her head over her grandson. "Dylan still believes that Greg isn't his son, doesn't he?"

Lana curled her legs under her. She slanted a quick glance toward the entrance to the sales floor. Brittany, never one to stand on ceremony, was liable to pop in on them at any moment. But Janette would probably keep her occupied creating a display for the new shipment of silver-plated rattles and banks that had arrived from England that morning. She wasn't as worried about being interrupted by Dylan and his father. They would most likely come the back way, down the stairs, and from where she was seated she would have plenty of warning of their arrival.

Linda looked at her when she didn't answer immediately. "Has Dylan told you about Jessie's...about their being separated at approximately the time she got pregnant?"

"A little," Lana said cautiously.

"And that he suspected she was unfaithful."

"Yes."

"She was such a mixed-up child. I won't speak ill of the dead. But...well, there are days I'm glad Dylan is free of his commitment. If only—" Tears brightened her gray eyes. They were the same color as Dylan's. The gray of a wild, hill-country sky on a stormy day just like this one.

Dylan had told her only the barest facts about his marriage. Heaven help her, she wanted to know more. She wanted to understand him. She wanted to make everything right so he would love her as she loved him. But he wouldn't thank her for this conversation with his mother.

"She was so mixed up." Linda Van Zandt seemed to be talking as much to herself and to Greg as she was to Lana. "Jessie wasn't herself. Greg's birth was difficult. And then we were so worried about him. He was so very, very tiny. Perhaps if I'd been kinder to her…" Two big tears escaped and slipped down her cheeks. "I didn't realize how unhappy she was…. Not until it was much too late."

Lana couldn't remain silent in the face of the other woman's pain and remorse. "Dylan feels the same way."

Linda wiped the tears from her cheeks. "Of course he does. He's a good man. He would have stayed with Jessie, and maybe one day—" She broke off and took a deep breath. "But Jessie died. And that can't be undone. Except—"

"Except?"

"For the way Dylan feels about Greg."

"He's much better with him," Lana said, giving Dylan's mother what comfort she could.

"But he won't love him as his son. And he is his son. I know it." Her words were heartfelt. Lana felt the mother's love, the absolute conviction behind them echo in her own soul. "His eyes are turning gray, like mine. Like Dylan's. Have you noticed?" Lana had noticed, but she was afraid it was wishful thinking on her part. But Dylan's mother saw the resemblance, too. Lana reined in her joyful thoughts. Linda Van Zandt wanted Greg to be truly Dylan's son even more than Lana did. "He has the same blond hair Christy had when she was a baby. Christy is my daughter. Her hair's as dark as Dylan's now. As dark as my own used to be. But it was blond when she was a baby. But Dylan's too blinded by hurt pride to see that.''

"He's trying very hard with Greg," Lana said, and knew it wasn't enough.

Linda clutched the baby to her and rocked back and forth. "I don't want him to be trying to love Greg. I want it to come from the deepest part of him, spontaneously and naturally, the way the good Lord intended.''

"That might take some time." But not so long as she feared it once would. Did she dare confide so much of her hopes for the future in Dylan's mother? They barely knew each other. And as far as Linda Van Zandt was concerned, she *was* only a friend.

Linda sat up straighter and wiped another wayward tear from her cheek. "I'm sorry. I'm not usually weepy. It's just—" she smiled, lifting her shoulders in an expressive shrug "—everything. You're right. It's going to take time. And it's going to take a good woman.'' She cocked her head. "Are you that woman, Lana?''

"I—''

Color flooded Linda's cheeks, and she smiled sheepishly. "I'm sorry. I shouldn't have blurted it out that way. It's just that the other morning, when I called... I—I got the impression that Dylan wasn't alone. Was I wrong?''

It was Lana's turn to blush, but she didn't look away. "No. I was there." But she hadn't been in his room since. Or in his bed, or even in his arms.

"I may be jumping to conclusions, but I don't see you as the kind of woman who indulges in one-night stands.''

"I'm falling in love with your son, Mrs. Van Zandt, but I don't know what Dylan's feelings for me might be.''

Linda's expression remained serious. She narrowed her eyes slightly and held Lana pinned to her seat with her gray gaze. "Dylan isn't a one-night-stand kind of man, either. He's good and honest and loyal, just like his father. If he made love to you, he cares for you.'' There was no hesitation as she spoke the words.

"I want to believe that," Lana said, horrified at the wistfulness that had seeped into her voice against her will.

"You're going to have to have a hell of a lot of patience to get past all the obstacles my son has piled up in front of his heart."

"I know." Lana ruthlessly suppressed the small army of niggling doubts that held sway in a dark corner of her mind.

Now Linda did smile. "Well, if you want my opinion— and you're going to get it whether you want it or not—I think you're just the woman for the job."

CHAPTER FOURTEEN

DYLAN LEANED BACK in his chair and let his eyes wander over the empty diner. How had they all ended up here at Austin Eats? Not that he hadn't enjoyed the meal. Shelby Lord was a hell of a cook. But the last thing he was in the mood for was a family get-together with the Lords. It brought home to him how things might be if his life wasn't such a mixed-up mess.

His parents had been on their way out of Oh, Baby!, headed to Cartersburg, when Lana had suggested they have dinner at Shelby's restaurant, reminding them of her invitation the day he'd taken her to their home. His mother had accepted readily. And so had his dad, so there was no way he could refuse without looking churlish and rude. And he had to admit Lana's sister had been an excellent hostess.

"Lana tells me the three of you are triplets," Linda said, giving the three Lord siblings a careful scrutiny. Michael had joined them after dinner, just as Shelby was closing the diner. They had the place to themselves. "The resemblance is certainly striking." It was, except that Lana's coloring was more subtle than her brother's or sister's.

"We have an older brother, too, Garrett. I'm sorry you couldn't meet him," Shelby said, rising to retrieve something from the cooler. "He has a ranch, and this is a very busy time of year for him."

"Don't have to tell me that," his dad remarked. "Grew up on a ranch myself."

"Dylan told me," Lana said.

"He did, did he?" Roger gave his wife a quick look over the rim of his coffee cup. Dylan knew that look. His mother had figured out something was going on between him and Lana and had told his dad. He remembered the phone call the morning after they'd made love. He'd told Lana then that Linda was hard to fool, and he figured he'd proved himself right.

"Have you saved room for dessert, Mr. Van Zandt? It's blueberry pie," Shelby said, coming back to the table with a laden tray.

"Call me Roger, please. And yes. I think I could eat a piece. We'd have most likely ended up getting a drive-through burger on the way home if Lana hadn't invited us here," Roger said as he accepted a piece of blueberry pie à la mode. "This is a damned sight better."

"We'll pack a hamper of goodies for you to take home," Shelby promised him.

"You mustn't go to any trouble," his mom said.

"It's no trouble."

"Well, thank you very much. I haven't had such a good meal since I broke my ankle. Except for that lovely picnic you packed when Lana and Dylan brought Greg to visit," she added hastily, taking the smallest piece of pie on the proffered tray. His dad made a sound of protest. Linda leaned forward and patted his hand. "Not that you haven't been taking great care of me. But it is nice to be out of the house. I'm going stir-crazy cooped up there."

"I'm glad you liked the food." Shelby acknowledged the compliment with a smile that was a brighter, bolder version of Lana's.

"It was heavenly. Thank you so much for inviting us, Lana," Linda said.

"It was my pleasure. Shelby's got a great place here."

"Yes, she does. And so well-located. Do you eat here often, Mr. Lord?"

"As often as I can manage." Michael turned the masculine version of that smile full force on Linda, and Dylan could have sworn she simpered. His mother, happily married to his dad for thirty-five years, was blushing like a schoolgirl.

Michael and his dad seemed to be hitting it off, too. They were both Cowboys fans, it seemed. It gave them a starting point. From there they moved on to the baseball playoffs and the stock market. And finally the mishap at the site the day before.

"Too damned bad," his dad said. "But one of those things you have to contend with in the construction business. Thank God no one was hurt."

"Thank God," Linda echoed.

"And there wasn't any structural damage to speak of. Dylan will be back on schedule by the end of next week."

If he could get the money to replace the elevator. That was a big if.

He'd been to the bank just a couple of hours ago. The loans officer hadn't been encouraging. Even knowing he had the full backing of Van Zandt Development had failed to make an impression on the man.

"Look—look! Greg smiled at me." His mother's exclamation cut into his thoughts and brought his attention to the others at the round table. "Dylan. Did you see him? He smiled at me."

Since Greg was sitting in his carrier directly in front of Linda, Dylan doubted anyone had seen the baby smile except his mother.

"No, Mom. I missed it." Greg had been holding his head up more strongly, and for longer periods of time. He was more active, kicking and waving his arms and legs, but so far he hadn't smiled—at least not for his father.

"Well, he did."

Shelby was there in an instant. Lana leaned forward for a better look. Her breast brushed his arm and her eyes met his for a fleeting second before she returned her attention to the baby. God, he wanted her. They'd had so little time alone together since the night Greg had taken ill, and no chance at all for intimacy with a fussy baby to care for each night.

But he wasn't about to give in to the clamoring need to have her with him. Not until he knew if he was going to have to take her up on her offer to loan him money. How the hell had he gotten into such a mess?

"Come on, sweetie. Do it again." Once more, his mother's voice interrupted his thoughts, and he was glad of the distraction. "You're a big boy now. You can do it."

Greg let out a mewling little cry, scrubbed at his eyes with his fists and promptly fell asleep.

"How do they do that?" Shelby wanted to know. "Fall asleep between one breath and the next?"

"They wake up just as quickly." Linda sighed and looked at the clock above the street door. "Oh, dear. Look at the time. Roger, we really should be going."

It took several minutes to say goodbye and get his mother and her crutches out of the diner and into the car. "Hand me Greg so I can give him one last kiss." Dylan did as he was told. His mother passed the baby to him as his father climbed behind the wheel. "Bring him out to see us, you hear? I'm getting my walking cast tomorrow, but I'm not supposed to drive for another week. If you don't show up at the house real soon, I'll be back. Doctors or no doctors.''

"Yes, ma'am.''

"And, Dylan. Don't worry about the project any more than you have to. Your dad and I will stand behind you all the way.''

He forced a smile. "I know you will.'' That was the problem. They'd stand behind him until he took them down with him.

"Let me know what you hear from the bank, son,'' his father said, leaning past his mother as he turned the key in the ignition. "We'll work out something.'' His words were confident, but there was a furrow in his brow that he probably didn't realize was there.

"Thanks, Dad.''

"Goodbye, Lana. Goodbye, Shelby. Michael, it was good meeting you.''

"Same here, Mrs. Van Zandt.''

The big sedan pulled into the thinning evening traffic. With a wave Michael headed to his own car, mumbling something about a report to finish reading at Maitland Maternity. Shelby stood in the doorway of the diner with her arms folded under her breasts.

"We should be getting back,'' Lana said. "It feels like rain.''

"If you wait until I finish locking up, I'll run you back to the store,'' Shelby offered.

"No, thanks. I'd like to walk.''

"Then I won't keep you standing here. Good night, Dylan.''

"Good night.'' She went inside the quiet diner and left them alone on the sidewalk.

A drop of rain hit him on the top of the head. Dylan squinted at the sky. The clouds had been thickening steadily all afternoon, but the rain had held off so far. "We probably should have driven the truck."

"Probably," Lana agreed. "But I wanted to try this pram." She held out her hands for Greg, and he handed the baby over so she could settle him in the big-wheeled, ornate carriage.

"Where did you get this thing, anyway? What did you call it? A pram? Looks like a baby buggy to me."

Lana laughed. "It's a top-of-the-line imported English baby pram. With all the bells and whistles. Chrome wheels. Spring suspension. Real leather. I couldn't resist it. Supposedly the royal princes were pushed about in one just like it. But Lord knows who'll buy it. The price is obscene." She leaned over and pulled the accordion-pleated top of the carriage forward, then snapped the clear plastic rain shield all around the sides. "There. His carrier and his diaper bag both fit inside. And when he's older there'll be plenty of room for him to stretch out and take a nap. He's snug as a bug in a rug, even if it pours rain before we get to the store."

Another warm drop of rain splashed onto Dylan's shoulder. "I think we'd better get moving or that might just happen."

But they didn't hurry. They strolled leisurely along the street. Once they turned off the busier thoroughfare where the diner was located, it grew quieter. Here and there couples and threesomes sat on stoops. Small trees had been planted in boxes along the curb. Flowers grew around their bases, and the scent of petunias clogged the air. Music drifted out of an open window or two, although the evening was muggy, and the sound of window air conditioners was louder than the music.

Downtown Austin seemed far away.

Lana must have been thinking along the same lines.

"You've done the right thing buying the building," she said, looking at the most recent sign of gentrification along the once working-class street—an upscale coffee shop.

"Yeah, as long as I haven't bitten off more than I can chew."

"Dylan—"

They turned the corner and crossed the street. The tables and umbrellas in front of the Crystal Unicorn were still on the sidewalk. He cut her off. "Would you like a cup of coffee?" Dylan asked. He was reluctant to have their time together end. He wanted her. And she knew it. But he had no intention of letting the situation get out of hand. They were safe here on the street, in full view of the neighborhood.

"I think I should be getting on home." A faint frown tugged at the corners of her mouth. She had felt his withdrawal, and it hurt her. But there was nothing he could do to make it right. Falling the rest of the way in love with Lana Lord was the worst thing he could do now. For all their sakes.

Dylan nodded. "All right. I have a few things to see to inside before I leave. I'll come with you and pick up the rest of Greg's things."

"I can take him home."

"No, I can manage." They were in front of the lobby entrance. He fumbled in his pocket for the keys.

"The rest of his things are still in the store, and I need to put the pram away. I'll bring Greg to you. There's no need to get him wet in the exchange." It was sprinkling fine, misting drops that were as warm as tears on his skin. The moisture shone like glitter in her auburn hair.

"All right."

"We won't be a minute."

She was almost as good as her word. He was standing in front of the empty elevator shaft, staring at the jagged hole the falling elevator car had torn in the walls, when she came back.

"Will you be able to repair the gate?" She touched the bent and twisted brass grate with the toe of her shoe. "It gave the lobby such character."

"It can be repaired." But it wouldn't be cheap. Once more he saw the disapproving frown on the face of the loans officer at the bank and wondered why his father's credit rating, as well as his own, had taken such a nose-dive. He turned his back on the gaping elevator shaft, which was cordoned off with the same bright yellow tape police used at crime scenes. There was nothing more he could do tonight.

Lana was almost as good at sensing his thoughts as his mother. "How did your meeting with the bank go?" she asked.

"They want my dad to co-sign any new loans. And they want proof of one hundred percent collateral." God, what would it be? Their house? Could he ask that of them?

"Have you told him yet?"

"No. I don't know what the hell I'm going to do." He spread his hands on the draftsman's table that was angled against the stairwell wall and stared at the blueprints with unseeing eyes.

"I meant what I said the other night, Dylan. I'll loan you the money."

"I'll bet your brothers will be damned glad to hear you say that," he said, unable to keep the bitterness from invading his voice. Michael Lord hadn't been as actively hostile as he had at their first meeting, but whatever headway they'd made tonight in the pleasant surroundings of

Austin Eats wouldn't survive once the younger man learned his sister wanted to invest her inheritance in Dylan's overbudget and behind-schedule project.

"We're not going any further with this conversation than we did the first time, am I right?"

"I can't take your money, Lana."

"Why not?"

"Because I—" He'd almost said, *Because I love you.* He clamped his mouth shut on the words and drew in a deep breath. "I don't borrow money from friends."

"Is that all I am?"

They were on dangerous ground. He had to be very careful not to betray himself. He looked at her, and her hazel eyes were filled with anguish. "You know you're more than a friend."

"Then let me help. Is your pride worth more to you than Greg's future?"

"I'll think about it," he said gruffly. He'd have to, but it galled him to be put in the position of penniless suitor. Or worse yet, some kind of gigolo, which was no doubt how her brothers would describe him. Better to let her think he didn't care for her at all.

Lana set Greg's carrier on the table, and he immediately started to whimper. She picked him up and cuddled him close. "I think he's hungry again."

"Are you sure it's not his ear?" What if Greg was getting worse? How much longer could he go on imposing on Lana?

"I think he's just hungry. But we—" She colored slightly and bent to kiss Greg's downy hair. "You should keep a close eye on him tonight. Ear infections are tricky things in little ones. They have a tendency to come back just when you think you've got them licked."

"As my mother has warned me at least six times today."

"She loves him so."

"And so do you." Another of those quicksilver visions of them as a family had flashed through his thoughts, betraying him into reckless words.

She looked at the sleeping innocent in his carrier. "How could I not?" She raised her eyes to his. "And what about you, Dylan? Can you love your son?"

Dylan, too, looked at the sleeping child. How could he tell her he still saw nothing of himself in Greg's tiny features? That he felt Jessie's betrayal every time he looked at his son, and that, try as he would, he couldn't get past it?

His silence was as condemning as his words would have been. She stepped away, half turned, so he saw her face only in profile.

"I'll be going. There's a bottle warmed and ready in his bag." Before, she would have stayed to feed him. Now she was going. He had hammered another wedge between them. Again, it was probably for the best. As taking Greg to his parents, as soon as his mother could care for him again, would be for the best.

"Lana—" If only he could make her understand how complicated it all was.

"Good night, Dylan." She moved toward the lobby door.

A figure walked by the tall windows that fronted the lobby and stepped into the open doorway. Lana stopped where she was.

"Good evening." The voice was low and cultured. "I'm looking for Dylan Van Zandt."

"I'm Dylan Van Zandt."

"My name is Tyler Rosebrook." He paused, as if waiting for some sign of recognition. Dylan had never heard the name before, but a cold, hard lump formed in the pit of his stomach. A premonition of dread. A faint, faint echo of his mother's gift?

"What can I do for you?"

The man came forward. He was dressed in a dark jacket and khaki pants. His eyes were gray, the same color as Dylan's. The color Greg's were turning. The stranger fixed his gaze on Greg's carrier. Lana took a step nearer to the child. He noticed her protective gesture, and a slight smile curved the corners of his mouth. He took off the Stetson he was wearing and inclined his head in a slight bow. "I assure you, the little one is in no danger from me."

"It's late," Dylan said. He didn't move closer to Greg's carrier, but he felt his muscles coil like a rattler ready to strike if the other man took one false step. "What do you want, Rosebrook?" he demanded. Where had he heard that name before?

"I believe you have something that belongs to me."

He could hear Lana's quick, indrawn breath beside him. She reached out and put her hand on Greg's carrier, as though she might snatch him and run. Rosebrook. Jessie had spoken often of one of her professors. His name had been Rosebrook, he remembered. Tyler Rosebrook. A cold ache started in his chest and spread outward, but he ignored it. "What's that?"

"Your late wife was Jessica Reilly Van Zandt, correct?"

"She was."

The stranger's smile grew a fraction more pronounced as his gaze settled once again on Greg. "Then, unless I'm mistaken, that child is my son."

CHAPTER FIFTEEN

LANA WANTED to pick up Greg's carrier and run from the building. Away from the man—with eyes the same color as the baby's—who was standing before her. He was a danger to her hopes and dreams for a future with Dylan and his son. She knew that as surely as Dylan's mother would.

The stranger lifted his eyes from studying the baby, met hers and smiled slightly. Lana shivered. His smile was affable enough, even charming, if she were inclined to think of him as anything but a threat. There was intelligence in those gray eyes, but beneath that intelligence was a ruthlessness that spoke of a man used to getting what he wanted in life, no matter what obstacles were placed before him. "Miss Lord? I believe we've met at some point in the past. I knew your parents." There was a hint of Texas in his well-modulated voice, but it was overlaid with the more clipped tones of an Ivy League background. He looked to be about forty, slim and elegant, casually but expensively dressed, his pale-gray Stetson held loosely between his hands. She could have met him at any of a score of charity drives or Statehouse functions, but she didn't think so. She would have remembered those eyes.

"Skip the Miss Manners routine," Dylan said bluntly. "And tell me why in hell I should believe a word you say."

Lana glanced his way. A muscle jumped along the hard line of his jaw. His hand, on the drafting table, bunched into a fist, then deliberately relaxed. He took a step forward, placing himself between Tyler Rosebrook and Greg.

"There's no use beating about the bush," Rosebrook answered just as bluntly. "I had an affair with your wife. The last time we were together was not quite ten months ago. We made love on several occasions." He gave Dylan stare for stare. "I believe Gregory Reilly Van Zandt to be my son, not yours."

"You're mistaken."

Lana didn't know if Dylan's denial came from his unrecognized and undeclared love for his son or from remnants of love for his dead wife. She wanted desperately for it to be the former, because she didn't think she could bear for it to be the latter.

"It's the truth, Mr. Van Zandt, and I think you know it. Actually, my involvement with Jessica began a number of years ago. I was her professor." Lana finally placed the name. Tyler Rosebrook, scion of an old-money Texas family that had founded a small, exclusive private college an hour or so outside the city.

"You seduced her, you mean."

Rosebrook's smile disappeared. "I'm not proud of having an affair with a student almost young enough to be my daughter." To Lana's way of thinking, he didn't appear embarrassed at all. "But Jessie..." His gaze flickered to Lana, then fixed once more on Dylan's set face. "She was a lovely and loving young woman. I'm afraid I let my heart rule my head when I became involved with her."

"You seduced her, promised her God knows what and then dumped her," Dylan said, biting off each word.

"I was a married man. By the time my divorce was

final, Jessie had married you. It was too late for us. Or so I thought. I loved her, you know.''

"I don't believe you."

Lana felt out of her depth. She had no claim on Dylan beyond loving him. No right to be there, hearing what this man had to say about Jessie. No desire at all to hear Dylan say he loved Jessie, too. But how could she leave Greg alone with two men who might come to blows at any minute? And she had no right to take him with her.

Rosebrook took a step forward, the veneer of affability scoured away by the force of Dylan's anger. "Believe what you want. It doesn't change the facts. The boy is my son. Jessie wanted me to have him."

"You're lying." Dylan hadn't asked her to leave. Lana stayed where she was.

"There was a letter waiting for me when I returned from Europe a few days ago. It was from Jessie. It must have been mailed just a day or so before her death. She told me about the baby—that she believed him to be mine. I've come to make a claim for my son."

"No." The word was torn from Lana's throat. She bit her lower lip to keep from saying more.

Once more Tyler Rosebrook turned his penetrating gray eyes in her direction. "I understand you've been helping Van Zandt care for the boy these last couple of weeks. I'm grateful for your help."

His arrogance was breathtaking. Lana was too stunned to reply. But at the same time she recognized a formidable foe. If he had truly only learned of Jessie's death a few days before, he had made it his business to find out everything he could about Dylan and his son in a very short time.

Dylan took a threatening step forward. "Why do you want the boy?"

"I loved her," Rosebrook said, but there was no hint of softness in the words. "I couldn't help myself. It's true I was married at the time we started seeing each other. But my wife and I had been separated for some months. She wanted to try one more reconciliation, and I agreed. I sent Jessie away. If I had known her brother was dying, how vulnerable she was, I would never have done so. But when I gave up trying to mend a marriage that was beyond help, it was too late. In the meantime Jessie had married you. I tried to put her out of my mind. I never tried to contact her."

"And then, last year, she ran away from me and went back to you."

"She loved me." The three words were spoken with perfect assurance that must have pierced Dylan to the core.

"But she didn't stay."

"No, regrettably. If she had, she might still be alive."

Lana felt Dylan absorb the blow. "Why didn't she stay?"

Greg had started to whimper, picking up on the tension in the pool of light around the drafting table. Rosebrook watched as Lana found his pacifier and put it in his mouth. Her hands were shaking. She felt his assessing gaze on her face. He went on talking as he watched her. She knew her love and anxiety for Greg, and possibly for Dylan, were impossible to hide. Deep inside she knew she'd handed Rosebrook a weapon to use against Dylan, and there was nothing she could do about it.

"My wife found us together," Rosebrook continued, not missing a beat. "Even though she wanted the divorce, she didn't want me to find happiness with another woman. There was an ugly scene. She saw a way to sweeten her divorce settlement. She threatened…all kinds of things. I didn't realize how fragile Jessie was. How much she took everything to heart. She ran back to you, it seems. When I didn't hear from her again I assumed it was because she had reconciled with you. I left the country. Now I realize it was because she was pregnant and probably didn't know whether I'd believe her or not if she said the baby was mine. She was wrong. If he is my son, I want him with me. Can you prove to me that he's not my flesh and blood?''

''At this moment I can't prove anything you say is, or isn't, true,'' Dylan said.

''I have Jessie's letter. You can read it if you want.''

''No.'' The word seemed torn from the very depths of Dylan's soul.

Rosebrook moved to his left and took a couple of steps forward. He nodded toward the carrier. ''May I see him?''

''You're close enough.'' The don't-tread-on-me tone of Dylan's voice echoed through the empty lobby.

''He's very small,'' Tyler Rosebrook observed. ''He was premature, I understand. So his date of conception is more in doubt than with a full-term pregnancy.''

''Yes.'' The word was bitten off.

Rosebrook didn't press his point. He didn't have to. ''But he's progressing well?'' He directed the question at Lana, not Dylan.

She forced herself to meet his gaze head on. ''He's doing well.''

''And Miss Lord here has helped take some of the burden of caring for him off your shoulders since your mother's accident a few weeks ago, am I correct?''

''You're damned well-informed for only having found out about Greg a few days ago.''

''I made it my business to find out everything I could about you, Van Zandt. I know you're head over heels in debt from this project, even before the unfortunate incident with the elevator, and from the medical bills for the baby and Jessie. I know you avoided visiting the child at the hospital as much as possible after Jessie died. I know you left him first with your mother, then with Miss Lord, a stranger, so that you can keep this project from ruining you and your father's business. I know—"

"All right," Dylan growled. "I get the picture."

"I'm not wrong in thinking that you've always harbored some doubt about Greg's parentage?"

"I can count," Dylan said.

"Then you believe me when I tell you Jessie and I were lovers."

"I believe you." Lana's heart bled for him. How it must hurt him to have to give voice to his deepest doubts about Jessie, about Greg.

"Do you also agree that the child would be better off with me?"

"I don't know you from Adam, Rosebrook. Why the hell do you think I'd give my son to you?"

"Because you know in your heart he's not your son. I can give the boy everything you can't, Van Zandt. He'll be my heir. The Rosebrook heir. The name means something in this state. I can give him everything he wants in life."

Their gazes locked and held. "What are you proposing?"

"I want him. It's as simple as that."

"You're so sure I'll give him up without a fight?"

"You'll do what's best for the boy. Let's not beat around the bush. You're in a hell of a bind, Van Zandt. Is that the way you want to bring up a child, teetering on the edge of bankruptcy? You've sunk everything you've got into this project." There was nothing affable about his smile now. It was feral, a predator's grin. "Sorry, poor choice of words." He glanced over Dylan's shoulder toward the damaged elevator shaft in the shadows. "It'll be the ruin of you if the insurance company refuses to pay up. Your parents' money's at risk, too. Not to mention Van Zandt Development's reputation—or what will be left of it if you default on your loans. Damned bad luck, old man."

"I'll bring this project in on time." But Lana knew Rosebrook had scored a point. Dylan was worried sick about the cost overruns and whether the insurance company settlement would cover the repairs to the elevator shaft.

"I'm sure your mother will be comforted by your certainty. But maybe it isn't just bad luck, eh? Maybe you're a damned poor contractor, to boot. I can't let my son grow up in want while you scramble around for every dollar you earn."

"I'll give Greg every advantage I can."

"Not good enough." Rosebrook snapped. "If you don't agree to a paternity test voluntarily, I'll get a court order and force you to comply."

"I'll be damned if I will." Dylan took a menacing step forward.

Lana held out her hand, pushed against his chest and felt his heart thundering against her fingertips. "Dylan, no." Fighting would only make things worse. Rosebrook would probably charge Dylan with assault.

Jessie's lover hesitated for a moment, his expression watchful, assessing, as though he realized he had pushed Dylan as far as he dared for the moment. "I think you'll agree to the test when you've had time to consider the alternatives. There's Jessie's reputation to consider, even if you don't care about your own. Greg won't thank you for smearing her name when he's old enough to understand what happened. And you can't afford to fight me in court. That's not boast, that's fact, pure and simple. I'll ruin you for sure and still get my son." He reached out so quickly Lana couldn't stop him and touched Greg's tiny foot with the tip of his finger. "And because in your heart you know it was what Jessie wanted."

THE RIDE HOME was a nightmare. Lana replayed the scene in the lobby over and over in her mind as she drove. Tyler Rosebrook had produced a card from his jacket pocket and dropped it on the table. Lana had stared at the heavy, embossed rectangle for a long moment. "Here's my private number. The test is simple and accurate. It doesn't even require your blood, only a swabbing of the inside of your cheek. I'd prefer we not use Maitland Maternity's facilities, although they're far and away the best. My personal physician will take care of everything. His name and number are on the back of the card." Then he had turned on his heel and walked out of the building.

Why didn't he want to use Maitland Maternity's laboratory facilities? They dealt with rich and famous people every day. Their discretion was legendary. But they were also ethical and aboveboard, and Lana wouldn't put anything past Tyler Rosebrook. If falsified test results would get him what he wanted, he'd move heaven and earth to obtain them.

Surely Dylan would come to the same conclusion. "Dylan—"

"I don't want to talk about it now," he'd said with a finality that was frightening.

He'd picked up Greg's carrier and diaper bag and reached for the switch to turn out the lights. "I'll follow you home," he said. "This rain will make the roads slick. Be careful."

Now, almost an hour later, he hadn't said another word. She couldn't stand the silence any longer. They were in the kitchen. She had made tea for herself, but it was cooling on the counter. She sat at the center island and watched as Dylan made Greg's bottles for the next day. When they'd arrived home he had carried Greg into their room and gotten him ready for bed by himself. Shutting her out of the nightly ritual she had come to love almost as much as the man and baby.

"Did you have any inkling Jessie's lover was Tyler Rosebrook?" she asked. She might as well get it out in the open. She'd learned enough about Dylan to know he would keep his thoughts and his feelings to himself if she didn't force the issue. The worst that could happen was that he would turn on his heel and walk away without answering.

"No." He was silent a moment then spoke again, his voice hollow, as though the words were pulled, reluctantly, from the depths of his soul. "All she told me was that he could buy and sell me a hundred times over. I guess she was right. I never put two and two together until he walked into the lobby."

"He's a very wealthy and influential man."

"I figured that when he said he knew you." He was standing in profile. She watched as he fitted the plastic sleeves inside the bottles and poured in the formula. His strong, tanned hands were sure and steady. Not once did he look up from his task.

She ignored the jab of pain his remark sent arrowing through her. "I don't know him. But my parents did. His father founded Rosedale College."

"I've heard of it. Small, elite and endowed up the wazoo with old family money, right?"

"Megan Maitland sits on the board of regents, I think. Rosebrook's a professor, as he said. English classics, if I remember correctly." And as ruthless and self-involved as the men of those times, she was coming to believe.

"The kind of man that would sweep a girl like Jessie off her feet."

She stood and went to him. She wrapped her arms around his waist and laid her cheek against his back. He stiffened slightly but didn't shrug her away. She listened to the strong, steady beat of his heart for a few moments before she spoke again. "Most women, let alone one as vulnerable and confused as Jessie, would be susceptible to Rosebrook's charm and sophistication. You couldn't know she was still in love with him when she married you. She probably thought it was over, just as you did."

He turned suddenly and took her in his arms. "Why are you championing Jessie this way?" he wanted to know.

Why *was* she defending a woman who had caused so much heartache for all concerned? "Because the Jessie you've described to me didn't have a chance against a man like Tyler Rosebrook. But mostly because of Greg," she said simply, meeting his storm-dark gaze. "I want the memories of his mother that you pass on to him to be good ones. No one who has lived her whole life wondering about even the smallest details of her mother's life could want anything different."

"God, Lana. What am I going to do? Rosebrook's right. There's no way in hell I can fight him in court. If I tell him to go to the devil with his demands, that's exactly where I'll end up. There's no way I can finish the building project and fight a legal battle against Rosebrook at the same time.''

"Let me hire you a lawyer. The best lawyer in Austin.''

"I can't do that, Lana. If he wants to fight me for Greg, he'll not only take me down, but my parents, too.''

"Your mother would fight him with the last cent she could beg, borrow or steal, with the last breath in her body.'' She looked into his drawn face and tried to smile.

"I know,'' he said. "Dad, too. They both would. And I would, too, if I didn't have them to worry about. But it's not only the money. It's what's best for Greg.'' He slipped his arms around her waist and drew her close, resting his chin against the top of her head. "He can give the boy the moon and stars,'' he whispered into the silence of the big kitchen.

"But what about love?''

His hold tightened convulsively on her. "He can't be any worse at that than I am.''

She leaned away from him, raised her hands to bracket his face with her palms. She'd told him she could wait for his love to match hers, but now, this moment, she wanted to hear him say the words aloud. If he loved her, she could fight his demons and her own—and win. "Oh, Dylan. Don't be so hard on yourself. You can love Greg. You can love—'' Her courage failed her, and she left the rest of the sentence unspoken, hoping against hope that he would say aloud the words she needed so badly to hear.

"Lana, let me love you. I need your warmth and your strength tonight. Don't go upstairs. Stay here with me.''

"I'll stay,'' she said. It was enough. It had to be. He lowered his head and kissed her as though they had been apart for a thousand days, a thousand years. She kissed him back. He still hadn't declared his love, but his mouth and his hands and his body spoke volumes. He scooped her up, and she felt light as a feather in his strong arms. He carried her into his room and undressed her in the dark.

She lay quietly while he dealt with his own clothes, listening to the quick, light breathing of the sleeping child in the crib nearby. Rosebrook's appearance and his incredible claim on Greg had followed too closely on the elevator mishap, that was all. By tomorrow Dylan would have put it all into perspective. Greg was his son. She was convinced of it. Dylan would never give him away. He was not that kind of man. She couldn't have fallen in love with him otherwise. She hadn't made another terrible mistake of the heart. She knew she had not.

His knee lowered the mattress. He lay beside her and gathered her close. His lips brushed her hair. His hands slipped over her shoulders and down to her breasts. She caught her breath on a sigh as his lips found her nipple and he drew it into his mouth. She held his head close to her heart. This was right. He was right for her. She would not doubt again. She had promised him patience, and she would keep her promise.

He shifted his body and lay full length between her legs. She pushed against him, wanting the completeness only their joining could bring. His mouth found hers again, and he pressed himself into her. She ceased to think or to worry, only to feel. And what she felt was love.

CHAPTER SIXTEEN

"LANA, what brings you over here so early?" Her rugged, handsome brother turned from the coffeemaker on a shelf behind his desk and offered her the cup he had just poured.

She'd planned it deliberately, arriving at his Maitland office before his secretary, so that she would have Michael's undivided attention. She smiled as she shook her head. "Thanks, no. I…I've only got a few minutes until I open the store, but I needed to talk to you."

"It must be important. It isn't even eight o'clock." He motioned for her to have a seat as he came around the desk.

"It is important."

"Fire away," he instructed, resting one hip on the edge of the desk as he cradled the coffee mug in both hands. "Lucky for you this is my second cup so I'm reasonably alert."

Lana was too upset to respond to his humor. "What do you know of a man named Tyler Rosebrook?" she asked. Michael was an ex-cop. He was head of security at Maitland Maternity. He had contacts in law enforcement, and in places much less savory. If anyone could confirm her fears about Tyler Rosebrook, it was Michael.

Her brother's dark brows drew together in a frown of concentration. He was a striking man, his coloring more intense and exotic than hers. He looked up and appeared to study the pattern of the ceiling tile for a long minute. "What's got you interested in Tyler Rosebrook all of a sudden?" he asked, dropping his head to pin her with his rock-steady gaze.

"I...I just wanted to know about him, that's all," she replied lamely. She couldn't quite bring herself, yet, to tell Michael of Rosebrook's claim to be Greg's father.

"He's a very influential man, or at least his older brother is."

"His brother?"

"William. He's the head of the family businesses. Tyler is the artistic one without much of a head for making money, just spending it. Eighty years ago their grandfather made the family fortune in oil, like so many others in Texas. He founded Rosedale College. The family's still active in its administration, but their real base of operations is here in Austin." His expression turned inward, as though he were scanning files in his mind. "Rosebrook's a professor of something or other, if I remember right."

"English classics, I think," Lana added.

Michael nodded. "But it's William who runs the show. They're into banking, oil, high-tech software development. They've got interests from Washington to Silicon Valley and everywhere in between. Why do you want to know, sis?" His frown deepened, and his expression grew hard and stern. "Rosebrook's not sniffin' around you, is he?"

"No. I've only met him once." But it was a meeting she would never forget. "What kind of man is he? What else can you tell me?"

Michael relaxed a little at her denial that Rosebrook had a personal interest in her. He took a swallow of coffee. "Good. He's too old for you. No children that I know of. Same for his brother. I guess the line dies out with them. He dumped his wife a year or so ago. And there've been rumors he's way too friendly with some of his students. He's never had to work a day in his life. I doubt there's anything he's ever wanted that he hasn't gotten.''

The last sentence struck like an arrow in the center of Lana's heart. ''Do you think he's ruthless enough to bankrupt Dylan Van Zandt?''

''Why the hell should he do that? Van Zandt's small potatoes. Under the radar, as far as Rosebrook and his kin are concerned.''

Lana took a deep breath and gripped the arms of her chair a little tighter. Michael couldn't help her if she didn't tell him everything. ''Dylan Van Zandt has one thing Rosebrook doesn't have. And wants very badly.''

''What?'' Michael grew still, focused, sensing the stark terror she had tried so hard to keep hidden deep inside.

''A son.''

''Jeez.'' Michael shifted his weight, gripped the edge of the desk and brought his face inches from hers. ''Are you telling me that Rosebrook is claiming to be the real father of Van Zandt's kid?'' She didn't question how he knew of Dylan's doubts about Greg's parentage. Shelby must have told him. They didn't keep secrets from each other; Lana wouldn't have expected otherwise. It made this conversation a little easier.

She swallowed hard to keep her voice from breaking. ''Yes. He says he was Dylan's wife's lover. He says the child is his. And now he's come to claim him.''

Michael's green eyes narrowed to slits. ''Van Zandt's not sure the child is his, right?''

Lana fought tears of frustration and hurt. ''Jessie, his late wife, had an affair with Tyler Rosebrook. She…she was intimate with both of them at about the time Greg was conceived. Dylan thought the baby was his. Until she told him otherwise.''

"And then she died.''

"Yes.''

"Has Van Zandt had a paternity test done to prove he's the father?''

"No. There's been no reason to. He feels responsible for Greg despite his doubts about his conception.''

"Legally the child is still Van Zandt's regardless of who the biological father is.''

Lana nodded. "If Greg *is* Rosebrook's son, he could tie Dylan up in court—for years maybe. Dylan can't afford those kinds of legal fees.''

"But if Van Zandt is the boy's biological father, then Rosebrook hasn't got a leg to stand on. Paternity tests are fast and accurate. This whole problem could be solved in a matter of days.''

"I don't think it's going to be that simple.''

Michael nodded. "Granted it won't be if the boy is Rosebrook's. But if he's Van Zandt's I don't see the problem.''

"I don't think Rosebrook will let it end there. I was there when he confronted Dylan with his suspicions.'' She shuddered at the memory of the complete self-absorption in Rosebrook's eyes. "And what you told me a little bit ago makes me even more certain I'm right. You said that neither Rosebrook nor his brother have children. That they're the last of their line. Tyler Rosebrook wants an heir, Michael. And he's set his sights on Greg. From what you've told me about him, I wouldn't put it past the man to be responsible for all the things that have gone wrong on Dylan's project at my building. Even the elevator failure.''

"This guy really made a bad impression on you, didn't he?"

"He scares me," she said simply. "He scares me to death."

"He can't force Van Zandt to give up his son," Michael said bracingly.

"Can't he? I think he means to do his best to ruin Dylan, ruin his whole family, so Dylan will give him the baby whether it's his child or not."

"Van Zandt didn't strike me as the kind of man who'd sell his own kid."

"He's not." Lana rushed to his defense. "He's a good man, Michael. But he's being backed into a corner by his creditors. He's hurt by Jessie's betrayal and he's worried sick that he'll take his parents down with him. He might feel he has no choice but to give Greg up to Rosebrook. And because it's what Jessie wanted." The last words ended with a sob she couldn't suppress.

Michael looked as ill at ease as any man confronted with a crying woman, but he pulled her into a hug. "Lana, I think I know why you care so much," he said gruffly. "But Greg isn't your baby."

"I know that." She rested her forehead against his shoulder, willing herself that there be no more tears. He reached behind him with the arm that wasn't wrapped around her shoulders and handed her a tissue from the box on his desk. When she had herself under control she stepped back and met her brother's concerned eyes. "But I want him to be mine. And I want Dylan to love his son as he should." She was quiet a moment, but she couldn't stop the words from coming. "And I want him to love me."

"Damn it, I was afraid of that."

"I didn't want to fall in love with him, Michael. It just happened."

"Does he love you?"

"I—" She couldn't lie to herself or to her brother. "I don't know. But in the end that doesn't matter. What matters is that Dylan admits Greg is more important to him than anything else in the world. So important that he'll give up everything, fight with everything he's got to keep his son. Somehow I have to convince him of that, and God help me, I'm not sure I can do it."

LANA SET a Peter Rabbit mobile gently spinning where it hung over the Prince William crib where Greg was sleeping. Dylan had been called away to yet another meeting with his banker. She'd sent Brittany home early, and Janette had taken the day off because her oldest was getting braces and the youngest had the sniffles. Lana and the baby were alone in the store. It was only minutes from closing time, and the weather was threatening thunderstorms. She didn't expect any more customers and was tempted to turn over the Open sign and call it a day.

She would stop by Austin Eats and pick up something to take home for dinner. If she didn't, she was certain Dylan wouldn't eat. Her appetite wasn't much better. Her stomach had been in turmoil all day, ever since her conversation with Michael. Her mind had been going in circles, too, searching for a way to make everything come out right, to put everything back the way it had been just days ago. Before Tyler Rosebrook had come into their lives.

When she had hoped, dreamed there was a future for her and Dylan and Greg as a family.

She bent to lift Greg from his bed, swaddling him in the baby Minnie and Mickey quilt that matched the crib sheet. He didn't waken but snuggled against the curve of her throat. She held him close, swaying gently, breathing in the sweet baby scent of him.

"You look very maternal, Miss Lord." The voice came from the doorway. She had been so absorbed in her thoughts she hadn't heard the chiming of the little silver bell that announced new customers.

She spun around. Tyler Rosebrook regarded her with those unnerving gray eyes. He was dressed casually in jeans and an open-neck shirt. "What do you want?" she asked bluntly in an attempt to hide her dismay at his appearance.

"I thought we might talk."

"There's nothing we need to talk about." She clutched Greg so tightly he wakened momentarily. She whispered soothing nothings into his ear, and he snuggled back to sleep.

"On the contrary," Rosebrook said, still watching her closely. "I believe we have a great deal to talk about. You don't mind if I close the door, do you? What I have to say is rather important. I'd prefer we not be interrupted."

She did mind very much, but she didn't intend to give him the satisfaction of letting her uneasiness show. "It's near enough to closing time. Go ahead."

He flipped over the Open sign and shut the door on a rumble of thunder in the distance. It had been hot and muggy all day, thunderstorms were predicted for the evening, and Lana wished she and Greg were safely tucked up at home or at Austin Eats. Anywhere but where she was, alone with the man who had the potential to cause her the greatest heartache of her life.

"We are alone, I presume?" Rosebrook asked, his gaze

sliding to the doorway leading to her office and the storage room.

"We're alone, as I believe you knew before you stepped foot in the door," Lana said.

Tyler Rosebrook acknowledged the challenge with a smile that Lana supposed most women would find charming. It sent chills up and down her spine.

"You're right. I knew you'd sent your employees home early. And I know Van Zandt is off meeting with his bankers. A meeting that will come to naught, I'm afraid."

"I don't believe that's any of my business—or yours," Lana said pointedly. Greg had begun to squirm, not quite waking but perhaps sensing the tension that sang through her body like a live current.

"But Oh, Baby! is your business. A very up-and-coming one."

"I work very hard to make it successful."

"Exactly. And it would be a shame to have to relocate."

"I'm not planning on relocating, Mr. Rosebrook. I have a long-term lease."

"With Van Zandt Development."

"Yes."

"But if Van Zandt no longer owned the building, the new owner might have other plans for the premises. The lease might be broken, and you'd be forced to vacate."

"Are you threatening me?" Lana asked bluntly. "It won't work." It took a distinct physical effort to keep her voice from shaking, but she managed.

"I would if I thought it might accomplish what I want."

"Threats won't work with Dylan Van Zandt, either." She wished she could have bitten off her tongue before she let those words escape, but it was too late. She had played into Rosebrook's hands.

"I agree threatening Van Zandt directly will get me nowhere. But there are other ways to get what I want."

"And what you want is this baby," Lana said very softly. "A son and an heir."

Rosebrook's eyes widened slightly, then narrowed as though acknowledging a hit. "Exactly, Miss Lord. I'll do well not to underestimate you."

"What if Greg isn't your child?"

His face hardened. "He's mine. I'm certain of it. But it wouldn't matter if he wasn't. He's Jessie's child, and she wanted me to have him."

"And you'll stop at nothing to get him. Even sabotage."

"Sabotage?" He looked puzzled. "Ah, you mean the elevator mishap?" He smiled, but the smile never reached his eyes. "I'm afraid I can't take credit for that. It was an accident, pure and simple. But the insurance company might not see it that way. There will have to be a very, very thorough investigation before the claim is settled. My brother sits on their board of directors, you know. It's...convenient."

"You just said it was an accident."

"I'd be a fool not to take advantage of it, now, wouldn't I? You were correct when you said threatening Van Zandt would get me nowhere. But threatening the well-being of his loved ones is another matter."

"He won't give up his son."

"You care a great deal for that little boy, don't you?"

"Yes." She was having trouble getting words past the tightness in her throat. "And I'll do everything in my power to help Dylan keep him."

"Van Zandt will never take your money. He won't stay

with you if he ends up bankrupting himself and his parents. His pride won't let him. And then you'll have lost both of them. No matter who his father is, Greg is another woman's child. He always will be.''

"What are you getting at?" she demanded, although she thought she knew already and she hated him for saying the words aloud.

"You'd be there to help Van Zandt pick up the pieces. You'd have the man you love. I would have my son. The two of you could have babies of your own. Lots and lots of babies. And all you have to do is convince Van Zandt to have the paternity test done at my doctor's office.''

"He won't agree to that. He'll know you'll falsify the results if you have to.''

"Of course he'll know. But he'll go along with it if he thinks it's the only way he can save his family from ruin and honor Jessie's memory.''

"Get out of my store," Lana said angrily. "Get out before I call the police to have you thrown out. I'll never, ever do what you ask.'' Greg was awake, frightened by her tone, and by how tightly she was holding him to her breast, to her heart. He began to cry. Rosebrook focused on the baby in her arms, but he made no move to come closer, to reach out and touch him as he had the night she'd first seen him.

"I've paid you the compliment of being frank with you, Miss Lord. Don't dismiss what I've said out of hand. We could be partners.'' He held up a placating hand at her sputtered denial. "Or at least reluctant allies. We can both have what we want most in the world if we play our cards right.''

"Get out," she said more loudly than before. "And don't come back.''

"I'm going," Rosebrook assured her, his hand on the

doorknob. "But you'll think about what I said even if you tell yourself you won't. And you'll see I'm right in the end. You can't save Van Zandt from himself. Or from me."

IT WAS ALMOST DAWN when Dylan awoke. How could he have slept so long and still feel exhausted? What little sleep he'd managed had been filled with nightmares. Dreams of blood and sorrow. He'd dreamed of Jessie weeping and of Greg, the best friend he'd ever had, turning from him in disgust because he'd failed to make Jessie happy and keep her safe.

Lana was asleep beside him. She had been there for him through the long, sleepless nights of the past week, offering her body and her love, and he had taken both to keep the terrors at bay. He lay still a moment, wondering what it was that had awakened him. Not another dream. He listened, then realized what it was.

Greg was snuffling and sucking on his fist. He was awake but not crying. It was the first time since he'd been with Dylan that he'd slept through the night. Dylan pulled on his jeans and got out of bed, then lifted his son from the crib before he started to cry and wakened Lana.

He carried the little one into the kitchen, wrapped in a warm cotton throw, and fixed his bottle by the light under the microwave. He held him in his arms and fed him the bottle, leaning against the counter, cradling him close so he would feel safe and supported—the way Lana had showed him. The way that had almost begun to feel natural and right—until the night Tyler Rosebrook walked through the door.

"Why the hell can't I love you the way I should?" he whispered. Greg opened his eyes when he heard his voice, but went on sucking at the small, flat nipple. "Your eyes are going to be gray. I thought that might be enough—you know, to prove you were mine.'' His head was still whirling with bits and pieces of nightmare caught like shingles in a tornado. ''But then Rosebrook showed up. And guess what, buddy. He's got gray eyes, too. And a ton of money to give you the best life a kid could have.''

Dylan looked at the dark kitchen with its tile floors, granite countertop, restaurant-size range and two big refrigerators. There was a butler's pantry and a safe for the silver. No Van Zandt he knew had ever owned such a thing. Rosebrook's house would be even grander than this one. ''All I've got to give you are doubts and debts.''

And he had plenty of both. Doubts about Greg's parentage and debts that were growing by the day. His creditors were starting to get nervous. He knew where the pressure on them was coming from. Rosebrook. The man was determined to get what he wanted, and he didn't have any qualms about how he went about it.

If Jessie's lover thought bringing Van Zandt Development to the verge of bankruptcy would convince Dylan to go ahead with the paternity tests, he was headed in the right direction. The last thing in the world Dylan wanted was to see his parents brought down with him. If Greg was Rosebrook's son, then the decision would be made for him.

But what if Greg wasn't Rosebrook's child, but Dylan's? He looked at Greg, waiting as always for some sign, some regeneration of the cascade of love and pride that had flooded through him at the first sight of the tiny scrap of humanity clinging perilously to life—love that had died at the knowledge of Jessie's betrayal, never to return.

He had told himself he would never have a paternity test done. He didn't want to know for certain and always that Jessie had betrayed him, that he was raising another man's son. Now he had no choice.

Jessie's lover had forced his hand. Would Rosebrook give up and leave them alone if the test proved Greg belonged to Dylan? Or did the other man want Jessica's child, a son and heir, so badly he'd stop at nothing to gain that end?

He thought of the calls from creditors he'd received the last few days. Men and institutions that had done business with Van Zandt Development for thirty years. Some were apologetic, some evasive, but all demanded payment immediately. Someone was putting pressure on them. And that would take a very powerful man. A man who would stop at nothing to gain his ends, including sabotaging the elevator shaft.

But so far three inspections, one by his own independent expert, could find no proof of foul play. Still, the insurance company was holding off, delaying settlement with one excuse after another. The insurance company where Tyler Rosebrook's brother sat on the board of directors. The result was damned near the same as if Rosebrook had cut the elevator cable himself.

Something alerted him to Lana's presence in the doorway. He looked at her. "I woke up and found you gone," she said. Her hair was tousled about her shoulders, and her lips were still swollen from his kisses. She looked like a woman who had been well loved…and who had loved well in return. But there was anxiety in her hazel eyes.

"Greg wanted his bottle."

She glanced at the clock on the microwave. "He slept through the night?"

"The first time."

She came toward him. She was wearing nothing but a sheet wrapped around her, and he felt himself begin to stir with a longing and hunger for her that he suspected would be with him until the day he died. "I thought I heard him several times during the night, but when I got up to check he was asleep. I must have been dreaming."

"I didn't get much sleep myself. I probably kept you awake."

"No, it wasn't that." She frowned as she looked at Greg. She reached out and touched the top of his head with the tip of her finger. "Tyler Rosebrook came to see me at the shop yesterday. Last night. Just as I was closing up."

"What did he want?"

"He wanted to talk to me about Greg. He asked me to help you make the right decision." The sadness in her voice and expression was almost his undoing.

"Goddamn it. Did he threaten you?"

She lifted her troubled eyes to his face. "No. But he's determined to have Greg. He'll stop at nothing."

"He's already putting pressure on my creditors. The insurance company is dragging its feet on signing off on the elevator accident."

He felt her gaze probe deep into his soul and forced himself not to look away. "You've made your decision, haven't you?" she said. He felt her draw away, not physically—not yet—but emotionally. He wanted to howl his anguish to the moon.

He looked at the child he suspected wasn't his, but what he saw was a reflection of the worry and stress that were beginning to etch new lines in his father's face, the sadness weighing on his mother's plump shoulders. He remembered the dreams of the night before. The way he'd failed Jessie as a husband and Greg as a friend. He heard Rosebrook's words echoing like a litany in his mind. *She wanted me to have him.* He knew he was walking into an ambush, but he was backed against the wall. "I'm going to let Rosebrook's doctor do the test. I can't see as I have any other choice."

CHAPTER SEVENTEEN

LANA'S HEART crystallized in her chest. She could feel the ice creeping through her veins, into her brain. Into her soul. Moments ago she'd awakened in Dylan's bed, replete and fulfilled. Now she had only to look at the resignation in his face, the stubborn determination to do what he thought was best, and all the happiness drained away, leaving her only a shell. "You can't mean that."

"Rosebrook could tie me up in court for years. We'd be fighting over Greg like a piece of property. He's got millions. I'm damned near broke. Worse than broke. If I can't get an extension on my loans I'll be bankrupt by the end of the month. If I can't get the insurance company to okay the settlement, my dad will be in damned near the same shape."

He wouldn't meet her eyes. He was talking dollars and cents, and she was talking love and commitment. They had never been further apart than at this moment. She clutched the sheet more tightly around her, feeling vulnerable and at a disadvantage in her near-naked state. She took a deep breath and forced herself to think calmly. Men saw things differently than women did. She had grown up with two brothers, she knew that. Stability and responsibility meant love and commitment to many men. They were not as much at odds as she had feared. And Dylan was committed to his family. She never questioned that for a moment. But she had to talk him out of this terrible decision, this sacrifice he was determined to make and would regret, she was certain, until his dying day.

"Your name is on Greg's birth certificate. There's no reason for you to give in to Rosebrook's demand for paternity tests."

"Jessie believed Rosebrook was Greg's father," he said flatly. "I've never felt about him as I should. The way my dad says he felt about the three of us when we were born. Maybe there's a reason for that, and maybe Rosebrook is it."

"Dylan, it's sometimes difficult for a parent to bond with a critically ill infant." His gaze narrowed. "I…I've done some reading." She fell silent a moment, marshaling her courage. "It's natural, Dylan. Those first few days you must have been afraid to love him. He was so tiny. So helpless. Wondering if he would be with you hour by hour. Especially after everything…because of Jessie's death. You just need time—"

He cut her off. "Don't psychoanalyze me, Lana. Greg deserves the best life I can give him." His voice was harsh and toneless. "Putting every other consideration aside, maybe the best is giving him up to someone else. Have you thought of that?"

"No." She clutched the sheet to her breasts to keep from reaching out with both hands to shake some sense into him. "Not if that man is Tyler Rosebrook. I…I don't trust him. I—" She broke off, unable to find words to voice her heartfelt reservations about Jessie's lover without sounding melodramatic. She needed to stay calm. To keep her arguments concrete and logical. "Blood isn't thicker than water. I *know*. My brothers and sister and I are living, breathing examples of it. Greg needs to be with you. With your parents. He needs to grow up with his cousins. He needs to have the memories of his mother and uncle only you can give him." She wasn't getting through to him. She could see it in the stubborn line of his jaw, the tension in his neck and shoulders.

"Memories don't make up for a father who's bankrupt and whose grandparents have lost everything they've worked their whole lives for. I don't want to discuss it any further, Lana. It's—" He shut his mouth so quickly she could hear his teeth snap together.

"You were going to say it's none of my business." She had to swallow hard to keep from crying. How could he dismiss what had passed between them so callously? Nearly blinded by tears, she failed to see the bone-deep pain that settled like cloud shadows in the depths of his gray eyes.

"Lana—"

"I love him, too, Dylan," she said softly.

"I know you do."

"But you don't love me." He made a low animal sound deep in his throat, but she refused to let it stop her. "At least not enough to let me help you fight to keep him."

"God, Lana. Would you believe me if I said I loved you more than life itself right now? I would, but it's not the time."

"It might never be the time. I thought I knew you, Dylan." She looked at Greg sucking hungrily on his bottle. "But I guess I was wrong. Horribly, stupidly wrong."

"Lana—"

"Don't. Nothing you can say right now will make a difference. I can't believe you would give your own child to a stranger."

"If he is Rosebrook's son, I have to."

"If you let Rosebrook's doctor perform the test, that will be the outcome, I'm convinced of it."

"I know that, too." He looked past her into the shadows, seeing what she didn't know, couldn't hope to understand if he kept her at a distance this way.

She reached out and touched the little one's satiny cheek. It was half killing her to walk away from Greg. How could Dylan consider for a moment giving him up? That question more than any other illustrated the distance between them that she couldn't hope to bridge with reason or understanding. The hopelessness that welled inside her almost stopped her heart in her chest. "You can stay here as long as you like," she whispered to hold back the sob that rose in her throat. "But I think it'll be best if I move in with Shelby until you find a place of your own."

"Goddamn it, I won't turn you out of your house."

"There's no place else for Greg that's safe and comfortable. Unless you mean to take him home to your mother?"

"I don't want my mother to know anything about this."

Lana's last hope died. She had counted on Linda Van Zandt's unquestioning acceptance of Greg as her grandson to pull Dylan from the brink.

"It will break her heart, Dylan." She would not tell him again that she loved him. She wouldn't beg. If he loved her, he would know they could make a family. That she would treat Greg as her own child.

"She'll understand."

Lana shook her head, too weary and heartsick to argue anymore. "No," she said. "It will break her heart. I know, because you've already broken mine."

"LANA, MY LORD, what are you doing here so early? It's not even six." Nonetheless Shelby was up and dressed. She answered the door of her town house with a cup of coffee in her hand.

"That's just what Michael said the other day. I'm sorry

I can't schedule my crises at more convenient times."
Lana started to cry. The tears that had been building inside
her all the way from home had reached critical mass and
were spilling down her cheeks.

"What's wrong?" Shelby set the coffee cup on a small
side table with a total disregard for its contents or the
safety of her carpet and put her arms around Lana.
"What's happened? Was there an accident?"

"Do I look that bad?" she asked, trying for a light tone
and failing miserably, if the look on her sister's face was
any indication.

"You look like you've lost your last friend in the
world. C'mon, tell me what's wrong."

"I may need a place to stay for a couple of days." It
was hard to get the words out with more tears threatening.

"What? Why leave the house? What about Dylan and
Greg?"

"He's still there. At least he was when I left. I can't
spend another minute under the same roof with him." She
put shaking hands in front of her face.

"Oh, Lana. Sit down. Oh, Sissy." It had been years
since Shelby had called her by her childhood nickname.
Her sister led her toward the couch, sympathetic tears glis-
tening in her eyes. "Did he hurt you? Should I call Garrett
and Michael? They'll take him apart limb by limb."

"No! It's not that. He didn't—" Lana took a long,
shuddering breath and forced her voice to stop shaking.
The last thing she needed was for Michael and Garrett to
come riding, hell-for-leather, to her rescue. "Dylan's not
that kind of man."

"Well, I didn't think so." Shelby handed her a box of
tissues and sat on the couch beside Lana. "He seems like
such a great guy. And I— Well, I thought you two were
hitting it off pretty well."

"I thought so, too." Lana tried to pull herself together. Shelby's town house was a short walk from the diner, but Lana knew she had only a few minutes to explain the situation before her sister would have to leave for Austin Eats.

"Then what in heaven's name happened to send you running out of your own house? This has got to be more than just a lovers' quarrel."

"Greg's father showed up," Lana said bluntly.

"No. Oh, Sissy. I'm so sorry. Are you certain? I mean is there—"

"Dylan's certain, that's all that matters." She balled the tissue up and closed her fist around it. "He's going to give Greg up to him."

"Oh, no." She didn't need to say anything more. Shelby knew how far gone Lana was with love for Dylan. And Greg. "Are you positive?"

Lana nodded. "He thinks he has to. To give Greg the kind of childhood we had. And because the other man says that's what Jessie wanted."

"Dear Lord, what a pickle."

"Isn't it." Lana started sniffling. She couldn't help herself. She plucked another tissue out of the box. "What am I going to do?"

"Have breakfast, for a start."

"I couldn't eat a thing."

"Yes, you can. You always eat when you're upset. We all do." Shelby stood and marched toward her little white and chrome kitchen.

"You don't have time to fix breakfast for me!" The diner opened in half an hour. The rest of the staff would already be hard at work.

"Of course I'm not cooking. What's the use of owning a restaurant if you can't get carry-in ASAP?" She picked up the phone and spoke so quickly and quietly Lana couldn't hear. She got up and wandered restlessly to the window. The sun was coming up. It was going to be a beautiful day. The hurricane in the gulf had stalled and then turned east, heading toward Florida, bringing cool, drier air down from the north.

"There. It's all taken care of." Shelby came up behind her with a second mug of coffee. "This will help. Ramon's sending over two Statesman Specials."

"Cholesterol heaven," Lana said, managing a smile.

"You bet your boots. No yogurt and fruit for us this morning. No wasting away into nervous collapse for the Lord crew allowed. We go down fighting. Right?"

Lana turned from the window, crossing her arms beneath her breasts to hold in the last of the warmth that existed inside her. She met her sister's concerned gaze head-on. "I feel like I've been shot right through the heart. A mortal wound." Breaking her engagement with Jason Fairmont hadn't amounted to a scratch, compared with the agony she suffered now. She'd lost Dylan's love. A love she must honestly admit he'd never offered her. And she'd lost Greg. Her arms ached to hold Greg. And to be held by Dylan. "I'm afraid the battle's already lost."

"Lana, don't say that. Here, take the coffee and let's talk this through." Shelby thrust the mug of hot liquid into Lana's reluctant hands, and the warmth of it did feel good. She took a sip. "There, that's better. Do I know the man who claims to be Greg's biological father?"

"I—" She wasn't certain she should reveal Tyler Rosebrook's identity even to her sister. Especially after the way she'd parted from Dylan that morning.

"Stop. Delete that request. Don't worry about breaking

a confidence. I should have said, is he the kind of man who should be raising a child?''

"It's Tyler Rosebrook,'' Lana said, making her decision. It was ridiculous to beat around the bush like this with Shelby. Her whole life she had trusted her sister with every secret she'd ever had.

Shelby pursed her lips in a whistle. "Okay. That question is settled. Rich and intelligent and connections all the way from here to Washington. Also, not a very savory reputation where women are concerned.''

"That's what Michael said. But Dylan doesn't know any of that last part. He's got every cent he has tied up in the building renovations. And the bank isn't too keen on loaning him more. He thinks it's Rosebrook's doing. I...I *know* it's Rosebrook's doing.''

"You do?''

"He came to talk to me. He said as much. He said his brother sits on the board of directors of the insurance company that's handling the elevator accident claim—''

"He'll try and hold up the settlement?''

"And pressure Dylan's creditors to call in his loans and ruin his family business as well as Dylan's project.''

"And Dylan, being a typical male, has put two and two together and come up with five. It's best for everybody to give the baby to Rosebrook, right? But what if Greg is really Dylan's child?''

"Rosebrook's doctor is going to perform the paternity test—''

"I see. You suspect the results will favor Rosebrook, no matter what.''

"Yes.'' Lana stared into her coffee cup. She might as well tell Shelby the rest. "Dylan thinks that's what Jessie, Greg's mother, would have wanted.''

"Ouch. That one's going to be harder to talk him out of."

"Do you think I can? Talk him out of it, I mean?"

"If the three of you being a family is what you want most in life, then I'd say, yes, it's worth having a go at it."

Lana smiled. She couldn't help herself in the face of her sister's determined optimism. "I've told myself over and over I could be patient. That I could wait for Dylan to deal with all the issues he had from Jessica's death and his doubts about Greg's parentage. But last night—" She paused, searching for the words that would describe the feelings that had surged up inside her. "It was like our mother abandoning us all over again." She spread her hands. "I know that sounds ridiculous."

"No, Lana honey. It sounds natural. And when you think of the agony Dylan must be going through, maybe you can sympathize a little with what it must have been like for her, with four of us to look after."

Shelby glanced at the coffee table, and for the first time Lana noticed the yellow legal pads and manila file folders scattered over the surface. "Is that the detective's report?" she asked, picking up one folder. Her hands were shaking. She put it down again. There was nothing inside she wanted to see.

"It's the list of names she's come up with. People who might have a lead on a couple of the sets of triplets she found. Garrett and I divided them up. She just delivered it yesterday. I...I haven't really had time to start looking through it yet."

Lana bowed her head again. "I'm sorry I was so adamant about not joining you in the search for her."

"It's okay, sis. Anyway, that's not our problem today.

You and Dylan and Greg are number one on the agenda. What do you intend to do?''

"Dylan loves Greg. I know he does. But he won't let himself admit it. If he did, none of the rest would matter. He would know it's best for the baby to stay with him."

"And with you," Shelby said, patting her hand.

"It may be too late for us." It hurt to say it. "But I can't let him turn Greg over to Rosebrook without trying to convince him he's wrong. Even if it means Dylan and I will never be together. It will be enough for me to know that Greg is with him."

IT HAD BEEN a hell of a couple of days. Dylan looked at the bright September morning with surprise. It was going to be a beautiful day. For all he would see of it. For all he cared, one way or the other.

He looked at Greg, fed and dressed to meet the day. The baby stared at him with solemn gray eyes. Rosebrook's eyes? Dylan's eyes? They would know soon enough. He had taken Greg to Rosebrook's doctor for the paternity test the day before. There was little doubt in his mind what the results would be. He'd made his bargain with the devil and he meant to keep his end of it, even though it would mean the loss of his soul and the woman he loved.

It was best for all concerned. "It is, little man," he whispered. "You'll be raised like a king. A lord."

Lana. He hadn't seen her since the morning of their quarrel. He'd made arrangements with Beth Redstone to leave Greg at Maitland Maternity's day-care facility, and he'd moved their things out of Lana's house and into the apartment above the Crystal Unicorn, which was the nearest to being ready to put on the market. It was big and empty and echoing. And Greg didn't like it. He'd been restless the last two nights, sleeping only as long as Dylan held him close to his heart.

Dylan hadn't slept at all. Even the warmth and softness of the baby in his arms hadn't been enough to vanquish the emptiness in his heart and in his thoughts. Lana was gone. Out of his life. It was better that way. She would never forgive what he was about to do for the good of them all, and he could never forget if he had to look at the reproach in her hazel eyes every day for the rest of their lives.

His cell phone beeped.

"Hello, Dylan."

"Mom?" Next to Lana, she was the last person on earth he wanted to talk to right now.

"You're already at the building, aren't you?"

"I came in early. How can you tell?" He had to drop Greg off at the clinic and then meet with the loans officer at he bank. He didn't have much hope of changing the man's mind about calling in his loans. Rosebrook had doubtless made his wishes on the matter perfectly clear, but Dylan had to give it a shot.

"There's an echo. I never notice it at Lana's." She let the sentence hang there for a moment. When he didn't respond, she launched into speech again. "I just can't shake this feeling, Dylan. You know how they are. But this one. Well, it's the strongest I've ever had. Are you sure everything's okay? Is Greg okay? He—"

He didn't give her a chance to finish. "He's fine."

"You're giving him his medicine?"

"Twice a day. Like clockwork."

"But there's got to be a reason for this awful feeling in the pit of my stomach. There always is."

"How are you feeling, Mom? Maybe it's some kind of side effect from your fall." He felt like a heel, dismissing her anxiety, but the last thing he wanted was his mother to stumble onto the fact that the man who was probably Greg's real father was in the picture.

"I'm fine. And it's not just nerves. There is something else."

"What's that?" The fine hairs on the back of his neck stood on end.

"There was a stranger in town asking questions about you and Jessie a few days ago. Sheriff Nelson stopped by the house last night to tell your dad and me. Questions about when she died. About how you two were getting along. About when Greg was born. I don't like it. Are you sure there's nothing wrong?"

"Everything's fine, Mom." God, he hated lying to his mother, but how in hell could he tell her on the phone what had happened? Better wait until all the decisions were made, the Rubicon crossed, before she knew there was anything wrong. "Look, I've got to go. I have an appointment with the bank and I'm already late."

"You'll bring Greg and come out this weekend, won't you?"

"I'll do my best," he told her.

"If you don't come here, I'll drive into town. I got my walking cast on yesterday. The only reason I'm not there talking to you in person this very minute is I promised your father I wouldn't drive till he gets back from Houston."

"Houston?" This was safer ground. His dad hadn't mentioned any trips to Houston the last time they'd talked.

"He went on business. Something about one of the subcontractors on the school project. But I'm of two minds—"

"I promise, Mom. We'll be there Sunday. Gotta run." He clicked the button and broke the connection. "Time to go, fella.'' Greg focused his big eyes on Dylan and smiled.

Greg had never smiled at him before, and his heart did a little tap dance in his chest. "Hey, big guy. Are you smiling at me?" The finality of the course he'd set for himself hit him like a sledgehammer blow. He would never see Greg laugh, or roll over, or learn to walk or ride a bike. When he did those things, it would be with Tyler Rosebrook by his side.

He strapped Greg into his carrier and didn't look at the baby's face again. *It wasn't a smile, you fool,* Dylan told himself. *Not a real smile, only gas.*

CHAPTER EIGHTEEN

LANA LOOKED UP from the display of Anne Geddes prints she was arranging on the alcove wall. The largest was a trio of fat, cherubic infants dressed as jack-o'-lanterns. Halloween was a little more than a month away. She'd already put a rack of tiny costumes on the sidewalk, hoping to lure impulse-buying parents on their way home from work on Friday afternoon. Greg would look adorable in the one shaped like a pea pod, with fuzzy green pompoms down his middle and a little green stem on the hood.

She stopped smiling. Greg might not even be with Dylan at Halloween. And even if he was, he wouldn't be with her.

She turned as the bell above the door chimed, grateful for the distraction of a customer. She couldn't keep her thoughts away from Dylan's dilemma or her own aching heart.

"Lana. I'm glad you're here. Dylan isn't next door. I...I came to see Greg." Dylan's mother looked flushed and anxious. She limped toward Lana, a cane in her right hand, the heavy walking cast on her left leg coming to just below her knee.

The older woman's unexpected appearance caught Lana off guard. She said the first thing that came to mind. "Linda, I didn't know you were planning on coming to town today."

"I wasn't. Until I talked to Dylan a couple of hours

ago. He sounded—'' She broke off and looked around the shop. "Where's Greg? Is he in the back room with your...with Brittany?'' she asked, pulling the name out of her memory.

"No, it's Brittany's day off." Lana was at a loss. "Greg's not here," she said, skirting the Prince William cradle and a table of porcelain snow babies at play in drifts of sparkling white cotton.

"Dylan took him to meet with the banker?" Linda's brow furrowed. "I don't understand."

"He's not at the bank with Dylan, either." So that was why Dylan had been wearing a suit coat and tie when she had looked out the window and seen him drive off earlier. Janette had come from the storeroom at the sound of the bell. Lana turned to the older woman, grateful for the small reprieve. "Would you watch the floor, Janette? I need to speak with Mrs. Van Zandt for a moment."

"Certainly." The quick glance of surprise that Janette sent her way was lost on Dylan's mother, who was maneuvering through the crowded showroom with the deliberate movements of someone unused to walking in a cast.

"We won't be long."

"Take your time. Is the Geddes display all finished?"

"Yes. But I was going to sort through the sidewalk racks and put them into some kind of order."

"Great. I'll do that. It's too nice a day to be inside." Lana was grateful Brittany wasn't in the store. She would never have taken the hint to give them privacy.

Lana held back the lengths of wooden beads that curtained the storeroom doorway so Linda could make her way through. She sank gratefully onto the couch. Lana brought the same cardboard box Linda had used as a footstool on her last visit and placed it under the cast. "Thanks," Dylan's mother breathed gratefully. "I'm go-

ing to have a stroke hauling this hunk of cement around
for the next month.'' She looked at the cluttered office
and break area, obviously noting that all signs of Greg
being there were gone. No empty bottles, Mickey Mouse
rattles or Winnie-the-Pooh receiving blankets. ''Where is
my grandson?''

''He's at the Maitland Maternity clinic day-care facility.''

''Oh?'' Linda frowned and looked at her skirt. When
she lifted her eyes her expression was puzzled and a little
hurt. ''I'm sorry. We shouldn't have imposed on your
goodwill for so long. I wish Dylan had brought him to
me. He's so little to be in a public day care.''

Lana rested her hip against the edge of her desk. There
was no way to tell Dylan's mother why Greg was at
Beth's day care without telling her about Tyler Rosebrook
and his claim on her grandson. Unless she told her only
part of the truth. That she and Dylan had had a falling
out and he'd taken Greg from her care.

It would hurt so badly, but she had to do it. Dylan
didn't want his mother to know about Jessie's lover, and
as much as she wished she could divulge his secret, she
had no right.

''You've quarreled with my son, haven't you?'' Linda
guessed.

''Yes. But I would still have taken care of Greg.'' She
wasn't so noble that she could keep from speaking up for
herself.

Linda's face crumpled. ''But it would be awkward. I
didn't mean to imply—'' She lifted a hand to her forehead. ''I'm sorry you and Dylan have had a falling out. I
was hoping—'' She hesitated. ''It's none of my business,
of course. But—'' She lifted imploring hands. ''There's
something else wrong, isn't there? Something with Dylan

and Greg." She touched her breast with the tips of her fingers. "I can feel it here."

"I—"

"Please don't make light of my premonitions. They're real."

"I'd never do that." Lana pushed away from the desk and sat beside Dylan's mother on the shabby old sofa. "I believe in premonitions. And ties of the heart."

"Tell me what's wrong," Linda pleaded. "Dylan's voice on the phone this morning... He sounded so distant, so unlike himself. And then there was that stranger asking questions around town." For a moment Lana thought she meant Garrett and Shelby's detective, but Linda hurried on. "This wasn't the first person asking questions about Dylan lately. There was a woman, too. A detective. It was just after he met you. I—" She colored to the hairline. "Well, we—Roger and I—we figured maybe you were—"

"It was my brothers," Lana said, smiling a little in spite of the terrible ache in her heart. "They were worried about me. Having Dylan living in my house, and all. But you're right. That was weeks ago."

Linda nodded. "I barely had a twinge then. But this time the sheriff stopped by. He and my husband went to high school together, you know, and he thought we'd want to know."

"Yes?" Lana prompted gently.

"This man was asking so many personal questions. About Dylan and Jessie. About Greg. I just knew something was wrong. It came to me this morning, after I talked to Dylan. It's all connected somehow. And what would be the worst that it could be?" Tears flooded her gray eyes. Dylan's eyes. Greg's eyes. "It hit me like a tidal wave. It's the other man, isn't it? Jessie's lover. He's found out about Greg."

"He came to the building the other night. He said he had a letter from Jessie, written just before her death, telling him about Greg. He says she wanted him to have the baby. And—"

Linda put her hand to her throat and closed her eyes. "This man wants my grandson. Dylan will never give him up."

"He feels he has no choice."

Linda's eyes flew open. "I don't understand. Greg is Dylan's *son*." She colored a little. "We...we never discussed it. But even if Jessie was unfaithful...well, I know she and Dylan reconciled right away. I mean, she told me later... Oh dear, I'm sure you don't want to hear this. But I'm certain Greg is my grandchild."

"It's all right," Lana said soothingly. Linda was right. She would rather not have heard the words. "Jessie's lover was Tyler Rosebrook. Do you know who he is?"

Linda paled. "Everyone's heard of the Rosebrooks in this part of Texas. That's the man Dylan is up against?" Her gray eyes widened with sudden understanding and alarm. "That's why there's trouble with the credit lines on the project, isn't it? And the insurance company holding off on settling for the elevator accident. It's this Rosebrook's doing."

"I think so. He's insisting on a paternity test. And he wants it performed by his own doctor."

"And Dylan agreed." The tears spilled over. Linda pushed the cardboard box from beneath her cast and struggled to rise from the sagging sofa. "Oh, this is more terrible than I imagined." She put her fingers to her lips to still the trembling. "He agreed to the tests and he's considering letting this other man take Greg away, isn't he?"

Lana felt her eyes fill with tears she refused to let fall. "I think he's already made up his mind it's inevitable. Rosebrook's threatened him with bankruptcy and—"

"Us, too." Dylan's mother finished the sentence for her. "Oh, God. I can't let him do this. I have to go to Greg. I have to have him with me. Then I'll talk to Dylan. He'll listen to me. I... Where is this place? Maitland Maternity, you said. I...I don't know my way around the city." She looked around distractedly, searching for her cane, which had fallen beside the sofa.

Lana picked it up for her. "I'll take you to Maitland," she said. "They know me. But I doubt if they would let you take Greg away without Dylan's permission."

"He isn't answering his phone or his pager," Linda said. She brushed at her cheeks, wiping the tears away. Her gray eyes hardened, and Lana realized Dylan's mother would be a formidable opponent if she felt she was in the right. "I don't care about their rules and regulations. I have to see Greg, now. I have to think of some way to help Dylan deal with this horrible Tyler Rosebrook person. I wish Roger were here, but he's in Houston on business. But first, before I do anything else, I have to see my grandson."

"Beth Redstone is the head of Maitland's day-care facility. She and I have been friends all our lives. She'll understand why you need to see Greg."

Linda grasped Lana's right hand with hers. "I am his grandmother. I'm positive of it. If only we can make Dylan believe, too. You have to help me, Lana."

"I'll take you to Maitland," Lana said, once more almost choking on her tears. "But as for the other—I've tried. Oh, dear God, how I've tried. But Dylan won't listen to me. He's convinced he's doing what's best for everyone concerned, and there's no changing his mind."

THE DRIVE to Maitland Maternity was a quiet one. Lana found a space near the door and commandeered a wheel-chair from the receptionist at the front desk. "It will be quicker this way," she urged when Linda protested she was perfectly capable of walking. It was a measure of the older woman's anxiety that she gave up without an argument.

The door to the day-care facility was standing open, and Lana could see Beth among a gaggle of preschoolers at the far side of the colorful, sunny room. Older children at work on crafts and games at low tables regarded them with interest for a moment or two, then returned to their activities.

"Where are the babies?" Linda asked, looking past the laughing toddlers jumping and turning somersaults on blue exercise mats.

"There, in that small room." Lana pointed to the glassed-in nursery to their left.

Linda turned in that direction as Beth extricated herself from her frolicking charges and came their way. She held out her hands. "Lana. I haven't seen you for ages. What brings you here today?" Her bright eyes were fixed on Linda's profile.

"Beth, this is Mrs. Van Zandt. Greg's grandmother." Lana hurried through the introductions.

"Nice to meet you," Linda said. "I want my grandson."

"I—" Beth looked to Lana for guidance.

"I know it's pretty irregular, but there's been… There's a family…" Lana fumbled to a halt.

"I see." Beth squeezed Lana's hand, telling her without words that her old friend knew more about the situation than she was letting on. And it was no mystery how that came about. There was Abby and Kyle, Megan,

Shelby and Michael. They all saw Beth daily. And it wouldn't be the first time Lana's love life, or her lack of it, was the topic of conversation among her friends and family.

"Please, I need to take my grandson," Linda said more urgently.

"If it's an emergency," Beth said, "then, of course, you may take Greg with you. But I will need to see some identification, even though Lana's here to vouch for you. Regulations, you understand. Fortunately, Mr. Van Zandt has listed you on Greg's enrollment papers as the person to call in an emergency." She turned to Lana. Her face softened, and a tiny smile curved the corners of her generous mouth. "And you, too, Lana."

"Me?" Her spirits rose from the ashes. Even though they had argued before he brought Greg to Maitland Maternity, he had listed her as a person he trusted with his son. Surely, surely that meant something. It gave her new hope. Perhaps there was still a chance to make him see reason.

Beth looked puzzled. "Why, of course. I thought—" She stopped short, aware that Dylan's mother was only a few feet away, although all her attention seemed focused on the nursery door. "Oh, Lana. Is something wrong?"

"I don't have time to talk about it now, Beth. I have to get Mrs. Van Zandt back to the shop."

"I understand." She leaned forward and gave Lana a hug. "Call me. Anytime, day or night. I'll always be there for you."

Lana hugged her back. "Thanks, Beth. I'll remember."

A few minutes later, one of Beth's helpers appeared with Greg in his carrier, the familiar camouflage knapsack hanging over her shoulder. "Here he is, all fed and changed and ready for his nap."

"Thank you." Linda held out her arms for the carrier and then seemed to realize what an awkward business it would be for her to carry the baby and his paraphernalia when she needed the cane to get around. "Drat this ankle," she said helplessly.

"I'll take him," Lana offered.

"If you'll just sign the daily log, Mrs. Van Zandt," Beth said, holding out the log and a pen. "Right there where it says Time Out. There now. We're all set. It was nice meeting you, ma'am. Greg's a darling baby."

"Yes, he is. Thanks for taking such good care of him."

Linda seemed anxious to be on her way, as though she was afraid Beth would change her mind and snatch Greg back. She sat in the wheelchair they'd left outside the door and held out her arms for the carrier. "It's a very nice day care," she said distractedly as Lana wheeled her to the car. "So light and airy. The children looked as if they love it there."

"Beth is great with kids. Running a day care has been her dream for as long as I can remember."

"I could tell you were good friends."

"We've been best friends forever. Of course, I don't see as much of her as I'd like since she's married."

"As soon as we're back in your car I'll try and call Dylan to tell him I have Greg. Just because he's acting like a fool doesn't mean I have to." Linda colored to the roots of her hair. "Oh, dear. I imagine you're thinking that's exactly what I'm doing. Well, I don't care," she said before Lana could make a polite demure. "Dylan isn't in his right mind if he's considering giving Greg up." Suddenly she looked very much like her strong-willed son. "I'm taking custody of my grandson until *my* son comes to his senses and everything's back the way it should be."

DYLAN DROVE BY the front of the building on the way to his parking spot in the alley. He spotted his mom and dad's car parked right in front of Lana's store. He wasn't even surprised.

"And the hits just keep on coming," he said, jerking off his tie and unbuttoning the top two buttons of his shirt. The bank had just called in his loan, and now he had his mother to deal with. That infernal second sight of hers was turning out to be too damned accurate where he and Greg were concerned.

How was he going to make his mother understand why he'd agreed to Rosebrook's demands? Why he was contemplating giving up Jessie's child to her lover's keeping. Explaining to her that he had Greg's best interests at heart wasn't going to wash. And if he said, "I'm doing it to save you and Dad from bankruptcy," she would turn from him in disgust.

She would tell him they would survive without the money. They would fight to keep Greg. They would start all over again if they had to, but they would do it as a family. He wasn't sacrificing his son for their sakes, she would say. She would look him straight in the eye and tell him in truth he was only trying to do penance for Jessie's death.

And maybe at the bottom of it all, he was.

"Dylan." Lana stood silhouetted in the doorway, the afternoon sunshine bright behind her.

He hadn't seen her for days. For an eternity. "Hello, Lana."

"I have something to tell you." She looked tired and sad and she wouldn't quite meet his eyes but stared at a space just past his left ear.

"You have my mother and Greg with you, right?"

"She showed up here a couple of hours ago. She

guessed what was going on. I…she wanted me to fill in the details, and I did.'' Lana raised her chin and looked him in the eye for the first time. ''She's so worried she insisted on taking Greg from the day care. She's making a nervous wreck of herself.''

''I'll talk to her.''

Lana almost smiled, a small curving of her lips that passed in an instant. ''She's not in the mood to listen to anything you have to say. She's determined to give you a piece of her mind.''

''God, I should have just kept driving.'' He pushed his hand through his hair.

''It didn't go well at the bank, did it?'' Lana stepped forward as she spoke. She laid her hand on his arm. He took a step away from her, held himself in check with all his will so that he didn't give in to the almost overwhelming desire to pull her into his arms and lose himself in her warmth and quiet strength. She misinterpreted his gesture as rejection and dropped her hand. He felt her pull even further into herself and was powerless to do anything about it.

''They turned me down flat.''

''I'm sorry, Dylan.'' Her voice was as coolly polite as if they were strangers. The finishing-school haughtiness she had told him only surfaced when she was upset.

He forced himself to concentrate on the ruins of his business, not the ruins of his heart. ''Not as sorry as I am. With that loan called in, all the other lenders will follow suit. I'm broke. I'll have to lay off my crew by the end of the week. I'd better go talk to my mom.'' He had to stick to his chosen path. It was too late to salvage the happiness and loving future he'd glimpsed with Lana, and he still had his parents and Van Zandt Development to worry about.

"Your mother and Greg are in the storeroom. I'll leave you two alone."

"Lana—"

"There's nothing more I can say or do. I hope your mother can talk you into changing your mind. But you're so damned stubborn I'm afraid she won't. Goodbye, Dylan." Her choice of words was deliberate, he was sure. She never intended to see him again. Lana walked out the door, turning toward the Crystal Unicorn, and two steps later was lost from sight.

Dylan waited a long minute and then made his way to Lana's portion of the building. He opened the door at the bottom of the narrow dark stairway and saw his mother sitting on the worn sofa in Lana's storeroom, her foot propped on a cardboard box, Greg in her lap. Her eyes were closed, her cheek resting on her hand. He came up on her quietly and looked at the child in her lap. Greg was staring cross-eyed at his fist. When Dylan's shadow fell across him, he blinked and then focused his eyes on his face. And for the second time that day he smiled.

And for the second time that day, that newly minted smile, his son's smile, lodged like an arrow in his heart.

"Mom." He could barely get the word past the lump in his throat.

"Dylan? I…I must have dozed off." She sat up, pushing her hair behind her ears. Her face got that mulish look it did when she was determined to have her way. "I came to get Greg. I just couldn't shake my feeling. And I was right. Lana told me everything about Tyler Rosebrook and his claim on Greg. I don't believe a word of it. He's your son, Dylan. Can't you see that?"

"I can't, Mom," he said wearily. "God knows I've tried, but I can't."

"You would if you'd only look with your heart and

not your eyes.'' He heard the pleading in her voice and wanted more than anything to tell her she was right. But he could not.

"I'm sorry, Mom. It's for the best this way. It's what Jessie—"

"Jessie is dead. And she isn't above hurting you even from the grave. I know I shouldn't speak ill of the dead, but it's true.'' She stiffened her spine, sitting up ramrod straight. "You're not thinking clearly. I'm taking Greg home with me until you come to your senses.''

"You can't do that, Mom. He's too much trouble for you with your leg in a cast.''

"No grandbaby of mine is too much trouble. Get that ridiculous notion out of your head this instant. And sit down. You're giving me a crick in my neck standing over me that way.''

He dropped to his knees beside the couch. He was too heartsick to argue with her. "We'll talk about it later, Mom. Right now I have to go tell the guys not to come to work tomorrow.''

She reached out and brushed the hair from his forehead the way she used to do when he was little. She hadn't done that for years. Her voice gentled. "The bank turned you down?''

"Flat.''

"That's something else we need to discuss.'' Greg was wiggling on her lap, his little head moving from right to left, almost as if he was following the sound of their voices. "I got in touch with your father in Houston. He'll be here in just a few hours. We'll work out something about a loan then.''

"It's too late, Mom. Rosebrook's way ahead of us.''

Greg reached out with both arms. Almost against his will, Dylan touched his satiny palm. The baby's tiny hand wrapped around his finger and clamped tight. Greg stopped wiggling. He focused on Dylan's face with laser accuracy. He blinked, then blinked again, and a smile split his cherub face. Fireworks went off in Dylan's heart and in his mind.

Linda lost her train of thought. She laughed softly, delightedly. She touched the tip of her finger to the corner of Greg's mouth. "Oh, Dylan, look. He's smiling at you."

Dylan spoke through the tightness in his throat. "It's gas, Mom. All the books say it's gas at his age."

"Good grief, how can you believe such hogwash? Look at his face. He's missed his daddy, and now you're here. His world is complete."

"It's not that simple, Mom."

But Greg kept on smiling and wiggling. Dylan couldn't help himself. He reached down and took the baby in his arms, cuddled him against his chest. Greg squirmed and cooed some more. He burrowed his warm little nose into Dylan's shoulder. He felt his son's tiny heart beat against the muscles of his chest. His breath shortened, and the hairs at the nape of his neck stood on end. He looked down. Greg's eyes were closed, but he was still smiling. Smiling at Dylan. At his father.

Dylan slammed a mental door on his emotions, but the tingling warmth of Greg's tiny body in his arms remained. He gave him to his mother and stood up.

It was too late to fall in love with his son now.

His mother was still talking, babbling excitely. "And when the business with the loans is settled, we'll deal with Jessie's lover. Better yet, call him this minute and tell him you've changed your mind. That Greg is *our* baby, a Van Zandt through and through, and we don't ever want to see or hear from him again."

"I can't do that, Mom. It isn't just about the money.

Although God knows how we could fight Rosebrook and his millions even if I let you and Dad do such a thing. You can talk till you're blue in the face, but my mind's made up. If Greg is Rosebrook's son, I'm giving him up to him.''

His pager beeped. The smile had left his mother's face, and she blinked back tears. She held Greg to her breast fiercely, protectively. ''Don't answer that.''

''It could be Dad,'' he reminded her, silencing the pager.

She shook her head. ''It's him, Rosebrook. I know it.''

''I have to talk to him.''

She raised her eyes to his, full of sadness and disappointment. ''If everything Lana's told me about the man is true, there won't be any question of the test results saying he's not Greg's father. He'll make sure they do.'' Her face hardened, and she looked past him just the way Lana had. There were tears in his mother's eyes, but determination was written large on her face. ''Mark my words. If you give Gregory to that man, I'll never speak to you again as long as I live.''

CHAPTER NINETEEN

DYLAN GLANCED at his watch. The day was finally over. His crew had agreed to finish out the week. He'd find the money to pay them by Friday afternoon if he had to sell his truck to do it. But in the meantime, the plumbing and electrical in the first unit would be completed, and he and Greg would be more comfortable staying there.

If he still had Greg at the end of the week.

His hands curled into fists at his side. He forced himself to relax. He could still feel the faint pressure of Greg's tiny fingers curled around his, the residue of the tingling sensation that had seared its way from his hand to his brain to his heart—and, more deeply, into his soul at the sight of such complete faith and trust. God, where could his head have been these past days? He'd let himself be ruled by guilt and indecision, and it wasn't like him. But that had all changed because his son had smiled at him.

It was a small miracle, but a miracle all the same.

His mother was right. He had to fight for his son.

If Greg was his son. He was human. The doubts still nibbled at him, and the echoes of Jessie's last words echoed in his mind.

He looked around, ran his hand over the smooth mahogany of the stairwell railing. It was a good, solid structure. The apartments would make good homes for half a dozen young families. He'd find some way to make it work.

The building was silent. He'd sent the guys home early so he could deal with Tyler Rosebrook in private. His mother's premonition had been right. The pager message was from Jessie's lover. He had the paternity test results and he would bring them by the building at Dylan's convenience.

"Dylan?" It was Lana's voice. She was waiting at the bottom of the staircase. He had been prepared never to see her again.

Yet here she was, another miracle, small but wonderful. After he'd dealt with Tyler Rosebrook, he had some serious fence-mending to do with Lana. He just hoped to hell it wasn't too late for that.

She was breathing quickly, as if she had been hurrying. There was a frown marring her features. She pushed impatiently at a strand of hair that had fallen into her eyes.

"What's wrong?" he asked.

"Are your mother and Greg over here?"

"No." Her anxiety was catching. He met her halfway up the steps and took her by the arms. "I left them in your storeroom." To answer Tyler Rosebrook's page. Then there had been one small crisis after another. He'd never gotten back to Lana's shop.

"Janette and I've been out front reconciling the cash register. Your mother looked tired. I wanted to give her some time to herself. But when your father arrived a few minutes ago, she was gone. She must have left through the delivery entrance. She's taken Greg and disappeared. Dylan, I'm sorry. I should have kept a closer eye on her."

"How could you know she'd take off like this? But where did she go? Her car's still parked out front. I can see it from here."

"She must have called a cab to the back entrance. She was so upset I don't know where she might have gone."

"It's not like her to do something so off the wall."

"No one's ever threatened to take one of our grand-babies away from her before."

His dad had come in from the street entrance and was standing below them, hands on hips, a pitying look on his face.

"I thought you were in Houston."

"Keogh flew me in."

"Keogh? The banker?"

"We were together in Nam. It isn't only you jarheads who keep in touch with their buddies. He always said he'd help me out in a pinch. Son, I thought you had more sense than to try and keep me from figuring out what Rosebrook was up to."

"I do have more sense, Dad. I'm just pretty damned slow to use it sometimes. We'll talk about it later. Right now we have to find Mom. She can't have gotten far. A woman with a cast on her leg and a baby slowing her down."

"Hell, boy. You sure aren't thinking straight," Roger Van Zandt said disgustedly. "This is your mother we're talking about. She'd get where she's determined to go if she had to crawl to do it."

"Have you tried her cell phone?"

"First thing. She's not answering. She's got more than an hour's head start, according to Lana here. She could have hightailed it to the airport and be on a plane halfway to your aunt Gracie's in Phoenix by now."

"She didn't have to do that. I'm not turning Greg over to Rosebrook today." He felt Lana stiffen beneath his hands and knew he'd worded the statement just about as wrong as he could. He let her go. He didn't have time to explain. Rosebrook was due any minute. Dylan had to find his mother and his son.

"Janette's gone to ask after them at the Crystal Unicorn and the bakery. Maybe they've seen her." Lana's voice was carefully neutral, but she had moved out of his reach.

"I'll take off for the airport as soon as we're shed of this Rosebrook fella." Roger met him at the bottom of the stairs. "Your mom will have my hide if I let you face him alone. We are going to be shed of him, aren't we, son?" he asked in a slightly less confident tone.

"Dad, it's more than a possibility that Greg is Tyler Rosebrook's son. We all have to come to terms with that." It was the one fact he couldn't dismiss.

"Blood isn't always thicker than water." Lana's words were soft but threaded with steel.

Dylan turned his head and looked at her. "That's not the first time you've told me that."

The darkness in her hazel eyes lifted momentarily. "Dylan?"

"I—" How did he say it? How did he tell her his world had changed from one moment to the next because his son had smiled at him and he had let himself feel the wonder of it?

"Van Zandt. Here you are. Although I must admit I hoped you would be alone." They all turned at the sound of Tyler Rosebrook's low, cultured tones.

"Rosebrook, I wasn't expecting you so soon."

"I have the test results." Jessie's lover held up a manila envelope. "Signed, sealed and notarized." The look of satisfaction in his eyes told Dylan as plainly as words what those results were.

For a moment the old doubts assailed him. His guilt over Jessie's death welled up and clamored for an act of contrition. His ears rang, and his heart hammered against his ribs, but he shut the echoing voices out of his mind. "I don't give a damn what those results say."

"The boy is mine, Van Zandt. I want him."

"Go to hell."

"Dylan." His name was little more than a whisper of hope on Lana's lips.

His father moved to stand at his shoulder. "You heard my son."

"I'll see you both ruined, Van Zandt. The tests are valid." Rosebrook's voice hardened with challenge. "The boy is mine. I want him."

"Not as long as there's breath in my body." Greg was his son whether by blood or by choice. He would fight to the death to keep him.

"You'll end up bankrupt and I'll still have my son."

"I wouldn't make threats you can't keep, brother."

They all turned at the sound of the new voice in their midst. Dylan had been so focused on his confrontation with Rosebrook that he hadn't noticed the long black limousine stop in front of the building. The speaker was a short, balding man tending to fat, but with an unmistakable air of wealth and power that somehow canceled out his less than imposing physical presence. "Ladies—" He motioned Dylan's mother and Shelby Lord forward with a sweep of his hand. Shelby had Greg in his carrier and his knapsack over her shoulder, and it was obvious she had left the diner in a hurry. She was still wearing her white chef's uniform.

"Roger. Thank goodness you're here," Linda said, moving toward her husband as quickly as she could. "How did you get back from Houston so soon?"

"I flew in with Keogh."

"Shel?" Lana took Greg's carrier from her sister and placed it on the drafting table.

"Mrs. Van Zandt came to the diner a couple of hours ago." Shelby hesitated. "Perhaps I should let her tell you what's happened,'' she murmured, making as though to leave.

"No, Shel." Lana reached for her sister's hand. "Stay with me."

Dylan held Lana's gaze for a heartbeat or two. "Rosebrook, you can say whatever you have to say in front of my parents and Lana." He smiled. "And her sister."

Lana didn't smile back. It was obvious she had no idea what he meant to do.

"Linda, what have you been up to?" Dylan's father demanded.

"Getting to the bottom of this," she said defiantly. "At first I intended to go to the airport and take Greg with me to my sister in Phoenix. But I thought they might want to see some kind of permission from Dylan to take him on a plane, so I changed my mind and had the cabdriver drop me off at Shelby's restaurant until I could come up with another plan. We had a long talk." She gave Shelby a wavering smile. "And, well, to make a long story short, I decided to beard the lion in his den." She gave Rosebrook a long, hard stare. "But he doesn't keep an office in Austin, and I didn't think I'd get very far trying to reason with a man like that, anyway, so I went straight to the top." She took a breath. "Dylan, this is William Rosebrook, Mr. Rosebrook's brother and the head of the Rosebrook Family Foundation. Mr. Rosebrook, my son, Dylan Van Zandt. And my husband, Roger."

William Rosebrook nodded a greeting. "Your mother is a very persuasive woman. She talked her way past two security guards and my executive assistant to get into my office. I believe at one point she threatened to go to the newspapers and have me charged with discriminating against a handicapped grandmother with a child in her arms."

Linda's cheeks grew pink with embarrassment, but she met the older Rosebrook's gaze head-on. "I may have gotten a tiny bit carried away. But my grandbaby's future is at stake. I would have talked my way past a hundred security guards to get to you if I had to."

"Madam, I do not doubt that for a moment." William Rosebrook gave her a courtly bow. He turned assessing gray eyes on his brother. "It seems you have some explaining to do, Tyler."

"Stay out of this, William. You have nothing to say in the matter."

"On the contrary. If what Mrs. Van Zandt has told him is true, you've compounded your disgraceful behavior with that poor young woman last year by aiming to set yourself up with an heir, and not in the usual time-honored fashion. I don't like to air our family linen in public, but you give me no choice. This hare-brained scheme won't work, Tyler. I won't help you contest Mother and Father's will. Their money goes to the foundation. There's nothing you can do about it."

Linda hobbled forward, took Greg from his carrier and plopped him in Dylan's arms. "There, you heard it from the horse's mouth. Giving Greg up to that man won't give him a life of luxury. He won't be better off with a stranger. He belongs with us. At the risk of repeating myself, so help me, Dylan, firstborn or not, if you give this child up, I'll never speak to you again." She reached behind her and took her husband's hand. "And neither will your father."

"Now, Linda—"

"Roger, I've made up my mind."

"It's all right, Mom." Dylan smiled at the child in his arms. Greg smiled back, wet and sloppy, beautiful beyond description. Just a smile—that's all it took. *You're my boy,* he whispered in his heart. *I know that now.*

He could look at Greg and see his son. His alone. He still resented the hell out of Jessie for what she'd put him through. He still felt the gnawing guilt and probably always would, because he'd let that resentment get the better of him and she had run out into the rain to die. But denying his love for his son was not the way to cleanse his sin.

The road to salvation lay in being the best father he could be, whether Greg was his child or another man's. Greg had been given into his care. He was Greg's father. He understood what that meant now. It was a lifetime commitment—an obligation of the heart. And it had happened not because he had told himself that was the way it had to be, but because Lana had shown him how to love again.

"I have the results of the paternity test Van Zandt and I took. I'm the baby's father, William, not him. It says so right here." Tyler Rosebrook brandished the manila envelope. "I can break Mother and Father's will. We'll both have more money than we can ever spend instead of the piddling trust funds they left us."

"I don't need or want the money. I won't contest the wills."

"The boy is a Rosebrook. It says so right here." An edge of desperation had crept into the younger man's voice. He shoved the envelope under Dylan's nose.

"You don't take any chances, do you?" Dylan settled Greg into the crook of his arm. He snatched the envelope from Rosebrook's grasp so quickly the man took a startled step backward. "I don't need to see the damned test results. It doesn't make a damned bit of difference what they say. This boy is my son, and no one's going to take him from me."

With a flick of his wrist Dylan sent the envelope sailing toward the Dumpster near the elevator. Tyler Rosebrook watched it disappear into the trash container. "I'll make you pay for this, Van Zandt," he said between clenched teeth.

"I don't care if I have to fight you all the way to the Supreme Court."

"You seemed willing enough to consider giving him to me forty-eight hours ago. What earth-shattering occurrence changed your mind?"

"It was earth-shattering, all right," Dylan said, unable to stop the grin that threatened to split his face wide open. "He smiled at me. Really smiled at me. For the first time. His dad. That's all it took."

"And Jessie's wishes mean nothing to you?"

"Jessie was scared and troubled. I'm not sure she knew what she wanted those last few days of her life. Being the cause of that unhappiness is something I'll carry with me for the rest of my life. But it makes no difference now."

Rosebrook's eyes narrowed as he shifted his gaze from the baby to Dylan. "It might to a judge."

"That's the way it will have to be." He looked at Lana, and her confused expression made his heart hammer in his chest. Had the realization of how much Greg meant to him come too late for them? He directed his words to her, not Rosebrook. "I'll say it one more time. I'll fight you every inch of the way, even if I end up in debt for the rest of my life. Greg is my son. He stays with me. And if she'll have me, I'm asking Lana to be my wife and to become his mother and help me raise him to be the kind of man Jessie, and his uncle Greg, would be proud of." He hadn't meant to come right out with it that way, but there was no turning back. "I love you, Lana. I should have told you that days ago. I was a fool not to. Tell me it's not too late for us. Say you'll marry me and make me and my son the happiest men on earth." He held his breath, waiting through a dozen little eternities for her to speak.

Her gold-green eyes searched his, and he let her look as long and as deeply as she wanted. He had no secrets from her now. He had bared his soul. If she still loved him, she would know that.

Shelby gave her a little push forward. "This is what you've been waiting for," she said sotto voce. "Don't blow it."

Lana ignored her sister the way Dylan had ignored Rosebrook. There might have been only the two of them in the lobby, in the world. "You mean it, don't you," she said very softly, reaching out to circle Greg's tiny fist with her fingertip. He opened his hand and grabbed on to her finger as though he meant to never let go. The same way Dylan wanted to gather her close and never let her go.

"Every word. I love you, Lana. I should have told you days ago. Weeks ago. Greg loves you. Say yes and make us a family."

"Shelby's right. This is what I've been waiting for. Yes," she said, clear and strong. "I'll marry you." She stood on tiptoe and kissed him on the cheek. Her eyes were tear-bright and shining like sunlight on river water. "I was afraid you would never ask," she whispered in his ear.

Dylan turned his attention to Tyler Rosebrook. Their gazes locked and held for a long, silent moment. He could hear traffic going by on the street outside. His mother sniffled, and his father handed her a handkerchief. Greg stretched and cooed. Rosebrook fixed his gray eyes on the baby. The gray eyes he'd given Greg? It didn't matter now. It would never matter again. "Get out of my building," he said quietly.

Rosebrook took a second prudent step backward. "I suggest you fish those test results out of the Dumpster, Van Zandt," he said. "I believe their accuracy is over ninety-nine percent certain."

"It makes no difference what the tests say." Dylan closed the distance between them, ready to throw Jessie's lover out of the building bodily, baby in his arms or not, but William Rosebrook held up a restraining hand.

"My brother's right in this case. You don't have to fish those test results out of the Dumpster, Van Zandt. I have another copy here." He reached into the breast pocket of his handmade silk suit and produced a smaller manila envelope. "I took the liberty of checking with my brother's doctor. It seems there might have been a mix-up at the lab. Most regrettable. I volunteered to bring you the corrected copy. I believe if you take a look at these results you will see that they prove beyond any doubt that Gregory Reilly Van Zandt is your son."

"WHAT ARE YOU smiling about?" Dylan asked in a sleep-roughened growl that sent shivers across her bare skin. Lana slipped into bed beside him and pulled the sheet to her chin. He promptly pushed it down and gathered her close. "And why are you wandering around in the middle of the night?"

The only light came from the moon shining through her bedroom window, but she could see the curve of his lips, the strong, clear line of his jaw. She lifted her hand to touch his face, assuring herself he was real. That everything that had happened that day was real, and not a yearning dream. He kissed the inside of her palm, and the sensations that arced between her brain and her nerve endings dispelled any doubt that she might be dreaming.

"I was up checking on…our son," she said, savoring the words. "And I was smiling because I wonder what people would say if they saw him sleeping in a dresser drawer. I do own a baby specialties shop. I have my reputation to consider."

"We'll move his crib here tomorrow." There was no question that they would be living in her house. Dylan knew how much she loved the old pile of brick and stone. It was the perfect place to raise a family, even if her soon-to-be-husband felt his pickup stuck out like a sore thumb among the BMWs and Range Rovers he passed on the street.

"After you drive to Houston to meet with the banker friend of your father's," she murmured, sliding her leg along the length of his, savoring the roughness of his skin against the softness of hers. Roger's army buddy had agreed to an additional line of credit. More than enough to finish the project.

"I'll be back before dinner," Dylan promised.

"And if there's any hitch in the negotiations…" she prompted, running her hands across his chest, and lower, to the hard, flat planes of his stomach.

He sucked in his breath and lowered his head to kiss her full on the mouth. "Then, Ms. Lord, I will consider your offer of a loan."

"You will *accept* my offer of a loan," she whispered against his lips as she pressed her full length against him. "We're in this together from now on, remember? You promised. No more stubborn, Texas-male pride where our future is concerned."

He rolled on top of her. "I promise. No more stubborn Texas pride. But lots and lots of Texas loving."

There was no more conversation between them for a long time. Much later, as the moon was setting and dawn streaked the eastern sky, Lana awoke to find Dylan stretched out beside her with Greg sleeping on his chest.

She lifted herself on one elbow and dropped a kiss on Greg's downy head.

"Did I wake you?" Dylan whispered.

"No," she said. "I never heard him cry."

"He didn't. I just wanted to hold him."

Lana blinked hard to stop the quick, joyful tears that stung her eyes. "I've been so worried," she said, thinking back on the past few days. "It was like one of those nightmares where you run and run and can't get any closer to the person in danger. That's how I felt, trying to talk sense into you." She laid her head on his shoulder and breathed in the scent of man and baby. "Did it truly happen so quickly? Was it just his smile?"

Dylan chuckled, and it reverberated low and deep in his chest. "Like a lightning bolt between the eyes. Everything came together. All the things you'd been telling me. It all made sense. It wasn't only responsibility I felt for him. Or guilt at Jessie's death, or even Greg's. It was love. Just like you promised to teach me."

"I didn't teach you."

"You showed me the way."

"I think Greg showed us both the way."

She lay quietly with her head on his chest for a few minutes, listening to the strong, steady rhythm of his heart, savoring the intimacy. She thought of Jessie, who had been so sad and mixed-up and who would never know the happiness Lana felt now. *I will love Greg for all my life,* she whispered in her heart to the dead woman. *I promise you.* She lifted up to touch Dylan's mouth with hers. "Let's get married right away so we can start making a baby brother or sister to keep Greg company."

"I think I can go along with that plan, partner."

"One every couple of years or so, until we have half a dozen."

"It's a tall order but I think I can rise to the occasion."

"I'm sure you can." He gathered her close, and she laid her arm gently across Greg's tiny bottom. She closed her eyes and let happiness wash over her like a cloud. She had everything she wanted. Everything she had dreamed of and hoped for and wished for all her life.

And because she loved and was loved in return, she had also learned something of compassion. Compassion for the woman who had borne her and abandoned her and Shelby and Michael and Garrett all those years ago. "I hope we find you, Mom," she whispered to herself. "So I can ask you why you left us for Aunt Megan to take care of. To tell you that I forgive you, because you must have been desperate and alone. And to tell you I love you."

EPILOGUE

SHE LOOKED AROUND the little apartment she'd called home for the past fifteen years. It was cozy and snug, and she had good neighbors. It was on a nice street, quiet and tree-lined. The nicest home she'd ever had. She would regret leaving it, but her time was running out.

The last round of chemotherapy had not arrested her disease as the doctors had hoped. She was growing weaker by the day. Her time on earth was slipping away. She had a few months at best, a few weeks at worst.

She went next door to the Hernandez apartment to say goodbye to Maria, who had promised to feed the stray cat that LeeAnn had adopted two years ago and to remind her friend one more time to forward any mail or messages that might come for her to the hospice where she was moving.

"I will miss you, LeeAnn," her friend whispered. "I will visit you when I can. *Vaya con Dios*. I will pray for you."

"Thank you, Maria. I'll look forward to seeing you." She knew very few people would seek her out in the pleasant, adobe-style hospice, but she didn't care. She had always been a solitary person. She did not fear being alone. Even now.

But more and more she found herself dwelling in the past, remembering those days when she had been young and strong and it seemed that even the challenge of four babies and minimum-wage jobs was an obstacle she and Garrett could overcome.

Garrett? Would she see him in heaven, dressed in the worn leather jacket he loved, tall and strong and handsome as sin, astride his Harley? He hadn't been a bad man, only a careless one. Surely he hadn't sinned so terribly he wouldn't be there waiting for her. She had tried to be a good person all these years, to make up for the one terrible failure of her life.

Giving her children away.

She had done what she could to try to right that wrong, little though it was. But nothing had come of her tentative efforts to contact her children. That Megan Maitland had delivered her box of love offerings she did not doubt. But over a month had passed and no word or sign had come from them. If they'd *really* wanted to, they could have tracked her down.

They wanted nothing to do with her, obviously, and she was too tired to make another effort to contact them. She wouldn't go to Lana's shop with the stork and the baby hanging from the sign, or the diner where Shelby held court behind the counter. She wouldn't try to find Garrett's ranch so far out of the city or seek out Michael at Maitland Maternity.

It was in God's hands now.

But, oh, how she wanted to see them all before she died. If she could listen to them speak, hear their laughter, see the color of their eyes.

If she could tell them she loved them just once more in this life, it would be enough.

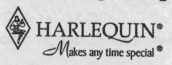

HARLEQUIN Presents

The world's bestselling romance series...
The series that brings you your favorite authors,
month after month:

Helen Bianchin...Emma Darcy
Lynne Graham...Penny Jordan
Miranda Lee...Sandra Marton
Anne Mather...Carole Mortimer
Susan Napier...Michelle Reid

and many more uniquely talented authors!

Wealthy, powerful, gorgeous men...
Women who have feelings just like your own...
The stories you love, set in exotic, glamorous locations...

HARLEQUIN Presents

Seduction and passion guaranteed!

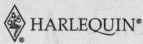

HARLEQUIN®

makes any time special—online...

eHARLEQUIN.com

your romantic life

━Romance 101━
♥ Guides to romance, dating and flirting.

━Dr. Romance ━
♥ Get romance advice and tips from our expert, Dr. Romance.

━Recipes for Romance━
♥ How to plan romantic meals for you and your sweetie.

━Daily Love Dose━
♥ Tips on how to keep the romance alive every day.

━Tales from the Heart━
♥ Discuss romantic dilemmas with other members in our Tales from the Heart message board.

HINTL1